# Four Seasons

# jane breskin zalben

**Alfred A. Knopf**
New York

THIS IS A BORZOI BOOK PUBLISHED BY ALFRED A. KNOPF

Text copyright © 2011 by Jane Breskin Zalben
Jacket photograph copyright © 2011 by Ericka O'Rourke

Visit us on the Web! www.randomhouse.com/kids

Educators and librarians, for a variety of teaching tools, visit us at
www.randomhouse.com/teachers

*Library of Congress Cataloging-in-Publication Data*
Zalben, Jane Breskin.
Four seasons / by Jane Breskin Zalben. — 1st ed.
p. cm.
Summary: Over the course of a year, thirteen-year-old Allegra Katz, a student at the demanding Juilliard School and the daughter of two musicians, tries to decide whether she wants to continue to pursue a career as a concert pianist or to do something else with her life.
ISBN 978-0-375-86222-9 (trade) — ISBN 978-0-375-96222-6 (lib. bdg.) —
ISBN 978-0-375-89405-3 (ebook)
[1. Piano—Fiction. 2. Music—Fiction. 3. Self-confidence—Fiction. 4. Family life—New York (State)—New York—Fiction. 5. New York (N.Y.)—Fiction.] I. Title.
PZ7.Z254Fo 2011
[Fic]—dc22
2010012731

The text of this book is set in 11.5-point Goudy.

Printed in the United States of America
February 2011
10 9 8 7 6 5 4 3 2 1

First Edition

*For Beanie—my heart sings for you, with you, and from you*

When words fail,
music speaks.
—Hans Christian Andersen

Music is the echo of the human soul.
—From *The Violin Maker*


**Antonio Vivaldi** was a violinist and a composer (1678–1741). He wrote *The Four Seasons* as a set of violin concertos in 1723. It remains among the most popular pieces of eighteenth-century Baroque music. Vivaldi based this cycle of seasons on sonnets he had written; the opening, "Spring," is the most famous. This novel takes place during four seasons of one year.

# Spring

## SPRING

Thunderstorms, those heralds of Spring, roar,
    casting their dark mantle over heaven,
Then they die away to silence, and the birds
    take up their charming songs once more.

—*From a sonnet by Vivaldi*

# Prelude

Just thinking about giving up the piano makes me break out in hives.

Big fat red ones.

But I think about it all the time.

My parents would disown me.

Miss Pringle, my piano teacher, might forget me. (That would hurt.)

Mr. Block, my school orchestra conductor, would be mad at me. (That doesn't count.)

And I'd never see Alejandro Sanchez again. (Which does count—major.)

So I'm going to continue lessons, even if it kills me.

And tell no one how I really feel: that sometimes music makes me sick.

And nothing that beautiful should ever, ever make you sick.

# March

We were either her best students or worst students,
but none of us knew which ones we were.
It was impossible to tell; it was probably a combination.
—Philip Glass, composer

Four hours of practice a day. At least. That's what they want
me to do. By "they" I mean the Pre-College Division music program I go to all day on Saturdays. It is part of a large conservatory, The Juilliard School. Everyone in the know always says
"The" and not just plain old "Juilliard." That "the" means it's
the only one of its kind in the world. And the truth is, it is.

Even though I aim for four hours, the kids who are
homeschooled, or forced, or just plain robots do at least five.
The ones who love to play and can't stop, six or more. But
I have so much homework from my regular school—where

7

everyone is "gifted" because it's private and the parents nearly poison each other to get their child in—that it's hard to fit in more than three. If my mother knew, I'd probably get chewed out—big-time. Maybe she does, for I believe that, like most mothers, mine sees and hears everything.

When Mom's not doing her voice trills at the piano, I squeeze in at least an hour or more of all twelve major and minor scales, which I count as part of my practice routine—even though I am *not* supposed to—along with the pieces I *am* supposed to learn. Miss Pringle, my teacher, picks them out for me for recitals and competitions and end-of-the-year jury evaluations, like the Chopin Prelude in E minor, which is one of the pieces I am studying right now. The prelude is paced and slow. The strewn-together notes make me ache every time I play it. It sounds so beautiful I struggle to hold back tears. By the tenth measure, the melody takes over and goes up ever so slightly in a minor key. My eyes start to become blurry, but I continue. Then, toward the end, I get this uplifting surge. It happens *every* time I play this piece. Not *hear* it, actually *play* it. I guess ol' Chopin does it for me like Billie Holiday does it for Ma.

My mother sings blues as good as Norah Jones, in cramped dark bars near streets named for letters of the alphabet. "Years ago, when it was called Alphabet City, it was like the Wild West," Mom told me. "But now that the Lower East Side's grunginess has gotten hip and upscale, everybody who likes my kind of music goes down there."

Mom's weekday shows start around ten or eleven at night, when downtown really starts to wake up. Since on school nights I'm in bed by then, I've never seen one. My mother trained as an opera singer. But that's a whole other story.

She says, "I need to perform to stay alive. I don't care if it's at some bar on Avenue C instead of the Metropolitan Opera House. Music's like breathing air."

Sometimes I half believe her.

Last night before she left, I asked, "When can I go to one of your gigs already?"

"Maybe on your thirteenth birthday, Alley Cat."

"But that's in June! Over two months away!"

"Patience is a virtue."

"Trust me, Ma, anyone who plays classical music has a whole lot of patience."

"If anyone knows, I know." She sighed and started to gather up sheet music for her accompanist. When she noticed me staring at the word *allegro* at the top of a song, she said, "You know we named you Allegra because Dr. Goldstein needed a catcher's mitt the night you were born." *Allegro* means a brisk and rapid tempo.

"Thanks for sharing that with me for the millionth time, Ma." I gave her a major eye roll.

She plowed on. "Allegro's the opening for the concertos of Vivaldi's *Four Seasons*. Dad was performing it the night you popped out. I guess you were destined to become a musician."

"Or a baseball player." I filled in one of Dad's lines in the familiar story, since he was away on tour.

My name might be Allegra, but mostly everyone calls me Ally.

9

Mom sometimes calls me Alley Cat after a dance Grandma does at the Y. Dad's mother has lived in her own place on the bottom floor of our brownstone ever since Grandpa died of a heart attack a few years ago. Grandma found him on their bedroom floor when she came back from her book club. She still feels sick about it, wondering, *Would things have been different if only I had been there?* She babysits me, if you could call it that—I'm *way* past the sitting age—when my parents are off doing their thing. I also suspect it's an excuse to come over because she's lonely without him, especially at dinnertime.

My father's the first violinist in a group called the Marduvian String Quintet, which means (a) he gets to play the hard parts, and (b) there are five—totally weird in the music world—instead of the usual four people in a group, which would have made it a quartet. Dad named it after my mother's family, Marduvian, which sounds more exotic than ours, Katz. Katz plants us in the heart of the Upper West Side. Near Zabar's. And lox and bagels. And walking distance from Lincoln Center—"the dream of all performing artists," say my mother and father.

Parents come to New York City from all over the world so their child can study with some hotshot teacher at Juilliard. Fifty to ninety young musicians get in a year, depending on who applies. A lot of families are pulled apart—where one parent stays behind with the rest of the family while the other lets their son or daughter follow a dream. Whose dream it is, I'm not always sure, but the one thing I know is that I'm lucky to live only ten blocks away. This is my schedule every Saturday:

Performance Forum, 9–10 (Not my favorite way to start the day.)

Choir, 10–11 (Everyone does it till high school. I sound like a frog.)

Theory, 11–12 (It is beyond boring. And I hate the homework.)

Lunch (What's lunch? I try to fit it in if I can.)

Chamber, 12–1 (Quintet: A violinist, a violist, a cellist, a bassist, and me.)

Composition, 1–2 (I love Dr. Rashad. He lets me eat in class.)

Solfège, 2–3 (Ear training. Required forever.)

Lesson, 3–4 (I have another lesson on Tuesdays after school.)

Master Class, 4–5 (It never, ever ends at five.)

Saturday afternoon toward the end of the day, I was heading upstairs for a private lesson with Miss Pringle when I got on the elevator and thought I would die.

"What floor?" Alejandro looked down at me with big doe-brown eyes as he flicked his long bangs off his forehead with a swift toss of his head.

"Five," I gulped as the elevator doors closed.

He pressed four, then five. We were alone until another boy got on at two. They bumped fists. "Hey, Sanchez, how's it going?" the boy said. Alejandro pulled one earbud away from his head so he and his friend could both listen to his iPod. The truth is, I had spotted Alejandro months earlier. Anyone would have. Major crush material. There had been a photo of

11

him in the Juilliard newspaper announcing a calendar of holiday events that featured his jazz band recital. He was playing his saxophone, wearing a dark suit, a black shirt, and a thin black tie. I cut it out and slipped it inside one of my music books. Then I'd open the page to see his picture, close it, and hours later pore over it again.

Alejandro was a few years older—sixteen? Seventeen? Maybe even eighteen? So I figured he probably didn't know I was alive. But when the elevator was almost at the fourth floor, he turned to me. "I really enjoyed hearing your piece in that open composition forum. Especially how you added the marimba and African drums. Interesting choices."

I blushed as my heart raced. He noticed me. *Wait till I tell Opal.*

Before he got off, he said, "My friends call me Alex."

"Or Sanchez," his friend teased, pulling him by the arm.

The temperature in the elevator felt as if it had gone up about one hundred degrees. I smiled to myself, thinking of Alex's olive skin and shiny black hair as it fell over his eyes— eyes I could totally get lost in.

When the doors to the elevator opened at the fifth floor, many parents were slumped in upholstered chairs dozing off; they got up at the crack of dawn so their children could arrive around eight-thirty. They drove or took trains or buses from New Jersey, Pennsylvania, Connecticut, Massachusetts. Some came in from Long Island or the outer boroughs. Those who were awake chatted mostly in Japanese, Korean, Mandarin, or, more recently, Russian, remaining in their separate cliques. I was a minority here, like Alejandro. Was he often left out of conversations, like me?

Behind the bank of elevators it was nutso. Pandemonium— one of the new vocabulary words on our flash cards in English. Younger kids were jumping up and down on couches clustered near the bathrooms, while violinists of all ages practiced in every imaginable corner. Some students went into bathrooms to rehearse, particularly the voice students, who seemed to get off on their voices bouncing off the slick tiled walls. I headed to warm up in one of the practice cubicles duplicated along a hallway as if by a cookie cutter. When I was done, two parents tried to grab the cubicle at the same time and began to have words in a language I didn't understand, as both their children looked on in silence. I left before I could see who won, and ran down the hall that wound around more practice rooms and classroom studios like the Yellow Brick Road. A librarian from the music research library came out to scold a few ten- and eleven-year-old boys who were playing handball against the walls. They raced around the corner and started to volley the ball again the second he went back into the library.

The door was ajar when I arrived at room 528. Eduardo, one of Miss Pringle's graduate students, was talking to her, and she motioned for me to come in. I often had my Tuesday follow-up lessons with him, as well as Saturday lessons that she couldn't make. "Now, I want you to find that Schumann we discussed," she said. "The Schubert, too. His Sonata in D Major. They're somewhere in the files in the living room. Or get them at Frank's Music. They would fill out that program you're doing next weekend. I want to hear them by Thursday—perfect. If you could also pick up some milk and juice . . ." He gave her a nod and smiled at me as he was leaving.

The Venezuelan government had honored Miss Pringle for bringing students back to the United States to study. Eduardo was one of her finds. She'd discovered him at fourteen singing on the street for spare change. He was living with his grandmother on the edge of a dirt road in a shantytown, in a shack with a corrugated tin roof, no running water, and a chicken. Miss Pringle saw something in him no one else saw and brought him to New York to train. Eventually he won a competition and got to play with the Orquesta Juvenil Simón Bolívar, receiving their highest award for achievement.

Many students besides Eduardo lived in Miss Pringle's sprawling apartment, coming and going, doing chores like laundry and cooking in exchange for room, board, and teaching. They had become her "children," and Eduardo lived with her like a son.

I glanced at my sneakers, perched on the brass pedals, as I sat on the piano bench, resting my fingers on the ivory keys, waiting for my lesson. Then I stared at a Chinese scroll of mountains clouded in mist on the wall behind her.

"Can you sight-read this for me before you play the prelude?" she asked.

I blinked, returning to the room as I glanced over the music. While I played, she sang along. "Da, da, da, d-a-ah!" Her voice went higher and higher as she began to clap out the rhythm. "Hold it longer here before you go up. At the G. Listen. The two eighth notes should be shorter. Then long, long, long," she barked, "starting now!" She continued to sing without coming up for air, and I decided she would have made an excellent swimmer. "Faster right here. Ya de de da dum. Too much. Wait! Wrong!" she exclaimed. She never played a single note to show me how to do it.

Still, I understood and went faster to the beat of her hands, which were like a metronome ticking its steady rhythm. She finally came to a halt. "Like that! Don't rush it. There's a rest," she demanded, pointing to it on the page. "Hold the chord a bit longer. There's a whole measure. Don't you see?"

I leaned in closer to the music as if I were nearsighted. *Yes, I see.*

"Well, you fumbled." She drank from her ceramic mug.

I started again, a few measures back, where I'd flubbed the chord.

"Notice you missed a note here, too." She pointed to an A-sharp twelve bars over. "One, two, three, four," she sang, counting out the rhythm again. "Tempo!" She thumped her hand on the card table next to her; the mug began to wobble as she showed me the rhythm as if I were a moron. "Are you good in math? Because it's all in the counting."

*Yeah, I'm great in math. I'm several grades ahead. Taking the SAT this year. You know, the SAT, in seventh grade! Duh.*

I corrected my mistake to sear the right note into my brain. Instead of that making me play better, I got worse.

"Let's go on to the next page in three-quarter time."

15

Miss Pringle began to clap again and do her ya de de d-a-ah routine.

"Round fingers!" she ordered, accentuating the *R* rolling off her tongue like ammunition. "Keep those hands high in the air. Wrists up! You're like limp linguini on a plate." She put a pencil under my wrists, lifting them until I got the right arc and my fingers looked like lobster claws on the keys.

We both sighed in unison.

"You learned something just now, didn't you?"

*Yeah. That you can sing and clap. And I can imitate seafood.*

As I opened the pages of my yellowed Chopin Prelude book and put it beside Bach's Two-Part Inventions, the photo of Alejandro Sanchez slipped out. Miss Pringle turned it over. "Who's this?" she asked.

"No one."

"No one?" she repeated, her eyebrows going up.

"Just a friend."

I tried to act casual. I didn't want to tell her he studied here, and that he had this unbelievable smile that could melt an iceberg faster than global warming.

Smoothing a strand of her thinning snow-white hair in place, Miss Pringle handed me back the photo. "Now, don't divert yourself from the music." This time I quickly tucked the photo inside an accordion folder along with my composition pad and theory notes. She pursed her lips. "And you're much too young, you know."

*Too young for what?*

"So, are you ready to give the prelude a trial run in master class today?"

"I'm starting to get a headache," I lied, giving her a false smile.

"Maybe it will go away?"

*I doubt it,* I thought. But I kept going, playing the prelude for her.

"You should use less pedal in certain parts. More in others. It's coming along."

She said nothing about my phrasing, my fingering, my expression.

"Maybe you need to do an easier piece. Although I've had eight-year-olds doing this one. You should be preparing a concerto at your age. Or at the very least a sonata. With several movements. Are you working on the Rachmaninoff? In C-sharp minor. I hope you signed up for a recital time. You know you'll be judged on how you did all year at the jury." How could I forget?

Our mid-May end-of-the-year jury was like reauditioning for the school. Every year. Any disaster that happened in the world, it went on. A tradition not just here but in pre-college programs everywhere. I don't think an earthquake or fire or flood could stop it. Well, maybe an earthquake. They might postpone a jury, but not cancel it. I had never heard of them actually kicking anyone out, but the fear was there for all of us. That jury evaluation hung over me like a cloud.

After my lesson, I ran downstairs to the office to get a date for a recital time at Paul Hall, while the rest of the class invaded Miss Pringle's studio like a swarm of bees. "Luckily, someone recently canceled their recital because they're playing out of

17

town on this date." The assistant to the head of Pre-College pointed to the second Saturday on the May calendar. "So you're still able to get a slot. Is this good for you?"

I nodded.

"You should have booked this earlier in the year. Like October. Did you forget?"

I couldn't say I'd forgotten. I was avoiding the responsibility as if it would disappear. Everyone assumed I had taken care of it. Like I had done for the last two years, planning when the term began, and preparing several pieces for the recital and then the jury.

The class was still emptying folding chairs from Miss Pringle's large closet by the time I returned, setting them up into triple rows for master class. A few older students sprawled out on a couch close to the piano, fooling around. Trying to hide from Miss Pringle's watchful eye, I slunk into the last row as a number of parents started filling up the back. They were supposed to remain in the lobby—a rule many parents broke. A few had small recorders to tape their children so they could go over their performances later. One father had a camera; he'd hit replay, like in a tennis match, and analyze every aspect of his child's playing before a big competition or performance.

Miss Pringle sat in one of those folding metal chairs off to the side near the door by her beat-up card table, her back against the wall, facing the piano. Mrs. Young, a parent, gave Miss Pringle a steaming cup of green tea that she had bought for her along with a red bean cake. She thought her son, Timothy, not quite nine, was God's gift to the universe. He had become teacher's pet. For the record, he wasn't even remotely a genius. With his thick black glasses and cowlick sticking out from his bowl cut, Timothy always crunched candy or kicked his leg against his metal chair when other people played, which managed to distract everyone but Miss Pringle. I knew he was going to pull something when Miss Pringle looked at me and said, "Ally, it's your turn."

I handed Miss Pringle my music to follow—although she knew every note in every bone of her body. She insisted we play as much as we could by heart. I took careful steps toward the piano, wiping both hands on my pants as I sat down at the bench. Even a cold March day couldn't stop beads of sweat from welling in my palms. I moved the bench slightly away from the keyboard, trying to get in a comfortable position. Then as I raised my hands above the keys, someone—and I'd put my entire allowance on Timothy—got a coughing fit, and I bungled the first few notes.

There are always coughs throughout an audience. That's why before you enter a concert hall they have those Lucite bins filled with little hard candies. But there's always one person who insists on unwrapping it during largo—a slow movement—and you can hear the cellophane untwisting from the stage. *Get used to it. This kid's training you for the audience from hell. You've been there: cell phones ringing, people walking out, coming in, slamming doors, squeaking seats, giggling with friends. Focus. Get inside your own head, Ally. Disappear into the music. Like Dad does. Like Mom does.*

I could almost hear Mom's voice, saying, *Slow down. You're not catching a train. Feel the notes. The pauses. All the spaces in between. Give it air. Breathe. Sometimes what's not played is as important as what is.*

So I took a deep breath like Grandma does on her yoga mat. In, then out.

Miss Pringle cleared her throat. "Would you like to begin again?"

I nodded. My hands began to sweat some more. I slipped at the same place I had screwed up during my lesson, but it was worse than before because now it wasn't only in front of my teacher, it was in front of all the pianists in my master class. Wrong notes built on each other, making me feel off balance as I made my way through the rest of the piece. It was the first time I'd played the prelude and not gone all mushy inside. I wanted to get through it without any mistakes, so I sacrificed emotion for perfection and ended up with neither.

"Comments?" Miss Pringle's eyes pierced me from under her prune-wrinkled lids.

I glanced over at my fellow students. Then away. Back down at the keys. Someone said my name and I gazed toward the hand that went up in the back. "You could work on the dynamics a bit more," Chisato said softly. "But I liked the emotion."

*What emotion? I had emotion?*

"Feeling is fine, but we must have technique," offered Miss Pringle.

*Well, so much for emotion.*

"Any other comments?" she asked the class's blank faces.

Miss Pringle stared straight at me. Everyone got quiet. "Well, this was not up to performance level. Don't you see, you need more time on a piece before you share it. It still needs work. Make it cleaner. Better intonation. I'd like you to get it ready for master class again before you even think of offering it in a performance."

As she hammered on, I screamed inside. *But I didn't want to do it!*

She scribbled away in her little pad and barely looked at me as she handed back my music. "I hope you're putting in the time." Then she turned to the class. "Four hours a day, minimum. And an hour of scales and arpeggios. Play a hard one for me in four octaves," she said to the next student, Hannah, who meekly inched her way past me and whispered, "I like how you played."

My lower lip quivered as I made my way back to my seat. Fury rose in me during the rest of the class, just like after Grandpa died. After the funeral Mom and I had gone to Central Park and walked barefoot on the Great Lawn while I told her a secret. When we came home, I overheard her telling my aunt. I can't even remember what it was anymore, but I remember the feeling: betrayal. I used to think *anything* Mom did would be the right thing, but it wasn't. It felt like a wasp sting I once got on the grass. Waking up to a truth sometimes hurts. Grown-ups don't always act like they should: grown-up. And sometimes they really let you down, and you get stung.

I ran for the elevator the minute master class ended. When it jolted to a halt at the fourth floor, mostly boys crowded on, holding trumpets, trombones, saxophones, and clarinets. They were happy, loud, and, unlike me, still excited after a very long

Saturday. I was glad Alejandro—I mean Alex—wasn't one of them.

Outside on the plaza, lights glittered in the distance from the Metropolitan Opera House. Cold rain lashed my face as I rushed toward Amsterdam Avenue, home.

"Anyone here?" I cried out, wiping the raindrops from my good jacket.

The house was dark except for a dimly lit lamp. I threw my backpack on the floor and kneeled to pet my cat, Beethoven, who was asleep under the piano on the worn Persian rug. Our other cat, Gus—named after Pythagoras—had died of old age earlier in the year. I scratched behind Beethoven's orange ears. He purred low rattling breaths, flipping onto his back, his paws in the air. He licked me on the nose with his coarse sandpaper tongue. "You want me to do the prelude? You've always been my best audience."

This time it went perfectly, and that was when I saw Grandma tiptoeing toward me, yawning, as if she had just woken up from a nap. She put her hand to her chest on the last note, like she was fainting, and asked the air, "How can a person play so beautifully?"

"Oh, Grandma." I started to laugh as I wiped away a few tears, which is a super-weird thing to do—laughing and crying at the same time.

She sat beside me on the piano bench at our secondhand Steinway. We took up the entire bench, banging out "Chopsticks" and then "Heart and Soul." I did the treble and sang the song, while she did the bass part. We sounded pretty bad and began to giggle as we belted out the words. I loved seeing her act silly.

"I wish I could do something creative like you and your parents."

"Grandma, no one on the entire planet makes a matzoh ball soup like you. I take that back. You make the best soup in the entire galaxy!"

"Ach. Talent like that." She waved her hand with a shrug.

"Talent like that is great! When I have your chicken soup, every cell in me fills with warmth. And when I'm sick or feeling down, it's the best medicine."

"Darling, give up music. Go into the diplomatic corps."

Grandma gave me a big kiss on top of my head and leaned on my arm slightly as she got up. "Come. I could use the help. These arthritic hands ain't what they used to be, and those Martians could use a nice fluffy matzoh ball. Best soup in the galaxy," she repeated, smiling at me. Then she lowered her voice. "I'll tell you a secret."

"What?" I asked, waiting for her to reveal something great.

"Parsnips. I whip parsnips into my matzoh balls. With a bit of seltzer. The key to the perfect matzoh ball. What can I say? I'm the Chopin of chicken soup."

If only she had given me the key to how to become a great pianist instead. The best one in the galaxy. Boy, would that make my parents happy.

The windows were a crack open in the parlor when I came downstairs Sunday morning. That's what we call it because it used to be a parlor long ago. It's where we keep the nine-foot-long piano, which I nicknamed El Grande after the extra-large lattes at our local coffee shop. Mom was dusting off her wooden metronome and paused with the dust rag in midair, mesmerized by a silver-framed photograph of Dad during a lawn concert in the Berkshires. She lovingly outlined his face, edging it with her finger as if it were a connect-the-dots page from one of my old coloring books. He looked all summery in his white tuxedo jacket, with his hair in a ponytail and his group playing under the stars.

"Hi." I came over as Beethoven did the cha-cha between my legs, nudging his furry head against my calves for attention.

"Hi, sweetie. Your father looks so young, doesn't he?"

I leaned in closer, staring at a younger version of him, without the gray in his hair.

"Seems like a lifetime ago." She let out a sigh and moved on to another photo, taken around twenty years ago when she was in *Aïda*. She was perched on top of a large gray elephant at the Metropolitan Opera House, wearing an embroidered silk costume with a feathery plume flowing from her coal-black wig. It still shocked me to this day that an animal so huge was onstage. I wondered what would happen if it had to go.

"Do you miss singing opera?"

She nodded and put her palm flat against her chest, taking in a deep breath.

"So why don't you go back to it?"

"I can't."

"Why not?"

"I just can't."

I leaned my head on her shoulder. Then I headed into the kitchen to grab some breakfast. A half-filled teacup sat on the countertop, its rim faintly smudged with the bright red lipstick she wore only when she performed. "Late night last night?" I called out to her.

"Yes. I was up after some hip-hop ukulele player. He had this backup guy who made sounds with his mouth like different instruments. It's unbelievable what a person can do with their vocal cords. Like those Mongolian throat singers."

"I wish I'd been there," I said as she came into the kitchen.

"Any plans for the day?" asked Mom. "Besides practice."

"Don't I get one day of rest?"

"Sunday's makeup for what you didn't get to during the week."

"You mean like studying and homework?"

She looked at me over her reading glasses, like, *Give me a break, Ally,* and began to straighten up the counter, tossing the wilted bouquet Dad had been given a couple of weeks before at one of his chamber music recitals at the 92nd Street Y. "Ah, the sacrifice we make for art."

"You're telling me," I said, shaking my head.

"So how did it go in master class yesterday?"

"It went."

"Yeah?" Her voice rose questioningly.

"It was fine," I lied. "I also got my recital date in May, right before the jury."

"I thought you had done that already," she said sternly. "Which hall?"

"Paul," I answered. "On the eighth. So tell Dad not to make any plans."

"Good. I like the acoustics in that hall. The sound is lush."

She seemed pleased as I followed her into a huge pantry that had been converted into a cozy soundproof studio Dad used for practice. On shelves were biographies of musicians and books on theory and history. Stacks of music paper, DVDs, demo tapes, and CDs were above a keyboard attached to a computer. Notes on fingering, dynamics, and phrasing were scribbled all over concerto scores. On the walls were oversized posters from international festivals—Spoleto, Aspen, Salzburg (birthplace of Mozart)—next to Mom's and Dad's framed degrees from The Juilliard School.

I looked at the music stand and the case holding the first violin Dad had ever bought—a cheaper 1910 German one that he sometimes used when he traveled and didn't want to worry about airplanes, humidity levels, and how they would affect the sound. But the spot where he kept his "good" violin—the one he used for really important concerts—was empty because he was in the Far East. Dad had saved up for years to buy it, then waited a year for it to be made especially for him by the violin maker who'd worked on Isaac Stern's Guarneri, re-creating its pattern. Dad guarded the Guarneri look-alike with his life.

"Did you finish your homework yet?" Mom asked, restacking a pile of music.

"Half. I'll do the rest tonight."

"Don't leave it to the last minute. You have a lesson on

Tuesday with Eduardo. You still need to prepare, even if it's with one of her assistants."

"I will." I tightened. "I'm meeting Opal today."

Mom rubbed my back. "Okay. Just remember."

"I know," I said impatiently. *Like I could forget.*

I felt like a ton of bricks had been lifted off my shoulders after I left the house. Opal was waiting for me with her dog a few blocks away on the steps by the front entrance to the Museum of Natural History. She and I had been together since third grade, when we started private school at exactly the same time—later than everyone else, who had made their close friends back in nursery school—after classes in each of our public schools had almost doubled in size and I started getting stomachaches.

"Opal?" I had asked when we met. I'd never heard that name before.

"It's southern. My mom said she'd been listening to way too many country-and-western singers while she was pregnant."

Then Opal revealed that her older sister was named Ruby. Ruby Rich—now that was a name to swallow. And their dog was Sapphire. "My parents consider us all gems," Opal had said with a tinge of sarcasm, even as a third grader, her eyes sparkling. We became fast friends.

Opal lived up to her name. She had smooth alabaster skin like her birthstone, with a sprinkle of freckles dusting her nose and rosy cheeks, and she burned the color of red-hot chili peppers. She didn't do music except in our school choir or when dancing to heavy metal and salsa. This was a plus, since I needed one friend on the face of the earth to be into something other than classical music made by a bunch of dead white musicians from hundreds of years ago.

Opal's main interests were boys, boys, and more boys—and art. Once she went to the Art Students League to take a class in life drawing and found a male model buck naked on a platform in the center of the room. Well, he was covered with a cloth, like some of the statues in museums that have fig leaves, but after that, Opal was more into abstract art.

"Hey." I pushed away a tiny pink braid coming out of the center part of her hair, resting amid her flowing red curls.

"Hey."

"Pink?"

"Got tired of the blue one."

"Sweet." I touched it again gently. "And why is your dog here at a museum?"

She grabbed my arm. "I've got a better idea than seeing dinosaur bones."

"Yeah, and what's that?"

"Follow me," she said, leading us across the street to Central Park.

"You'd better not spell trouble, Opal Rich!" I yelled after her.

We walked into the park toward the Boathouse. People bundled in ski jackets and overcoats were having brunch, sipping hot chocolate by the lake. One man was fishing on a rock. I couldn't imagine what for—a dead rat? The Upper West Side's skyline filled the background as the sun glinted between trees and buildings. Opal took out her cell phone and snapped the picture-perfect moment.

"Okay." I pulled my woolen hat down lower over my ears. "Now what?"

"You'll see."

"You're *so* mysterious. I hope we don't end up on the six o'clock news."

She rolled her eyes. "You don't trust me?"

"Well . . ."

"Thanks a lot!" She gave me a rabbit punch.

As I was following her over a meadow scattered with lamp-posts, asphalt paths, park benches, and well-trodden trails, Sapphire strained at her leash to chase a squirrel, and we came upon Bradley Clark, a new boy in our grade, walking a dog. Opal smiled at both dogs as they began to circle each other.

"Good boy, Sasha." Bradley tugged at the leash, pulling him away. "He's not mine. He's a neighbor's. I'm helping out."

"You do dog walking?" I asked.

"I do a lot of things," he said evasively, kicking at a tuft of dried grass. "Gotta go." He lifted the hood on his sweatshirt over his wavy blond hair, and we walked in opposite directions.

When he was out of range, Opal said, "Brad's a scholarship student. He lives just with his dad."

"Are his parents divorced?"

"I'm not sure what happened. Something with his mother."

I thought of what a pest mine sometimes was, feeling guilty as I thought this. "How do you know?"

"Rumors. Everyone knows."

"I didn't."

Opal smiled at me. "Of course not. Your head's in the clouds. With music. These things aren't on your radar. That's why I love you, Ally." She threw her backpack on a flat rock, unzipping it. "We're here."

"What's here? A walking tour of igneous rocks?"

Opal handed me one end of a string. "Hold this." Then .she began to unravel a huge ball of twine. Attached to it were itsy-bitsy brightly colored plastic clothespins holding small labels she had clipped from the inside of shirts, sweaters, pants, dresses, and skirts. *Made in Honduras, Nicaragua, China, India, the Philippines* . . . the list went on. Now I understood why she'd gone after the back of my new Gap T-shirt and jeans with a pair of scissors.

"What *are* you doing? A political statement?" I yelled out as she continued to unfurl the twine, labels dangling in the wind like proud flags on a clothesline. She walked further and further away. "Or are you trying to compete with the United Nations?"

She smiled and didn't answer me.

"Opal!" I shouted, my curiosity mixed with frustration as she pulled the string taut and tied it around a thick branch.

"I'm doing an installation!" she shouted back.

"A what?"

"Art."

"Art?"

"My sculpture teacher thinks it's brilliant!"

"Your *sculpture* teacher?"

When she returned, she fastened my end of the string around a strong tree limb. "I'll help you out sometime," she said as she finished the knot.

"How? You'll wheel my piano onto the stage? You can't be

a page turner because you don't read music. Even if you did, I'd have to play without it."

"I'll listen and clap and hoot and be proud you're my best friend."

"Oh, Opal. Don't hoot." I playfully tugged at her braid. "It's not a rock concert."

"Like I'd ever." And she tickled my nose with the tuft at the end of her braid.

We stood on the rock, watching her labels flapping in the breeze. One by one, other people noticed, too. They stopped, stared, and read. A mother held her daughter's small hand in hers. When she bent down to whisper something in her ear, pointing to Opal's string stretched out between two different trees, her nose nuzzled the soft curve of her child's cheek and the girl giggled without a worry in the world. I caught my breath.

We hung out all afternoon until the sun began to set. Opal and I took one last look at her installation before we quickly ran away. I thought of how much fun this had been, and how everything I did took so much effort, with months and months of preparation. In school we had learned about a nomadic ethnic group from the islands off the coast of Burma who lived as much as six months of the year on boats carved from tree trunks. They had no words in their language for *want, wish,* or *hope.* What would I do without those three words?

## April

Asked the secret of piano-playing, I always make sure the lid over the keyboard is open before I start to play. The notes I handle no better than many pianists. But the pauses between the notes—ah, that is where the art resides.
—Artur Schnabel, pianist

It felt like the world was passing me by.

I couldn't go for hot dogs at Gray's Papaya with Opal after school.

I couldn't hang out when she wanted to watch movies and eat popcorn.

And slumber parties on weekends. What were those?

Plus I was going to miss the opening of Opal's group art exhibit. (It was on a Saturday.)

Sacred Saturday (not to mention the other days of the

week) was devoted to one thing only, which reminded me of the old joke: "How do you get to Carnegie Hall?"

Drumroll, please. "Practice."

"You sure you can't come downtown with me after school? Just this once," Opal pleaded. "You could see the show before it opens. I made a pig from spare bicycle parts and other found objects. Sort of a Neo-Dada thing going on."

"Neo what?"

"Forget it. It's out there. I put a slice of bacon next to it. Very Damien Hirst."

"Who's that? An animal rights activist?"

"A world-famous artist."

"Another political statement?"

Once again Opal smiled at me without answering.

"Sorry, I wish I could come, but I can't. I've got a lesson."

"With the dragon lady?"

"No, with one of her assistants."

"The cutie from Caracas?"

"Opal." I rolled my eyes at my boy-crazy friend. "Yes. With Eduardo."

After the super let me into Miss Pringle's building, I walked up the stairs because the elevator seemed to be stuck. Then I knocked on the door of 4B. Santiago, a graduate student, opened it. I followed him into the kitchen past Eduardo, who was finishing up another lesson. Santiago opened the ancient-looking refrigerator and took a swig from a half-gallon carton of orange juice. "Want something?" He slid an apple pie off a shelf.

I shook my head. The sound of music poured out from

various bedroom doors. Then I took out my prelude and went through the motions of playing it, moving my fingers quickly across the gold-flecked red Formica tabletop.

"You've got style!" Santiago teased as he dug into the pie with a fork.

"You think it was too soft?" I teased back. "Or could I use more sound?"

"Nah." He took another bite, swallowing. "Why ruin it? Forte is way overrated."

When I heard Eduardo's student leave, I gathered my things and went into the living room. Every square inch was covered with music. There must have been books on every composer from every century. And what wasn't actual music was music-related. Music boxes. Porcelain figurines of flutists, violinists and singers. Teacups from famous musical cities like Prague or Vienna. Chiming clocks. Miniature pianos. Note key chains. You name it, Miss Pringle had it crammed onto shelves and floor space around her huge piano, which took center stage.

Eduardo smiled at me as I came in. "Heard it didn't go so well in master class."

I glanced awkwardly at my hands as I sat down at the piano.

"We'll work out the kinks today." He settled on a stool by my side.

I rolled my head from side to side to ease the tension.

"Good," he said, smiling. "Breathe."

I stretched my fingers, loosening them up with a few scales, and began my piece.

"Watch the quarter notes. Then the rest." He leaned over slightly. "Again."

So I did it.

"One more time," he suggested, his hands folded in his lap, listening.

I placed my hands at either side of the bench when I was done.

"Think of sound like color. Here could be a red. Exciting. Crescendo. Getting louder and louder. And here," he pointed to another measure, "lower down. Diminuendo. Calmer. Like a pale aqua blue. A wave lulling in the ocean. Paint a picture of the music. Music is also textured and multilayered."

I imagined a lake smooth as glass mirroring pine trees, mossy green, and held a note with the pedal to make the image and sound last a moment longer.

He gave me a huge grin. "One last time for the road."

I played it again, the picture etched in my mind.

"Very good—you were listening to me. Let's hear your Rachmaninoff now. You want to show the jury the best of your present repertoire so that your personality comes through in your interpretation of the composers. Can you do that for me today?"

"I'm trying." I got quiet inside before I began. Once I started, I couldn't sit still.

"Not bad, not bad at all," he said with a wide smile when I was finished. "I like that little dance you did on the piano bench while you played. Very frisky."

"What dance?" I asked, embarrassed.

"It's a lively piece. It's okay to express yourself. Mozart

isn't Rachmaninoff. And Rachmaninoff isn't Mozart. Start thinking who you like to play. Who *you* enjoy."

Self-conscious, I sat very, very still. I knew I loved to play Rachmaninoff.

"I'm going to play this at my recital before the jury evaluates me in May. Okay?"

"Ask Miss P." He nodded and put his hand gently on my arm. "Move aside."

I stood next to the piano bench. He began to play Rachmaninoff's Piano Concerto no. 3 in D Minor, op. 30. Then I eased over to the only vacant club chair in the room—the one Miss Pringle sat in when she gave lessons—and sat down in awe until he finished.

"I've been studying the Rach Three for over a year. Technically it's a killer."

"Rach Three? Is that the one you just played?"

He nodded. "If I don't conquer this piece now, it could take me years, but if I stay with it, then maybe I can do it as a soloist toward my master's degree."

"You were kind of moving, too," I said bashfully.

"I was, wasn't I? It's almost impossible not to be with old Rocky." He smiled. "The pianist Artur Schnabel had a teacher who put coins on the back of his hands to control his playing." Eduardo fished in his pocket and placed a dime on the back of each of my hands. At first I thought he had completely lost it. Then he flicked them onto the floor. "Get rid of those coins."

So I decided to play my piece for me. For me alone. And this time my heart sang.

\* \* \*

When I came home after my lesson, my father's coat and um-brella were hanging in the hall. "Dad?" I shouted, noticing his black violin case alongside some beat-up luggage with tags from different airports in Asia. "Dad!" I cried out, running into his outstretched arms, the hair on his arms tickling my face as he threw them around me. "How was the tour? I thought you weren't coming home until Sunday!"

He pressed his lips together, looking over at Mom. "Our last few concerts were canceled. Reviews were mixed. Not enough tickets were sold."

"Sorry." I felt bad for him, but happy he was here, since he was gone so much.

"Some critics can be so petty and small-minded. What do they know? Do they actually play?" Mom let out a sigh. "Do they see your arms, shoulders, and wrists ache like an athlete's from all the work? Or notice the bruise on your chin from playing for hours at a clip?" He always had a bright red mark on the left underside of his face that never seemed to vanish. That's how I could tell which violinists or violists practiced and which didn't.

Dad sighed, too. "They don't realize we pay rent, or not, depending on their good or bad press. They don't lose sleep after a bad review. Not one wink. Do they even care?" He rubbed his forehead, his face tired and pale like the translucent paperwhite narcissus flowers in the pot on the windowsill behind him.

"Whoa, Dad, you need some time off." I hugged him tighter.

"We were exhausted anyway. And jet-lagged. It's okay, Ally."

Mom looked at him sadly, then turned her gaze to me. "How was your lesson?" she asked as she tore up some lettuce leaves.

"Good. Eduardo's very helpful," I said, happy to change the subject.

"And Miss Pringle isn't?" my mother asked, turning around. "Maybe we should have you tape the lessons so you'd remember what she says and wants."

I glanced at my father, like, *Should I?*

"Don't look at me. I have enough trouble taking care of myself. Your mother's in charge of lessons."

"*I'm* in charge? Thanks a lot, Doug," my mother said. "I didn't know that. I thought we're both in charge of *our* child's education."

"Elana, calm down." He came over and put his hand on her back. "It's not like she's playing Alice Tully Hall with the Philharmonic. It's just a lesson."

My mother glared at him. "Everything's important, even *just* a lesson. Remember? You'd know that if you were around here more." She stiffened as soon as those sharp words slipped out.

"Okay, I'm going to sleep," Dad muttered, unbuttoning his shirt.

"What about dinner?" Mom softened her tone. "I made your favorite—eggplant. With pasta in pesto sauce. And roasted fennel and peppers."

"Wrap it up. Maybe later. Or tomorrow night. I had a snack on the plane."

A silence hung in the air. Mom and I ate our meal. I felt

awful. It was my fault. Over a lesson. A stupid, stupid piano lesson.

The next day, while I was in the middle of third-period English, I asked for a hall pass and rushed to the girls' bathroom. On one of those indestructible brown paper towels from the dispenser, I jotted down a string of notes that had suddenly come to me, and hid it under my sweater before returning to the classroom to continue a grammar lesson. I liked making up things in my head. I could see the notes, hear them, even away from the piano. I was hoping I could study composition privately with Dr. Rashad in the fall—if he'd do that.

At ten minutes after three Opal watched me rearrange choral music on the stage of our school auditorium for the fourth time in five minutes. "Where's everyone? I wish Mr. Block would call choir rehearsals during regular school hours." I mindlessly fiddled with the piano keys, playing the notes I had written on the brown paper towel, which I flattened out to read. "Rehearsals eat up my practice time. May eighth is my Juilliard recital."

"Ally, stop getting so bummed out. Chillax."

"Did you just say *chillax*?"

"Chill and relax." Opal tapped the stage floor for me to sit down beside her.

"Those two words aren't on my vocabulary list."

Our legs swung above the empty orchestra pit. "You're not scared to play here, are you? You could do it in your sleep. The spring concert's just a school thing."

"With teachers, the principal, and parents. Not to mention *my* parents."

"And cookies and lemonade. And the dumb chorus. Come on, you've performed at Lincoln Center."

"In a chamber group."

"So?"

"This one's in front of people I see every day. It's different."

"Yeah, easier. I'll get you a burlap sack to hide in, in case you screw up." Then she got serious. "Everyone wants you to do well."

"Not in my world. We're always under a microscope. Everyone's *so* critical. And the kids are so talented."

"Shut up." She elbowed me. "You're so talented, too!"

"Right." I grimaced. "There are the stars, who win all the competition prizes and get to play everywhere. And then there's the rest of us."

She looked at me. "Are you serious? You're in Juilliard. How many kids get in there a year?"

I sighed. "Ten to twenty pianists in the entire world."

"That many?" she teased, knowing it was so few.

I poked her.

"You've always been the girl with the golden hands."

I gave her leg a playful nudge with mine, and she nudged me back.

"Sometimes I think these golden hands are preventing me from having a life."

"Hey, they also got you to meet that cute guy."

I gently swatted her arm. "What cute guy?"

"There's more than one? The sax guy."

"The *what* guy?"

"S-a-x. With an *a*, not with an *e*. Any progress?"

"He's fine," I answered her, hoping I'd see Alex again this coming Saturday.

"Fine? What am I, your mother? More information," she said, pumping me.

"What's there to tell? We bumped into each other. There were a zillion people around. Or I've seen him in the distance in the cafeteria on the zero-minute break I have."

Opal shook her head.

"And on top of that, there are all these skinny girls from the School of American Ballet posing in first position, looking gorgeous in their short chiffon skirts and leotards, sipping Diet Cokes or air."

"If you like sticks. Maybe he prefers a little something to grab on to?"

I gave Opal a poke. She poked me back. "You need to be alone with him."

"I don't think he really knows I exist. In *that* way."

"So make him know."

"He's way older."

"Like how old? Don't tell me it's like one of those weird Internet things you hear about on the news."

"Opal," I groaned. "Not *old* old. I mean about three, four years older."

"Big deal. I'm almost fourteen and you know I've got a thing for my sister's best friend, Eric. He's about that age."

Opal's parents had held her back a year in kindergarten. Her birthday was in a few days, so sixteen or seventeen didn't seem like the world to her. And she had already been on a few dates. She considered the boys in our grade either too short, too dorky, or too immature. But Eric Gagosian didn't give her the time of day, and like me, even though her head knew it was insane, her heart held out a glimmer of hope. His jeans rode low and he had a Japanese ideograph tattooed near the base of his spine above his butt.

Ruby had a matching tattoo. They had gotten it together when they both aced three of four AP tests, which looked super-impressive on college applications. Eric had applied to Cornell, Ruby to Yale, plus fifteen other schools when neither of them got in early admission in December. They'd hear any day now, and Opal's parents were like nutcases, waiting. Ruby broke out from nerves.

The red zits on her nose only added to her anxiety level, particularly when Opal started calling her "Rudolph." Opal said to me, "I'm gonna puke if one more dinner table conversation revolves around GPAs, APs, or SATs," plus a few other letters of the alphabet Opal added that I can't repeat.

At three-thirty the entire orchestra and choir finally arrived, with Mr. Block following close behind. A paisley silk scarf was draped around the neck of his coat, his eyeglasses balanced on his bald head. He tapped his baton on the podium for the orchestra's attention. I went over to the piano, playing an A, as they tuned their instruments. Mr. Block said, "People, today marks the first rehearsal for our spring concert. I expect all of you to make the evening a great success, and for you to be on your best behavior." He glared with his beady gray eyes at Matt, who was throwing spitballs into the orchestra pit and standing next to Bradley with the rest of the chorus in the bleachers. Then Mr. Block swept his hand up in a grand gesture, like the conductor he was, toward the large gilt-framed portraits of past headmasters arranged on the dark paneled walls. While he blah-blah-blahed about "discipline" and "commitment" and "honoring school tradition," Matt mimicked him from the side. I tried not to chuckle but couldn't help breaking into a broad grin. "Miss Katz? Do you have any input to offer here?"

I glanced down at the keys, away from Matt's silly expression. *Get on with it.* As if Mr. Block could hear my thoughts, he raised his baton and the first violins began the introduction. The second violinists, seated rows behind them, came in, and then he motioned on an exact beat for the sopranos to join them, shaking his fingers slightly as more voices followed, his hand trembling along with the vibrato of the violins. When the alto, tenor, and bass sections were all singing together, Mr. Block pointed to me. Luckily, I was right on time.

After an hour we broke. Opal and I went down the hall, where several boys were drinking from the water fountain. "Hi," said Bradley, looking up from the spout, water dripping from his lips onto the front of his plaid flannel shirt. He wiped his mouth with the back of his hand and moved away with an embarrassed smile. "Your turn."

Suddenly Matt pushed ahead, sneezed on the spout, and began to laugh.

"Gross." Opal backed away in disgust. "Now you know

why I always say date older, Ally." Opal offered me her half-filled water bottle. "It's a petri dish of bacteria on that fountain."

After we returned to the auditorium, the rest of the rehearsal was a joke compared to the Pre-College Symphony at Juilliard. The orchestra read through the second part of the program like they were speed dating. Half of them weren't in tune with the choir. And the altos sounded just awful. My cat could sing better.

As everyone was packing up their music and instruments, Bradley came over. "Sorry about the Matt thing earlier. By the way, you sounded great."

"Oh, thanks. Mr. Block wants me to do a solo."

"A solo?" he asked with a cute grin. "Let's hear one."

I looked around uneasily and didn't budge.

"Go on. Hardly anyone's here."

I composed myself, closing my eyes, then opening them, and my fingers began to glide across the keys. When I was done, the room was still. From the back of the auditorium came a burst of applause and a few stray whistles. Bradley was clapping the loudest, and I felt all warm inside.

"Want to go for a slice?" he asked.

"A slice?" I asked, distracted, gathering my choral music. "Of what?"

"Bread." He widened his eyes. "The kind with tomato sauce, cheese, meatballs or sausage. They call it pizza in some parts of Italy. Even some parts of the United States."

"Oh, *that* kind of slice. But it's nearly five-thirty."

He glanced over at the clock in the auditorium, like,

*Okay,* and I glanced at him back, like, *Not okay, I've gotta practice.* He gave me such a sweet smile.

"I should call home first."

I called my parents and heard the answering machine. *This is Elana Marduvian,* said my mother in a deeply serious operatic voice as my father added cheerfully, *And Douglas Katz. We're out on a gig or rehearsing, so please leave a message when you hear the C major chord.*

"Hi, it's me," I said to no one. "I'll be home soon."

"Need a chaperone?" Opal asked as we headed down the steps.

"No," I said adamantly.

"Is this your first official date?" she whispered in my ear.

"Get lost, Opal," I whispered back, giving her a jab.

"Playing the field? What about the sax guy?"

I gave her a look.

"To quote one of my mother's old record albums, 'If you can't be with the one you love, love the one you're with.'"

"Opal, it's just pizza."

"You hardly ever do just pizza. You were a wreck, I recall, about taking time for one measly choir rehearsal."

"Maybe it's time to make the time?"

"Maybe someone's getting a wee bit feisty?"

"Maybe someone is," I declared.

Opal waved as she headed to the subway station to catch a train downtown and mouthed, "Have fun!"

As Bradley and I walked to Ray's Pizza a couple of blocks away, he asked, "How long have you been playing the piano?"

"Since as long as I can remember. Too long."

"How long is long?" he persisted.

"I started at four. When I was six, I began Juilliard."

"Phew. That's a long time."

"I know. If you start later, like ten, you're over the hill."

"You're kidding me."

"I'm serious. Nine or ten's late."

"You must be committed."

"How do you mean that?" I joked.

Bradley shook his head. "You must have been amazing to be accepted so young."

"I'm okay."

"I heard you today. You're more than okay."

I gave him an awkward smile. Yeah, I was more than okay. But everyone wants to be the best. Including me. And since I wasn't the best, and wasn't sure if I would be someday, even with more practice, I didn't know how that sat with me.

He opened the door to Ray's. Steam clouded the plate-glass window. Beads of water trickled onto the speckled linoleum floor. "How's it going?" said a short stocky man tossing dough in the air like a whirling dervish. "What'll it be?"

"Should we get a pie?" Bradley asked.

I pulled a lone five-dollar bill from my pocket.

"I have money," he offered.

"That's okay," I insisted. "A slice will be fine, Bradley."

"Three slices to stay. One with spinach," he ordered. "And it's Brad."

I smiled at him.

"Any soda?"

"A water . . . Brad," I added.

"Bread and water? Hmm. You haven't been in prison lately, have you?"

We slid into a red vinyl booth, the rips in the seat mended with duct tape, and sat opposite each other, our knees barely touching, waiting for our pizza to heat in the huge oven.

"Not the kind with bars."

"What kind, then?"

"My own." I took in a breath, wondering why that had slipped out.

He gave me a curious look. "What are you talking about?"

"Nothing," I said.

"It didn't sound like nothing."

I sighed, hoping he would let it go.

"No, really, what did you mean by that?"

"I think you're as stubborn as me, so I guess I'll have to answer you."

He smiled.

"Lots of kids I know have careers by my age."

"Really?"

"Even younger. They play with huge orchestras. Have managers and agents dealing with recording contracts and bookings."

"That's heavy."

"If you don't have a career or are not going after one, you're not a rising star."

"Does everyone have to be a star?"

"Yes. Or at least everyone has to try to *become* one—a soloist."

"Can't you just do it because you want to? Isn't that enough?"

I laughed. "Then you're just another kid with some talent. It's hard for you to understand unless you're actually *in* Juilliard."

"You must really love music if you've put in all those years."

I blurted out, "I'm not so sure anymore." I twisted the end of a paper-straw wrapper. "I never have free time. I'm afraid to tell my parents I'm thinking of giving it up."

"You can't tell them? They're your parents."

"You don't get it. They'd *never* understand. Their whole life is tied up with music. That's what my family does. It's our family business."

He smiled slightly. "I get that."

I looked into his eyes. "It would crush them. Especially my mother." My voice lowered. "I bet if you were in my situation, your mother would feel let down, too."

"She passed away two years ago."

I felt awful for what I had said. "I'm sorry." I didn't know what else to say.

"We used to live in upstate New York. My parents rented a few acres, did organic farming. Dad would come in on Saturdays to the city and sell his produce at the Greenmarket over on Union Square. He couldn't stay up there after Mom was gone."

Brad drifted, looking out the window at passersby. He remained quiet. So did I.

"After she died," he went on, "I went to live with her

younger sister in Idaho. She's head of a peace coalition. My uncle's an environmentalist who hunts."

"You don't say." I gave him a mischievous smile.

He smiled back. "Tell me about it. They serve moose burgers for dinner and have a moose head on their dining room wall."

I made a face. "Something he killed?"

Brad nodded. "I missed my father more than ever. Especially his cooking."

I understood what it was like to miss a father.

"When my dad got back on his feet here in the Big Apple, I came to live with him. He took out a loan and started his dream restaurant. When he was younger, he had been a line cook, a grill cook, and then a head chef, so he opened a small place in East Harlem, nothing fancy, and renamed it Frisée. That's frilly lettuce that looks like it had a bad hair day. We live right above the restaurant. His food's delicious because he only uses stuff grown locally, like he grew on our farm. Now he does it all. The meals. Desserts. And taking care of me."

"Everyone needs someone to take care of them."

Brad wiped his eyes. He wasn't crying, but still, they were moist.

I handed him a napkin and he rubbed his eyes. "Guess we're not strangers anymore."

"Guess not."

"My mom was the person I talked to." He bounced one of his legs nervously in place, jangling the keys in his pocket. "Tell your mother about the piano."

"I can't." The words lingered in my throat.

Much to my relief, the pizza maker called us over to get our slices.

When we sat back down in the booth, I asked him, "Do you have something you like to do more than anything else?"

"Kind of, but I usually work after school. Today's my day off."

"What do you do? Besides dog walking," I teased.

"I read to this old woman who's losing her eyesight. Get her mail, the newspaper, prescriptions at the pharmacy. Sometimes I go shopping for her. Take out the garbage. Borrow audiobooks from the library. And, as you've seen, walk her dog. Small stuff for me. Big stuff for her. I put in a few hours every day after school. And I also work in my father's place on the weekends. I do prep work when I'm not mopping up. I dice onions, shallots, garlic—anything in my path—into teeny pieces."

"I'll have to watch out for my fingers."

Brad laughed. "He's going to teach me how to do sauces and bake French tarts. I know this sounds crazy, but I love old copper pots, whisks, battered wooden spoons, iron skillets, you name it. I can't get enough. It takes me somewhere else." When he talked about cooking, his eyes twinkled and he looked happy again.

"I know exactly what you mean." I thought of the prelude.

"You should come sometime." He sprinkled red pepper flakes on his second slice.

"I'd like that. It would be fun seeing the restaurant."

"It would be." His face lit up. "Food's a lot like music."

"How's that?" I tilted my head midbite, the cheese oozing off.

"If you don't start out with good ingredients, you don't get good results."

"So you need a really fresh egg to make a great omelet."

"Exactly." He grinned. "Of course, a few herbs couldn't hurt."

*What herbs could I bring to my music to make it great?*

The phone was ringing when I got home, and I ran to pick it up. Opal was at the other end. "What's the skinny on your first date?"

"*Date?* Opal, we just ate. And talked."

"About what?" she pressed on.

"Tell you later. Gotta go. I haven't practiced today yet." I quickly hung up, hearing my mother's high heels clicking across the parquet floor.

She stood with her hands on her hips. "Where were you?"

"Out."

She looked at me as if to say, *I knew that.* "It's way past seven."

"Orchestra rehearsal."

"Orchestra rehearsal? You play the piano. What orchestra?"

"School. I told you last fall that I'm playing in the choir concert this spring."

"But did you tell me you were coming home late tonight?" my mother asked.

"I left a message on the answering machine. Check if you don't believe me."

She gazed over at the blinking red light on the machine. "All right, but don't let it get in the way of your real music."

"What does that mean, my 'real' music? We're not making music in school?"

"You know what I mean. You've got a recital in May to prepare for."

"You sound like Miss Pringle."

Mom gave me a look as she picked up the mail. "And it's Wednesday. You have another lesson coming up on Saturday."

"Remember, I'm taking the SATs this Saturday. For the talent search for the Johns Hopkins program."

"In the morning, I thought. Your lesson's in the afternoon."

"I'm not sure how long the whole thing takes."

"Try not to miss your lesson or master class. You know you're not allowed a lot of time off from Pre-College."

"Okay, Mom. I know."

Opal's birthday party was Saturday around four, and I wouldn't miss that for anything.

"I realize you have a lot of interests. . . ." My mother's voice trailed off.

"If I do well on this SAT, my math teacher said I could go to their special institute in Baltimore this summer."

My mother accidentally dropped the mail on the floor. "What about the festival Miss Pringle's starting with a bunch of teachers from the piano and the string departments? It would give you time to concentrate without being pulled away by other things."

I stared blankly at her. "Like math?"

Everyone went where their music teachers went over the

summer. And my last three summers had gotten mixed reviews. My first year, age ten, I came home a week early with pneumonia, which got me away from the pyromaniac cellist whose mission, it seemed, was to cast me in *Lord of the Flies* because I was the youngest. The next year, I had fun hanging out with no parents around, but when it got hot and sticky and we had to practice all day in un-air-conditioned sheds with moths and spiders and the pool got coated with algae, the fun wore off. All that was left was Ping-Pong. At twelve, I began to think maybe there were other things in life besides just piano. And now that I was turning thirteen, I knew there were.

"Let's see how you do," my mother said noncommittally. "Did you eat?"

"I had something. I'm not hungry. I'll just practice."

After I was done, I headed upstairs and studied the SAT prep review until I went to sleep with logarithms dancing in my head. I had barely practiced—only two hours to stay in shape—because I knew I'd be skipping my lesson and master class.

The following day, I cut gym and health and went home early. Sometimes the principal let me do that before a big concert. So it wasn't totally out of line that the school might think I was preparing for one now, which in fact I was. When I opened the door to our brownstone, I heard Grandma chanting "om" to the sounds of a bell ringing. Unless she had a Tibetan monk with a gong stored in the basement, I figured it was on one of her meditation tapes. I guess she liked to practice ahead of time, too. Thursday evening she had a beginners' class in yoga and always came home smelling of incense. I snickered to myself, thinking of her in activewear on her yoga mat, as I slunk upstairs like our cat and got out of my school uniform. I spread my math textbooks all over my bed and didn't leave the room or even answer Opal when she sent me a text.

Grandma brought me a sandwich before she left for her yoga class, and threw me a kiss. "Don't work too hard."

Dad was probably at some rehearsal. I barely looked at anything other than the sample tests online until I sensed my mother standing in my doorway. "What?" I looked up from my laptop.

"Did you practice yet today?"

"I'm studying for Saturday. Am I allowed?" I said sarcastically, and began to stare back at the screen, reviewing some equations. "Can I have a little privacy?"

She came toward me and I tried to act busy. Then she kissed the top of my head, pressing her lips against my forehead. Her kiss felt different from Dad's or Grandma's or anyone else's. We were connected like one of Dad's violin strings—thin, unbreakable, unless you cut it with a sharp knife. But after a while those strings frayed and tore.

Friday morning Brad caught up with me before homeroom. "How's it going?"

"Going. I'm taking the SATs tomorrow."

"For that science thing?"

"Math," I replied. "Luckily, we don't have to do the writing part."

"You like math? I'm really bad in it. I'd rather cook."

"I love it," I admitted. "The problems are like figuring out a difficult piano piece."

"They say math and music are linked on the same side of the brain."

"Yes, they do. But you also need math to cook," I said.

"Not higher mathematics. No one has to know calculus to make a meat loaf."

"But if you measure the ingredients wrong, it could taste like a bowling ball."

"I've made a couple of those. One fell on my toe and almost broke it."

We both laughed as the second bell rang and we parted.

The day seemed to drag on. My body was in class; my mind was elsewhere. Opal said at the end of the last period, "Earth to Ally. Are you receiving?"

"All circuits are on overload."

Without saying a word, she nodded, understanding where I was at.

Opal tried last year with the PSAT but didn't make the cut. Her sister told her she was among the top 10 percent of dummies in the nation, but Opal said, "Does it test creativity? How would Picasso have done? Or the White Stripes?" Opal's favorite group. And when Ruby got a perfect score on her math and English SATs combined, Opal called her a nerd and informed her, "Albert Einstein didn't speak until he was three years old." To which Ruby replied, "Everyone and their uncle brings out that one to justify why their kid has the IQ of a cauliflower and the verbal skills of Jell-O."

"And," Opal continued on like a bulldozer, "he failed an

exam to become an electrical engineer, and couldn't even find a teaching job after graduation, so his father hooked him up in a Swiss patent office pushing papers."

"More like scribbling equations on his lunch hour, which became—what is that theory again? The quantum theory of light!" Ruby exclaimed. "Winning him the Nobel Prize in physics! So much for losers."

"My point exactly!" screamed Opal at the top of her lungs. "You just never know how some people turn out!"

I loved Opal's spunk. Now we hugged each other and she shouted, "Good luck! See you tomorrow after the exam?"

"Your birthday party trumps master class any day."

She crossed her heart with her forefinger. "I won't tell a soul."

"Not even if you're tortured?"

"Only under tickle torture."

And we both went to tickle each other, trying our hardest to cover our armpits.

When I got home, my parents were getting ready to perform, so it was just me and my grandmother. I knew she'd totally get that all I needed was to study and not practice. After I'd been cooped up in my bedroom for hours, she knocked at my door, then took me to her living room, which faced the backyard garden, where she had a small stone statue of a Buddha sitting on a bed of pebbles. It was almost pitch black inside, except for lit candles surrounding two yoga mats. "Sit," she ordered. "And breathe."

We both sat cross-legged. I tried to follow each pose she

got into while vocalists chanted "Hare Krishna, hare, hare" from the CD player in her bookcase. Before each position, she gave its name: "Downward dog . . . Halloween cat . . . cobra . . . pigeon . . . camel . . . fish."

"What's with all the animals?" I finally collapsed on the mat.

"Laying like a lox." She wiggled flat out like a fish out of water.

"Are you serious?" I asked, thinking of the salmon in the deli case at Zabar's.

From the expression on her face I knew she was teasing, and we both burst out laughing, holding our stomachs until we ached. When we came up for some air, she stayed on her back, holding the soles of her feet together and rocking back and forth like a newborn. "This position is called happy baby."

I imitated her until we both started giggling like crazy again.

"Or upward doofus baby," I added.

"Or downward diaper baby," she countered. "This session is disintegrating fast."

"And it's not very Zen-like."

Grandma sat up. "But I feel more relaxed. I'm in touch with the inner baby in me." We laughed together as we went into her tiny kitchen. As she opened her refrigerator, I noticed a Post-it that said: *Ally's recital, May 8, 4 p.m.* We had tea and two big bowls of lentil soup, with ice cream sundaes afterward at her counter. "Now get a good night's sleep and stop being such a worrywart."

So much for relaxation techniques. At one in the morning,

I got up with butterflies in my stomach. There are those who are test takers, and then there are those who aren't. And I was one of the latter.

Two sharpened number-two pencils were lined up on my school desk beside a brand-new white eraser and a backup pink one, ready to fill in the blank bubbles on the computerized sheets. I had a bottle of water, a packet of tissues, and some Life Savers. The name of the candy wasn't lost on me. My hands began to sweat even more than when I was playing the piano, so we're talking Niagara Falls here. I could hear the *thump thump* of my heart in my ears. Math and science geniuses from all over the city were doing this. *And why am I here again?*

So, with my pencil in hand, I began. My mind went blank. I glanced up at the large clock above the blackboard, the red second hand ticking, changing from seconds to minutes. Well, this felt familiar. And I was no Einstein.

People left early as I sweated it out to the very end. I was the last to finish. I couldn't have felt more relieved as I exited that test room. The nagging part was that I knew the butterflies hadn't ended with this one exam.

Opal's parents were artists who'd rented in a loft building in the Meatpacking District before lofts became fashionable. They had lived in their neighborhood back when the air reeked of slaughterhouses and carcasses hung in refrigerated trunks idling on cobblestone streets. Opal's mom said that platforms once mounted with sides of beef now held sculptures and paintings or were entrances to clothing stores and spas no artist could afford. Opal called it "Hollywood on the Hudson."

I pressed the outside intercom, then waited for the buzzer at the glass door. When I got inside, I took the freight elevator up to the top floor and slid open the elevator door. I walked into a cavernous space without any walls. There were huge white columns and a high ceiling of dark wooden beams. Opal's father had built a staircase to a porch-like second floor hanging over the living room. To the ceiling he had attached a swing that skimmed a rug Opal's mother had made on a loom. On a long flea-market worktable Opal's mom wove tiny wall hangings, which she cleared off each day so they could eat their meals at night. Today, friends and family stood around it, munching crackers and cheese and guacamole.

Opal had invited the entire homeroom class. She was off in the corner with Brad, and they waved me over. I handed her a package wrapped in tangerine origami paper tied with a silver thread. She hollered over the noise, "Ally, you shouldn't have!"

"A best friend can't come empty-handed to a birthday party!"

"You being my best friend is enough of a gift."

We both stuck our fingers down our throats in a gagging gesture.

Before Opal had a chance to open my present, a relative pulled her away to say hi to some cousin. She called over her shoulder, "I'll be right back!"

Brad smiled at me. "How did the test go?"

"I finished."

"That's something."

"Doing great on it is something."

Someone turned up the music, and a bunch of our friends began to dance together in a group as Brad and I watched Opal join them. He began to talk, and I leaned in closer, hardly able to hear him. "Do you want to go up on the roof?" I shouted above the band.

"What?" Brad shouted back over the volume of the bass drums.

I gave him a big smile, tugging his arm. "Follow me."

We passed through the busy kitchen to a steep staircase that led to the roof of the building. Green plastic grass covered part of the blacktop. Geraniums cascaded from terracotta urns. Brad and I walked underneath a trellised arbor out to a narrow terrace the length of the building. We stood by a railing at the edge. I couldn't look down since I was afraid of heights, so I glanced straight ahead over the decks and water towers dotting other rooftops.

"Have you said anything to your parents yet?" he asked.

"About what?" I pretended I didn't know.

"About maybe quitting."

I shook my head.

"Why not?"

"Because."

"Because?"

"Because I said so." When those words slipped out of my mouth, I realized I didn't want to be pushed by one more person in the world.

"Sorry, I was just asking." He put his hands up like he was backing off.

"I'm waiting for the right time. They don't even know I'm here missing my lesson and master class."

"When's the right time?"

"I don't know. I don't know what I want. Sometimes I just want to be left alone with my piano, with no one judging me. No one saying I'm good or bad or need work. I want to be doing it just for me."

Brad took my hand and led me away from the terrace to another section of the roof with a glass greenhouse that didn't have any houseplants. There was a heater with a single bed and several throw pillows Opal's mother had made. A bird's nest, pieces of driftwood, shells, antique bottles the color of beach glass smoothed by the sea, crocks jammed with brushes, colored pencils, and pens were scattered on shelves. Wicker baskets on the shabby desk held watercolor pads.

Across from the greenhouse was a grill where Ruby was cooking marinated zucchini and yellow squash while Eric flipped Tofu Pups and chickpea burgers. She waved a hot dog in the air. Brad and I made our way over to her as she squealed, "I got in!" nearly dumping bowls of coleslaw and pickles and a bag of buns onto the roof deck. "And so did Eric!"

"Except you'll be in New Haven and I'll be in Ithaca," he said wistfully.

All I could think of was that this was the best birthday gift Opal could have. She'd no longer have to hear about so-and-so's GPA and who was a tenth of a point ahead of Ruby. But more important, maybe she'd begin to shine with Ruby gone next fall.

"That's great!" I told them, popping a sweet potato chip into my mouth.

"Yeah," Brad added. "That's big. I'd like to go to the CIA."

"A lot of people from Yale work for the Central Intelligence Agency," said Ruby.

"The Culinary Institute of America," Brad corrected her bashfully.

"Oh." Ruby handed him the spatula. "Then maybe *you* should be doing this?"

Eric pulled it back, pressing the grilled vegetables as flames began to flare.

Opal came upstairs wearing the necklace I'd gotten her in a thrift store over on Columbus Avenue. "It's *so* fifties!" She fingered the little "diamond" heart.

"I knew the moment I saw it, it was *so* you."

After we ate, we went downstairs. Opal's parents started to sing "Happy Birthday," and everyone joined in. Opal blew out the candles on the sheet cake, handing each candle to Ruby, then cut the cake. I couldn't help noticing that written in blue on the vanilla icing was *Happy Birthday Opal* and the outline of a bulldog—Handsome Dan, the mascot of Yale—with *Go Yalie!* in a bubble like a comic strip. A double celebration.

"Can you bake a cake?" I whispered to Brad.

"Sure. Why?"

"Because everyone deserves their own party."

He squeezed my hand. "Everybody does."

When things began to wind down, Opal opened her

presents as Ruby listed who'd given what. Then Opal's parents and sister, along with Eric, started to clean up. When Opal tried to help, her mom protested, "It's your birthday. We'll do it." So Opal waved good-bye, allowing Brad and me to pull her away. We took the subway uptown to 104th Street, where Brad lived.

Loud Latin music echoed from apartments with smells of spicy cooking wafting out onto the street. Neighbors on webbed plastic beach chairs chatted by front stoops while others played dominoes in a pocket park.

Brad brought us through an unmarked door of a small four-story brick building into his father's restaurant. The place wasn't crowded in the front, but out back past the kitchen was a slate patio and an outdoor heater with some couples scattered around little tables. Ivy climbed a chain-link fence at the end of the garden by a small stone fountain.

"Oh, good." Mr. Clark wiped sweat from his brow. "You're here for the dinner rush." He handed Brad an apron smudged with sauce.

Opal and I exchanged looks. Then she jumped right in. "Do you have any extra aprons?"

Brad shook his head, but Mr. Clark grinned and began to search in the lockers where waiters and cooks kept their things. He handed us two extra aprons.

"But it's your birthday," Brad said as he grabbed Opal's apron back from her.

"Think of it as a performance piece," said Opal. "And we are the stars!"

I tied the starched white apron around my waist. Brad

diced carrots while Opal and I filled bread baskets and water glasses. Brad's father looked pleased, especially with Opal, who was working like she was born for the task. As the evening wound down and customers lingered, the three of us flopped onto stools in the kitchen, but it was a good tired.

Brad pulled out a well-used cookbook smudged in gravy and icing. A note was tucked in a page with a recipe: *This is my favorite cake even though it comes out lopsided every time I make it.* He lined up the ingredients. Meanwhile, Opal put on a CD she found in a stack on the butcher-block top and began to dance with her hands in the air to the screeching hypnotic beat of a synthesizer. My ears nearly blew off when she slid in 50 Cent, blasting it over the grind of the electric mixer frothing egg whites. We danced and baked at the same time. I had a feeling that Mr. Clark would have preferred a Puccini opera, but he took it good-naturedly.

As the cake layers baked in their round metal tins, I saw Brad touch the recipe. Was he remembering baking this with his mom on one of his birthdays, or hers, or his dad's, in a warm kitchen that smelled of orange zest and cinnamon? I could count on one hand the number of times I had baked with my mother, and I never had with my father. Brad's eyes welled with tears. I touched his arm. Opal being Opal, she flicked some coconut flakes onto his cheek. When he didn't respond, she stuck her forefinger in the icing and put a dab on his nose. This time he wiped it off, licking his finger. Unable to resist a taste of good icing, I began to lick the whisk, and Opal took the wooden spoon. Mr. Clark, who was out front

64

schmoozing with the customers, came back when the cake was done, and we iced it. Brad topped it with fifteen candles—one for good luck. The moist layers were still warm, causing the frosting and candles to slide every which way, but Opal got a chance to make her very own wish and blow them out without sharing the limelight. The only thing she did share was the cake.

As we waited for the train to pull into the station, Opal nudged me with her elbow as two old women came toward us on the platform. One was wheeling the other in a wheelchair. When the train arrived, they switched places! The one who'd been pushing sat down, and the other one began to wheel her inside the subway car.

"That's us when we're old. You'll take me to a museum," said Opal.

"And you'll take me to a concert," I replied.

Opal put her arms around me. We hugged each other as the train doors closed.

I hoped my birthday in June was as wonderful. The one where I'd hear Mom sing.

When I got home, my mother was pacing the living room floor, her eyes looking wild. "Where were you? You didn't call. I've told you to at least call."

"I'm sorry." I glanced over at my father, who didn't seem too happy, either.

And Grandma gave me a look that said, *Ally, you should have called.*

"I forgot. Sorry," I reiterated. "Things were running late."

"Things? What things? I called Hannah's mother. Unfortunately, they weren't home. Neither was Miss Pringle. And no one was picking up in the office after six. I was beside myself!" She looked at me frantically. "You did this the day of your school choir rehearsal, too. You've got to let us know if you're going to be late."

"I wish you would stop telling me what to do!"

"All we're telling you is to act responsibly," said Dad.

"And this wasn't responsible behavior," added Mom. "This is *really* late!"

I noticed the clock said way after ten.

"Your parents love you," said Grandma. "They were scared. We all were."

"I said I was sorry. I'll call next time," I grumbled, turning to head upstairs.

"Did you eat dinner?" Mom began to go toward the kitchen.

"I'm not hungry." I was stuffed from the party and all the cake and nibbles at the restaurant. I could have used a stomach pump more than a hot meal.

"Why don't you get ready for bed and come downstairs before you go to sleep?" Dad said.

When I came down in my pajamas, my parents were watching a black-and-white foreign film with subtitles. Mom's head was leaning on Dad's shoulder, and without saying a word he moved over on the couch to make room for me. I curled up between them. Mom offered me popcorn from a large ceramic bowl on her lap, and I took a few kernels in our silent peace agreement even though I was still full and had already brushed my teeth.

"So how was the SAT?" Mom questioned me.

"Hard. But I finished."

"And class today?" she asked between crunches.

"Master class went over." I looked the other way.

"Guess everyone's getting ready for their performances."

"Yeah, you know how it is," I said to her.

"I certainly do," my mother said, scooping another handful of popcorn.

"You know rehearsals and stuff can sometimes go on until ten."

"Yes, I know that, too. But that's usually on a Friday night, right?"

*Caught.* I smiled uncomfortably.

Why couldn't I tell Mom and Dad that I hadn't gone to class? That I'd gone to Opal's—and Brad's—instead? If only I could be honest and tell them. Why couldn't I say something as simple as that?

# May

Rhythm is something you either have or don't have,
but when you have it you have it all over.
—*Elvis Presley, singer*

Alex was jamming with a bunch of friends on the plaza near
Juilliard. His saxophone case was open, filled with crumpled
dollar bills and loose change. People stood around. The coolest
thing was hearing his group improvise. They were totally out
there. I'd never heard a sound like that before. Alex had
sound in his soul. It showed as his long lean body swayed to
the wail of his saxophone during his solo riffs. The music
swallowed me up, tingling in every cell, every neuron, every
synapse. I never wanted the music to end. Because most of all,
I didn't want to stop watching Alex.

Bin-Yu, a violist from Shanghai, stood beside me,

spellbound. Miss Pringle walked by without even a glance as she headed toward the Juilliard lobby. She was too busy talking to another teacher who taught cello.

Alex gave a little wave in my direction. I was thrilled that he had even recognized me in the crowd. I was about to wave back when I saw that he was actually waving to a ballerina standing in a confident pose, not me. Her gauzy pale-pink skirt undulated gracefully in the breeze against her slim but muscular legs as she waved back at him.

Bin-Yu leaned over and whispered, "The hot new thing. A friend of mine who's in the ballet orchestra asked her out, but she blew him off. He told me she's already been invited to be part of American Ballet Theater next year, with a one-year contract into the full ballet corps, because she won a gold medal in a competition."

*Flavor of the day.* I sighed. I couldn't compete in *anything.*

"How old is she?"

"Seventeen, I guess. I heard the competition's for dancers ages seventeen to twenty-four."

I felt disappointed. Deeply, deeply disappointed.

Once they began to play again, I watched him watch her when he looked up from his sax. Before the set ended, she motioned good-bye, probably rushing off for some *pas de deux.* Shortly after that Alex stopped; I still put a dollar in his case.

"Come on." He tried to shove the money back into my hand.

But I shoved it back. "You guys were great."

The slight touch of his fingers on mine sent quivers down my spine.

"When I hear you play in public, I'll give you some change in the tip jar."

"Yeah, the next time I play piano in a cocktail bar," I said.

"That should be in a couple of years, right?" he teased me.

What did he mean by that—"a couple of years"? Was he telling me I was young and out of his league? Or maybe I was being overly sensitive, hanging on his every word.

"See you around," he said as we walked inside the lobby.

"Don't know about that. I'll be stuck in a practice room for the next few weeks. Got my jury."

"Oh, yeah. My string and percussion friends are on overload right now, preparing."

"You could say that."

Alex put his hand on my shoulder, and I felt another flutter. "Be strong."

If only.

Morning classes seemed to slide into the afternoon, and at the end of chamber music rehearsal I asked our coach, "Would you ever consider having us play original pieces?"

The bassist paused as she packed up her bass. "Mozart wasn't original?"

"You mean like new music?" the violist asked.

"Well, y-yes," I stammered.

"Who did you have in mind?" asked our coach. "Philip Glass? I know he has written ensemble work, but a quintet? For our instruments? I'd have to look into that."

"I don't know if I could play modern music," the violist said doubtfully. "I'm used to romantic and classical composers."

"What about Aaron Copland? You play him," the bassist said to the violist.

*Here it comes. The musicians' version of sports. Instead of fighting over a stupid ball, they're going head-to-head over who's better: Beethoven or Mozart? Copland or Stravinsky? It's like talking about apples and oranges.*

"Never mind." I began to pack up my chamber music. "It was just an idea."

Our coach tapped me on the shoulder. "Whose music were you thinking of?"

I hesitated. "Mine."

"Have you worked out the parts for everyone in the group?"

"Not yet. I started to."

"I'd like to see it when you're done." She smiled at me. "Consider it your first commission. Whenever you complete it. Take your time. Even if it's next year."

I smiled at the music coach, then rushed to Dr. Rashad's classroom.

"I got my first commissioned piece!" I cried out to him as he was waiting by the door welcoming students as they toppled into the room.

"Congratulations!" he exclaimed.

I showed him the scribbling of my piece on the brown paper towel I had used in school, and how I was working out

71

the notes on proper sheet music paper. I waited for a response as he looked over all the parts. Then a smile broke out on his face. "There's a famous modern composer who teaches here on the graduate level. He doesn't start with his compositions on a musical staff. He uses a marker on unlined paper." I grinned at this. "Then he graphs the flow of the music."

"Like in math?"

"More like how an architect thinks of a building. Starting first with the plans."

"Not the mortar and bricks."

"Exactly. Of course, you need to have a foundation. The same applies to music." He paused. "The Beatles didn't really know how to write music, yet look at what they left us—all those great songs. Many composers know a melody, but they have to learn how to flesh it out with the instruments of the orchestra."

"I'd settle for a quintet."

"Then you have to learn how to write a manuscript. The dynamics. With the right instrumentation. And learn to transform these simple notes you put down into something with color and expression, so that the spirit of the melody comes through in an inspired form. You have to learn how to be a good orchestrator if you want to be a composer."

"Will you show me how?"

"I'm happy to show any young composer how to reach her potential."

I smiled to myself. He actually called me a composer.

My next class, solfège, was canceled, so I used the time to

practice before master class, because Miss Pringle always picked on the people whose recitals were coming up. Master class was beginning by the time I slid into a seat. Roberto, a junior in high school, announced he was going to do three movements of a Haydn sonata, an étude, and a transcription by Franz Liszt of a Wagner piece from the opera *Tristan and Isolde*. My mother would have loved hearing that.

Miss Pringle cut him short. "Next time you play for someone, Mr. Laurence, even if it's in master class, wear a sport jacket or a suit. I want you to know what it feels like to perform professionally, when you'll be wearing a tuxedo." She flashed a little smile. "So come back next week with a bow tie at the very least."

What if Roberto didn't own a sport jacket or suit? A tuxedo cost money to rent. And who wore a bow tie other than a professor or weirdo? What difference did it make if someone wore a suit or not? Wasn't it the playing that counted?

The next boy dropped his stack of music on the floor as he got up from the bench. "Play again next time *without* the music." She made a tsking sound, shaking her head as he scrambled to pick up the music and reorganize it. Then in a sweet voice she addressed Aya, a girl much younger than all of us, whose mother had dragged her halfway across the world from Tokyo. "Do you have the first movement of the Beethoven piano concerto ready for me?"

Her mother bowed her head slightly with a bashful smile. "*Hai.* Yes."

"Lovely." Miss Pringle beamed as Aya's mother straightened

the bow on her daughter's ruffled organza dress. With a gentle grin and light touch, she edged her child toward the piano, again half bowing her head to Miss Pringle.

"Just what we need," whispered Hannah, "another eight-year-old prodigy. She won a bronze medal last week in Houston. And another one in Dallas two days later."

Aya aced the first movement and was getting ready to do the second one when Miss Pringle put up a hand to stop her, smiling, showing her it was enough.

I prayed I wasn't picked to go next.

Miss Pringle put down her little pad. "Anyone else have something for today?" She glared straight at me. "You have a recital next week. Let's hear some of yours."

My mother, father, and grandmother tiptoed in and sat in the back of the room next to Hannah's mother. *Oh, great.* Miss Pringle smiled at them. I couldn't look at anyone. Especially my family.

"Ally?" She put her hand out for my music, waiting for me to rise.

As I squeezed through the row, the door opened again. Eduardo was standing there alongside Alex. I thought I would die. What was Alex doing here? He glanced over at me, and I became paralyzed.

Miss Pringle gestured for me to sit down at the piano. "Go on, dear."

Each step to the front of the room felt like an arduous journey. I hadn't practiced enough this past week. I wiped my hands on my cotton Indian skirt. My mother cleared her throat, and I stopped. "Sorry," she said respectfully, "but wouldn't it sound better if the music stand was slipped off the piano? You don't really need it." Miss Pringle, who had my music on her lap, gave a nod of approval, and with Eduardo's help I slipped off the wooden shelf on top of the strings, putting it down off to the side. Then I began to play. Mom was right—it opened up the entire sound, making it richer, deeper, less muffled. My mind went out of the room, into the music, then back again as I finished.

After a noticeable beat of silence, Miss Pringle said as if she didn't know, though she had to have known, "Remind me, what else are you getting ready for the jury?"

"Of course the prelude. The Rachmaninoff. In C sharp minor. Opus three, number two. A Bach. And a Gershwin."

"A Gershwin? When did we add a Gershwin? That's not classical music." Her eyebrows furrowed. "Which one again?"

"*Rhapsody in Blue*," I said in a hushed tone. "We picked it out months ago. You're supposed to have a twentieth- or twenty-first-century composer."

"But that's so light and jazzy. That's not acceptable for a jury! What are we going to do about it at this late hour?" She grimaced and shook her head.

Where had she been during my lessons? Why hadn't she said something then?

"Oh, Allegra. Do something that shows technical skill."

"Gershwin's rhythm and fingering show a level of proficiency."

After I played, she said, "The Rachmaninoff needs work. The Bach's coming along. The Chopin," she sighed, "well,

75

you've got that down now. You should; didn't you begin that last year?"

My cheeks became hot and flushed. I wanted to disappear.

Eduardo jumped up and grabbed my music from Miss Pringle. As he returned it to me, he whispered, "Coins, Ally. Coins."

I tried to eke out a smile, but it was hard. Really, really hard. I couldn't hear anyone else as they played during the rest of master class. All I could see was my mother's face. Disappointment? Sadness? Anger? All of the above? And at whom? *Me?*

At the end of class, the walk from Miss Pringle's studio to the elevators felt like eternity. As we waited for them to come up, my family was quiet. Eduardo broke away from a group of some kids, and Alex followed him. "You okay?" Eduardo asked me.

I sort of shrugged. "Yeah."

He patted my shoulder. "Breathe."

My father put out his hand to shake Alex's. "Are you in Pre-College, too?"

"I'm in the Jazz Studies program. Saxophone. I'm a good friend of this guy over here." He and Eduardo looked at each other and smiled.

"We come from the same country. Sometimes he fills in if we need a sax when I do a gig, especially at a wedding or bar mitzvah," Eduardo added.

"Oh. More Charlie Parker, John Coltrane, Wynton Marsalis," said my mother.

"Than Hindemith and Bach," Dad added with a chuckle. "Alto or tenor sax?"

"Both."

My parents looked impressed.

Grandma, who could fit her knowledge of music in a thimble, ignored their conversation. "Darling, you were fabulous!"

I stared downward.

When we got to the lobby, Eduardo whispered to me, "Ally, Miss Pringle is old school. That's the way she was taught, and she isn't going to change," while Alex said to my family, "Nice meeting all of you." Then Alex turned to me. "Your master class was a real eye-opener. Eduardo suggested I see what goes on in your famous teacher's class. Or should I say infamous? Try not to sweat it."

"Thanks for the support."

"Later." Alex bumped his fist against mine, like he had done with his friend.

"Later." I tried to grin.

As soon as my family was outside, my mother began to tear up. Was it because of me? Or a memory she had of her own master class? My father's interest had been caught by a poster for the Chamber Music Society as we passed the glass lobby of Alice Tully Hall, but when Mom started patting her eyes with a tissue, he must have noticed, and he put his arm around her, leading her away from the shadow of the imposing building. I watched my parents huddle together as they crossed the avenue, and it gave me a pang in my chest.

Grandma hooked her arm in mine. Now my eyes were filled with tears, big gloppy ones. We waited by the traffic light. She squeezed my hand. "This, too, will pass. Being a teenager is like having a long-lasting case of chicken pox, but eventually, after all the itching and scratching, it goes away, with maybe a scar or two left as a reminder."

"Aren't there vaccines now?" I wiped away my tears.

She inhaled. "Honey, there are no vaccines for adolescence. Or life in general. You just have to live it and learn along the way." Grandma patted my hand. "I'm still learning." She looked up at the sky, smiling. "What a night. The sky's so clear."

I stared at the constellations and then at my parents. *Why is it that the people who are supposed to be the closest to us are sometimes as far away as the stars?*

When we got home, I ran upstairs and took a long hot bath with lots of bubbles. After I got out, my mother was lingering in the hall outside. As I dried my hair with a towel, I could see that she looked pale.

"What?" I looked at her in the bathroom mirror.

"I can't watch again what I saw today." When she spoke, her voice faltered, and her breaths were uneven.

"And what was that?"

"You suffering."

"I'm sorry, Ma," I said, feeling guilt, although she seemed to be suffering, too.

"There's nothing for *you* to be sorry about." She put her hand to her chest.

Was this a good time for me to say, *I'm going to quit?*

"You know that girl Hannah in your class? Her mother called."

"Called *here?*" My voice went up, surprised.

"Yes, while you were in the tub. She doesn't like the way Miss Pringle treats some of her students. After the jury is over, she's seriously thinking of having Hannah switch teachers for next fall. Would you like to switch, too? I could look into it."

"Hannah's very talented. She *can* switch, easily."

"So are you, Ally."

"I don't want to audition for a new teacher and start all over."

"Who said you'd be starting all over again?"

"I'm used to Miss Pringle's methods."

"And what methods are those?" she asked with a small smile.

"Ma, you know how hard it is to go from one studio to another—fitting in a new lesson time at a reasonable hour. I know some kids who take theirs late at night. I'd also have to start with a new assistant teacher, with different kids in my master class. Everyone gossips. They'd want to know what happened after studying with Miss Pringle for six years."

I thought of what Opal had said to me, how I didn't notice or care about those things, but I did when it involved music. That was where it counted.

My mother looked at me. "Who cares what anyone thinks?"

What came out of my mouth surprised me. "I do."

* * *

Sunday morning, Opal came over to lend me one of her more fabulous outfits—her purple crepe dress—for my recital. When I put it on, it was short on me and swung lightly as I walked, but I felt as if I belonged in that dress—that I could stroll the entire length of Manhattan and everyone would turn and stare and say, *Who's that girl?* Still, I asked, "Should we lower the hem an inch or two?"

Opal checked me out as she lay on my bed surrounded by stuffed animals. "Hey, you look cool," she said admiringly, "like one of the Dixie Chicks. And they say and do exactly what they want. Leave it alone."

I went into my closet and took out a pair of tap shoes from Capezio, with delicate thin straps crisscrossing the ankles. "What do you think of these?"

"They're beige." Opal scrunched up her nose.

"So?"

"So, blah. I'm going to dye them mauve to match the dress." Opal put the shoes into her backpack.

"You're a born artist."

"Would ya say? When you're done wearing them, I'm using those babies."

"For what?"

"My next installation."

And we both giggled at the thought of Opal's new work of art: my heels.

After Opal left so I could practice, my mother passed by my room and saw the dress laid out on my bed. "What's this?"

"I decided not to buy a special outfit. It seems silly to get all bent out of shape over an hour of playing."

"Let me take you to some trendy boutique on Columbus. My treat!"

"The dress is Opal's. So in a way it will be new."

"Oh, Ally, you know I love Opal, but her taste is so . . ." She exhaled. "Way out."

"Ma." I rolled my eyes, which was becoming a habit. "It'll be fine."

"But you know how the other girls dress when they perform."

"Yeah, I do. They look like wedding cakes."

She cracked a smile.

"I'd worry more about how I sound than what I wear."

"What do you mean?" Mom eyed me nervously.

"You know exactly what I mean."

After a bunch of back-to-back lessons every day with Eduardo and Miss Pringle, I had my final extra lesson before my recital with Miss Pringle on Thursday afternoon after school. I had breakfast with Bach, lunch with Rachmaninoff and Chopin, and dinner with Gershwin. Nothing else was on my mind. Not school. Not food. Not sleep. I challenged myself until my fingers, wrists, neck, and shoulders ached.

"Let's go through the order of your program," Miss Pringle suggested when I finished playing through all the pieces. She had timed the length of each one, since we were allowed about an hour to perform our repertoire. I always went way over.

"I'm thinking of the Chopin first, then a Bach invention. Next the Rachmaninoff, topping off the program with the Gershwin—if that's okay, since I did prepare it."

She tightened her lips into a thin line. She had already commented on that one.

"Should I review Massenet's Meditation from the opera *Thaïs*? You always like us to have something prepared for an encore."

"I doubt there'll be enough time. Anyway, it's for violin, and so gushy."

"I love it. I did an arrangement for the piano from my father and mother's music. It's very short and moving. Like a lot of movie music."

"I wouldn't know. I don't have time to go to the cinema."

*Neither do I*, I thought. "A lot of movie music being written is wonderful. Mozart or Chopin might have been film composers if they'd lived today."

Miss Pringle made a face, but I knew Dr. Rashad would have agreed.

"Take off from school tomorrow and practice all day."

"But I have a math test in the morning."

"You need to prepare. I wish you were homeschooled like many of my students."

"I guess I could do a makeup test after the weekend," I mumbled. "I'm sure my mother would write me an absence note."

"Good. Then you can do the proper preparation."

This time I knew she was right. I wanted to do well in both. That night I e-mailed my friends as a reminder about my "gig" at Paul Hall, since I wasn't going to be in school on Friday: four o'clock Saturday afternoon. My mother and grandmother had asked a few people, and my dad had invited his quintet. Of course the people from my master class would be there—it was an unspoken expectation. There would be a reception in Miss Pringle's studio after the performance. Some parents did it up big at a restaurant or in the private catering space off the main cafeteria, inviting every family member down to aunts, uncles, and cousins. We kept it low-key. Mom preordered sushi trays. Grandma baked oatmeal and ginger cookies and cut up fruit for a platter. I offered to help, but she said, "I'm not taking any chances with those fingers!"

On Friday, my mother and father pretty much left me alone to practice, but every so often one of them would pass by the piano, grin slightly, and then continue on to another part of the brownstone. They didn't criticize or comment or make suggestions. It was too late for that. It was my time alone to put in the work.

The big day I woke up early, not feeling ready after an awful night's sleep—a virtual repeat of the SATs, watching the numbers tick by on the digital clock on my nightstand. By eight in the morning, the smell of fresh coffee was coming from the kitchen and I was already blow-drying my hair. Then I put on some blush and tied a black velvet ribbon with a crystal pendant dangling from it around my neck.

I skipped classes—it was allowed for warm-up. Mom carried Opal's dress across Broadway in a plastic garment bag while I carried my purple shoes that Opal had dropped off. I changed out of my jeans in the greenroom offstage. After I was dressed, Mom and Dad hugged me and my father handed me the ironed white handkerchief he used against the chin rest on his violin when he performed. It didn't seem to work too well; his red mark seemed raw, even darker. They left ten minutes before I was supposed to go on. "So you can get into your own head," whispered Dad.

"Break a leg!" Mom told me as a way of wishing me good luck. "No fingers!" She smiled at me, but I could see the tension behind her eyes.

I paced the room and kept wiping my hands on Dad's hanky. Then I heard a knock at the door and thought, *Who's this now?* When I didn't answer, Eduardo pushed it ajar, poked his head in, and handed me a slip of paper with a quote from Chopin: *Bach is like an astronomer who with the help of ciphers finds the most wonderful stars. Beethoven embraced the universe with his spirit. I do not climb so high. A long time ago I decided that my universe will be the soul and heart of man.* Before Eduardo closed the door, he said, "Climb high and never lose your soul. Promise?"

"Promise."

When he closed the door, I stepped out of the shoes Opal had painstakingly dyed, and slipped on my leather cowboy boots. No heels. No frill. No diamond hairpins. Just me. I don't know why exactly it was so important for me to do this, but it was. I had worked hard, eating, sleeping, and breathing my program. Maybe this was my way of saying to myself that I was not going to lose my soul. *This is who Ally is—the real me. Take it or leave it.*

I strutted out onto the stage thinking of the great perform-ers who'd walked across this stage in a similar moment. I saw Mrs. Young, in the audience, put her hand on Miss Pringle's forearm to hold her down in her seat. Miss Pringle looked as if she were going to have a heart attack. Roberto not wearing a tux paled in comparison to me looking as if I belonged in an all-girl band instead of at some stuffy recital. Was she going to drag me off? Make me strip? I had read about a female ensemble that performed nude. They were all over twenty-one and, I imagine, not particularly shy. (If I were in that group, I definitely would play the double bass. It's huge.) Then I looked at no one. All that mattered were the piano keys and the wonderfully dexter-ous fingers that had played on them recently before me—the future Chopins, Rachmaninoffs, and Bachs.

The entire performance was a blur—all I remember is that by the time I had gotten warmed up and begun to enjoy it, it was over. But I knew I'd played with more emotion than I'd ever realized I was capable of feeling. Was emotion the "herbs" Brad had talked about that day at the pizza place, giv-ing the music that something extra to make the composer's notes come alive?

Not everyone from master class had showed up. Still, at the reception, the important people were there: Dad's group, Mom's friends, and, most of all, mine.

I was shocked to see Alex strut through Miss Pringle's door, flash me a grin, and head straight toward me. My heart began to pound. "Hi," I said.

"Eduardo wanted me to let you know how sorry he is that

he couldn't make the performance. Right after he saw you, some family stuff came up—his grandmother. That's why he isn't here at the reception."

I hadn't realized Eduardo wasn't in the audience until now. "That's too bad."

"Well," Alex said, beginning to edge toward the door, "be happy it's over."

"*This* hurdle. Next is the jury."

"Any crime you committed I should know about?" he teased me.

I gave a little laugh. "You know this is like a warm-up for the jury."

He patted my shoulder. "You'll do fine." I felt his hand there.

Opal rushed to my side, smiling.

"Alex Sanchez," I said, "this is my friend Opal Rich. From school."

Opal looked as though she had been introduced to Prince Harry at high tea in Buckingham Palace. I had to pinch her even though she knew not to make a complete fool of herself. "He's as cute as an actor," she said, practically swooning, right after he left. "I take that back. Better."

"What's better than an actor?"

"Musicians." She giggled. "Musicians are real hot."

Brad was standing off to the side, watching us. I was about to go over to him when Hannah came over to congratulate me. A minute later I looked in the direction where Brad had been, and he was gone. Back to the restaurant? But he'd left a plate of cupcakes he had baked and a gift on the card table. I slipped his gift in my purse.

Miss Pringle was smiling as she bit into a pastry, but she never came up to me to say, *Ally, that was a great job*, or *Ally, good*, or even *Ally, that was a major improvement*. Nothing. Nothing at all. And she left before the reception was over. *What did I expect?*

At least my family gave me a thumbs-up.

Mom wove her way over to me. "Miles Davis once told Billie Holiday she didn't need any horns because she sounded like one. Well, that was you today."

"We're very proud of you. I'm glad you're my daughter. I think I'll keep you," my father joked as I groaned.

"D-a-d."

"I'm *kvelling*," Grandma told me, beaming.

Miss Pringle and Grandma were around the same age and lived only blocks from each other—eight, to be exact—but they were miles apart.

When the last person said good-bye, we packed up the empty platters and went home. Dad picked a dead vine off the clay pot out front. He and I hadn't planted the morning glories or pansies we usually did in the spring—he'd been too busy trying to get into summer festivals—and it was too late in the season for any seeds to take.

I played the disc of my performance, burned only hours before in the engineering lab above Paul Hall by a music technician. As I listened, I opened the square envelope that accompanied Brad's present and read the card:

*I'm glad we met and are in most of the same classes. Remember how we learned in science*

*about meteors—something that moves at*
*spectacular speed, a fiery streak in the sky*
*passing through the earth's atmosphere? Well,*
*you're like a shooting star.*

I wanted to fly uptown and say, *Don't say those things about me. I don't deserve them. Meteors light up the sky, but when they come down to earth, they are dull, ordinary rocks, almost nothing at all to look at.*

Instead, I tore open his gift—a book from a used-book store. The binding was worn leather, the title in gold foil with some letters missing. Its cream-colored pages were ragged at the edges. He must have saved up to buy it with the money he earned from helping out that old woman. *How many walks did that dog take for this? How many dinners did Brad have to make?* It was about Mozart's sister, a forgotten genius—the "other Mozart"—overshadowed by her brother, the child prodigy. I turned the pages, reading, as I hit replay over and over again, and somehow understood exactly how Mozart's sister must have felt. I cringed with each tiny mistake on the recording. There were only three off notes, but it felt like when I got pimples on my face—looming the size of mountains.

Hitting a single note that stings the air—a note that makes you flinch if you're in the audience, where you slink down in your seat, embarrassed for the person, but think at the same time, *That person sucks*—well, it's worse if you've actually *played* that note. The humiliation is off the charts. There wasn't a hole big enough for me to crawl into. Where was Opal's burlap sack when I needed it?

Eduardo canceled Tuesday's lesson. He left a message on our machine. "I'm so sorry I missed your recital, but I had to. Personal things. I got behind and have to rehearse for my own graduate school jury. I'm also helping out with the May auditions for the Pre-College Division. Heard you did fine. Actually, the word on the street is you did really well! Keep up the good work." His words filled me. I smiled, deciding I'd use the lesson time to go over the recording that had been made during my recital, so I didn't mess up in those spots for the jury.

At my next lesson, Miss Pringle plunked her tea-filled mug on her wobbly card table along with a cranberry muffin. "How do you think the recital went?"

I stared at her sullenly. "Okay, I guess."

"Let's look at this following week as an opportunity to do better. You played . . ." She stopped herself. "We need to turn up the heat so it's flawless."

*Is she calling me a failure because it wasn't perfect? I didn't butcher the recital. I made a couple of flubs. Not like that time in master class. She probably didn't want to praise me before the jury—afraid I'd get complacent. Confident. I could use a compliment. Or two.*

"Put in at least six hours a day. Eight, with breaks, if you can."

"I have school. It's near the end of the year. Papers. Tests."

"This is school, too, you know."

She said nothing about my outfit. Thank God.

I went only to the classes that I had to go to. Opal e-mailed me the homework. Otherwise, I left school early and came home to practice the rest of the day and evening. I missed a choir rehearsal with Mr. Block. The school orchestra could manage without me, bumbling their way along. I didn't let up until the day of my jury.

You want to play for the big honchos after lunch, when they are fed and happy. They're harder at the beginning, when they're all rested and have had their caffeine fix. At the end of the day, they are rushed, tired, and irritable, so it can go either way. I was fourth that day.

*Six teachers seated in a row. Now seven: one arrives late. My lucky number.*

*Seven pairs of eyes behind an extra-long cafeteria table covered with a linen tablecloth. We're in a classroom. Blank staves of music are lined on the blackboard waiting for notes and measures to be filled in next fall.*

*Cups of tea in white china cups. Not Styrofoam or paper. Silverware to stir.*

*An urn of coffee. The smell makes me nauseated.*

*A pitcher of ice water. Cubes pressing against each other. I'm thirsty.*

*Pencils, pads, sheets of paper for grading each student. Or comments.*

*There are four women. Miss Pringle sits at the end. Two over seventy, like her. Or are they eighty? I can't tell. One is wearing a hearing aid. A hearing aid? This isn't funny. The fourth is about forty. I've seen her around and heard she's a concert pianist. There are three men. One young. One middle-aged, a little older than my father. He smiles. Then there's a new teacher from a conservatory* in Moscow. His hair is wild—going every which way. He looks temperamental. I try to smile.

Miss Pringle can't score me because she's my teacher and has to act impartial. Instead she critiques my technique, expression, tonality, musicality. But she's here to judge me, same as they're judging me—and her. How I play reflects on how good a teacher she is. Even who your teacher is—how long they've been on the faculty—counts. Mom calls it a pecking order. So maybe Miss Pringle is nervous, too, about how she'll look in front of her colleagues. Mom also says, "It's politics," whatever that means. I guess it's like lunchtime, who gets to sit next to whom in the cafeteria— the popular group or the losers. Opal and I sit off together near the salad bar. Whispering in the corner.

I've practiced so many hours, weeks, months, years. Twenty minutes and it's over. Like when I auditioned. Twenty minutes! Done. My entire year judged. They know in two, maybe less. They've heard it all. All the biggies. Eduardo thinks I'm good. I can tell by the way he treats me. There are many people who are really good, but great? Can I become great?

What is greatness? How do you describe talent? I love nectarines. Opal loves cherries. Does that make one fruit better than the other? So how can anyone really be judged? Isn't it who's doing the judging of whom? It's so individual. And do "they" always know? I hate them scribbling away taking notes, some not even looking up at me, how my face changes at a phrase or chord. A teacher at the jury table swings her leg in a beat different from the one I am used to for the Rachmaninoff. Does she want to throw me off? So I won't do as well as her students? They do that, the teachers— competing against each other, too.

*Opal told me about a painter who lived long ago, Van Gogh. He died penniless. His work is worth millions and is in museums all over the world. I think of the composer Tchaikovsky, who did* The Nutcracker. *When his most famous violin concerto premiered—the one Dad loves to perform—the critics walked out. Tchaikovsky got so depressed he wanted to give up. And now every single student plays that piece as a rite of passage. The sound tugs at my heart when I hear violin students practicing it in the halls on Saturdays. I have to remember these stories so there's hope.*

When I came out, my parents eagerly rattled off questions.

"How did it go?" Mom asked.

"It seemed okay."

"Well, were they grinning or frowning?" She nearly jumped on me, probably having flashbacks to her own juries.

"Neither."

"Poker faces." Dad nodded to Mom, and she acknowledged his nod back.

"I hope I at least get a B."

"Let's pray for a better grade," my mother murmured, "than a B."

Other students were pacing the corridor outside examination rooms as I packed up the music that I had been practicing with before the jury. Doors opened and closed briskly, echoing blips of piano sonatas, fugues, preludes, concertos, intermezzos, or violin partitas and caprices with intricate double stops. Faces exited those rooms sad, happy, nervous, arrogant, or relieved. I felt nothing. Wiped out.

Suddenly a door flew open and Timothy Young's mother,

who'd had her ear pressed up against the door, nearly fell inside. Timothy came out, smiling broadly.

"They like you?" his mother asked impatiently, pouncing on him.

"They were all smiling," he told her as she bobbed her head, grinning.

"Ah, good. Good." She looked as if she had won the lottery.

"Of course they were smiling," I said, glancing over. "Your fly's open."

He quickly looked down, embarrassed, and zipped up his pressed black pants. "I was so scared, I had to pee right before the jury," he admitted, running in the direction of the bathroom again.

I felt bad I had said anything. Even Timothy Young, child genius, got scared.

# June

The musical universe is based upon mathematical
principles of harmony.
—Pythagoras, mathematician

The results of the SATs came before Memorial Day. Most parents were panting by the Internet, like Opal's when Ruby took hers a year ago last March, but not mine. I didn't tell them the date the results would come. June 1 was *my* deadline. Right before my birthday. Not because I did badly—because I did so well. I knew Mom would get freaked out about my confusion. *Do I do music or math over the summer?*

When I showed her my SAT scores along with the letter of acceptance from Johns Hopkins, she looked at me dumbfounded. Unlike my father, she didn't understand higher mathematics and had pledged after high school that she'd never take another course involving numbers as long as she lived. And she stuck to that decision, putting her all into becoming an opera singer. You still need to know some math if you don't want to get cheated at the supermarket, though.

"Well, that's wonderful."

I wondered if she meant it.

My father said, "You knocked it out of the ballpark."

I smiled modestly, looking from my mother to my father.

My algebra teacher, Ms. Johansen-Williams, flipped out when she heard I made it into the Johns Hopkins University Center for Talented Youth. It was the geek version of *American Idol*. "Top fifth percentile in the country!" she shouted with glee, then observed my lack of excitement. "What's up, Ally?"

"The piano. I do that every summer."

She tapped her pencil on a stack of blue exam booklets. "I've seen you at the school concerts. You're wonderful," she said with a smile. "Do you know Pythagoras? The Greek mathematician from about 500 B.C.?"

"My family used to have a cat named after him."

She nodded. "He said there are three types of music: ordinary music made by an instrument, unheard music made by each of us between our soul and body, and music made by the cosmos. To Pythagoras, the laws of music governed the universe. So an instrumentalist and the cosmos might sound the same note."

I thought of how my mind disappeared into both music and math.

Ms. Johansen-Williams got up from her desk, took a book off a shelf, *Music of the Spheres*, and read me a passage:

"Pythagoras's discovery of the arithmetical basis of the music intervals was not just the beginning of music theory; it was the beginning of science." She looked up at me. "The genius of the man was the way he joined both." She closed the book, handing it to me. "Keep it for as long as you want. I'm sure whatever you decide will be the right decision for you."

"I hope so. I just don't know what that is."

"Let your heart tell you. Go with your gut. Pythagoras changed the way we look at harmony. Harmony means agreement and peace. You'll find it."

A few days later, a manila envelope with my name was on the countertop by the rest of the mail—my music report card. Glaring at it, I poured a glass of milk and bit into a pretzel from the Ball jar next to the tea bags. *Procrastinating.* Another flash card word. I carefully began to lift the flap of the envelope without tearing the transcript, then paused; finally I ripped it open the rest of the way, like a Band-Aid off a wound.

> Composition A+
> Performance Forum A
> Solfège C+
> Music Theory A-
> Chamber Music A+
> Piano B
> Jury B+

I examined the computer printout, then folded it in thirds, placing it inside the envelope for my parents to see later.

I couldn't pretend it hadn't come; someone had left the mail there. I slipped the sheet out and looked at it a second time. Pre-College Division. Permanent record. Name. Student number. Birth date. Course. Grade. Piano, B. I felt numb. Jury, B+. Not even A-. I wanted to cry, but I didn't. Couldn't. I went to my room. Beethoven followed, purring, jumping on my bed, curling up in a ball beside me as I curled up in my own ball and fell asleep.

I woke up to Grandma's voice raised over my mother's. Were they fighting? "I don't care if she got into both programs. She should relax. Do nothing this summer! Music? Math? What's next? Brain surgery?"

"I don't think that's your choice to make," Mom said sternly.

"Nor yours," Grandma replied with a critical edge to her tone. "It's hers."

"I know that!" Mom hollered back. "You think I don't know that?"

"She rehearses Friday nights. Leaves here on Saturdays at the crack of dawn, staying in stuffy practice rooms till it gets dark, cooped up like a chicken in a henhouse. No window. No day or night. It's like Las Vegas in there!" Grandma grumbled. "A girl her age should have fresh air! She should go to the park. Meet a friend. Ride a bike!"

Of course, when Grandma said that, I thought, *What if I fall and break my hand?*

"When is she supposed to be a normal kid?" Grandma ranted on.

"I did it. So did your son!"

"And look where it got you!"

*Boy, that must have dropped a bomb.*

"Not everyone grows up to become a famous opera singer," said Mom.

*Here it comes*, I thought as my mother began to hyperventilate.

"That doesn't mean the passion is less. Maybe it's more, because there's all the struggle without the glory. That's a lot harder to do. And there's a lot of us doing it!"

"We're on the same side." Grandma lowered her voice. "Ally's."

"I know," my mother sniffled. "I know."

Then it got real quiet. I strained to hear them as I scratched Beethoven's tummy.

"I don't want Ally to feel this is an all-or-nothing decision like it was for me."

*Huh?*

"I realize she's interested in many things. The world's open to her. But when it comes down to it, we're alone. I hope music becomes a lifetime companion whether she makes it a profession or not. Music can be there as a friend," my mother continued.

"Not always. You of all people should know that. It can also let you down."

"Music never let me down. The business surrounding it did. And some of the people in it. The ride—actually *doing it*—is exciting," my mother challenged her.

*Except when you want to get off the ride. Right in the middle.*

I sank lower under my quilt, warm and protected.

*What should I do? For me. Not for anyone else.*

The answer that should have been easy wasn't.

Last New Year's Eve, right before midnight, Opal and I had tugged at both ends of party poppers wrapped in pink tissue paper. They made a loud bang. That's what I felt like—a party popper pulled at both ends, being torn apart.

When my father came home, late, he tucked me in. "Mom told me everything. You know Einstein was a violinist *and* a mathematician. Eventually he chose one. The same period in the early nineteen hundreds, Einstein's Theory of Relativity was published, Arnold Schoenberg, a composer, changed the laws of music with his twelve-tone atonal scale. His revolution in music was as profound as Einstein's was in physics. And they became good friends. Both broke down barriers in the way people think. So in a way, they did the same thing."

"I get your point. I still got a B," I whispered, as if I had gotten an F.

My father scooped me up in his arms. "You did your best. Isn't that enough?"

The next morning, just as I was logging on, Opal screamed into the phone, "Happy birthday, alligator!" I noticed on my computer screen she had copied the addresses from the e-mail that I'd sent to everyone announcing my recital and apparently had informed them it was my "special day." She'd also found Alex Sanchez's e-mail address and included him.

"I'm going to kill you, Opal Rich! Your fourteenth birthday might have been your last!"

As the day progressed, birthday greetings continued to arrive. Brad did one of those singing e-mails with red balloons all over the screen. Hannah wrote:

```
Getting u a T-shirt: I Survived
Solfège.
```

I sent:

```
Not a lot of people are going to get
that.
```

She answered:

```
I Survived Sight-Singing? Better?
```

Alex IM'd me:

```
What birthday is this one?
```

I didn't tell him my age in case he thought I was older. I IM'd him back:

```
What r u doing this summer?
```

He replied:

```
Seeing friends in Mexico. Playing
gigs. A wedding in Puebla. And u?
```

I answered him:

```
Big?
```


None of them could make my mother's performance that night at the Bloated Pig, a pub downtown, although Opal invited me to sleep over the following night. Mom said, "Sure," since I was finally free this Saturday. There was a part of me that was glad tonight was going to be just me and my mother.

As I sat alone at a tiny round table in the dark mahogany bar with bright red walls, a waitress wearing black fishnet stockings and a gold stud in one nostril plunked down a Diet Coke and a lemon wedge on a toothpick next to my napkin. "On the house," she said with a wink, lifting a generous plate of curly fries and a few pigs-in-blankets off a tray. "Anything else, give a holler." She swirled around to take orders from a bunch of hipsters at the next table who looked to be in their twenties.

More people came in as I nursed my drink through a straw. Some scruffy tech guys in a booth near the back were adjusting the sound level on the mixing board to my mother's voice while she tapped the microphone: "Hello? Hello? Can you hear me back there?"

On a small raised black stage, she sat on a stool under muted red and blue spotlights, which made her hair and skin glow like a movie star's. She wore gold hoop earrings and a simple tight-fitting brown sleeveless dress with a creamy leather belt that showed off her curves. Her stockings glittered when she crossed her legs. It was strange seeing my mother looking glamorous, not acting like a mom—nagging or reminding me to practice—but rather like a person out in the world.

There was a guy on acoustic guitar, an accompanist on keyboard, and a third in some sets on the fiddle. That's what she called it—not a violin—when she gestured and said, "And let's give a hand to Stephan on the fiddle." It was beat-up and scratched—different from my father's with its smooth dark orange-brown varnish.

Mom closed her eyes when the lights dimmed in the audience. She held on to the mike, singing from a deep place, letting down her guard. I looked around at the audience enjoying her set, their gazes fixed on her, and it filled me with pride that she was my mother. People stood in the back, the place packed to the bar. On the final song, when she hit a high note that was so clear it resonated throughout the room, I got goose bumps. She smiled brightly after the applause, took a sip of water, and did an encore song—a bluesy version of "Happy Birthday," real soft and slow. When she finished the last note, she headed straight toward me. I handed her a hanky from the small embroidered purse slung across my chest, the way Dad had so often done for me after a performance.

"Thanks, sweetie." She dabbed her brow.

"You were so cool, Ma."

She grinned as if I told her she had aced an aria in some opera. Then she took off her antique silver-and-turquoise bracelet and slipped it on my wrist. "Your father gave it to me on my opening night as Mimi in *La Bohème*. I wear it for good luck."

"Did you have good luck with it?"

She smiled without answering. "I want you to have good luck. Keep it."

"Are you sure?"

"I couldn't be surer."

I leaned over and gave her a hug. She briskly wiped the corner of her eye with the dry end of Dad's handkerchief. I felt so close to her, I almost told her how confused I was, but she looked so happy I couldn't. It was our night and I didn't want to spoil it.

When we returned after midnight, Dad was vegging out on the couch, surfing TV channels with the remote. His group had played in some church, Mozart's String Quintet no. 4 in G Minor and a piece by John Cage, a modern composer who said music was mathematical. Dad noticed the bracelet on my wrist.

"Is it okay? I know you gave it to Mom."

His brow wrinkled. "It's more than okay." He touched the turquoise stone. "Your wrist is like your mother's. Thin and delicate. It fits you both."

Grandma had baked a mocha-and-apricot layered birthday cake but was fast asleep downstairs. She'd left a note by the cake stand that said, *Eat!* So it was just my parents who sang softly to me in the kitchen at the butcher-block table. I blew out the candles, hoping a wish would come to me.

Saturday I took the train down to Opal's. I stopped in a market and picked up a brownie. As I walked over to Hudson, the sun felt delicious. Opal had once accused me of having a vampire thing going since I was hardly ever outside. Shielding my eyes from the glare, I thought, *The light! The light!* and laughed, but I didn't feel like a vampire today.

When I got to Opal's, she informed me, "Ruby the Rott-weiler was out late partying—a case of senioritis now that she's been accepted into college. You and I better head for the river, since she's snoring like crazy. I've poked so many springs in her mattress from the bottom bunk, it's amazing we're still speaking."

"I imagine you can hardly wait for her to leave."

"Then you can sleep over without us camping out on the living room floor."

"But I get the top bunk." I handed Opal half the brownie as we walked.

"Whatever." Opal took a humongous bite. "Guess who got in touch with me."

"Eric?"

"Are you serious? Eric Gagosian doesn't know I'm alive."

"So who?"

"Brad."

"Brad?" My voice went up an octave.

"Yeah, Brad."

"I didn't know you two talked."

Opal looked puzzled. "It's not like we don't talk. He was at my birthday party."

"I know that. Of course I know you talk in school. I don't mean *talk* talk. I mean outside of school. On the phone. Texting. Like that." I watched a sailboat go by on the Hudson River, avoiding her gaze.

"Sometimes, yeah."

"I didn't know that." I wondered if she was keeping anything from me.

"Now you do. It's not a big deal."

"What did he want?" I asked cautiously.

"To know if I was going to be around this summer."

"Really?" I said, thinking, *Really!*

"His father thought I was a great help the night of my birthday and asked if I wanted to work a day or two a week at the restaurant. Doing stuff like we did."

"Oh." I picked at an uneven stitch on my sweater. "So what did you say?"

"Duh. A job offer? I said yes. It'll pay for art supplies and extra lessons."

"That's nice," I said, but I felt hurt. Why hadn't he asked me?

As if Opal read my mind, she placed her hand on my arm. "Ally, I'm fourteen. I can get working papers. That's why they asked me and not you."

"Brad isn't fourteen yet."

"It's his father. Who's gonna know? The Department of Labor?"

"At least you've got a plan for the summer. I have to decide by this weekend."

"I bet you could work off the books with us even though you're underage."

The thought was tempting. Filling water glasses. Sweeping floors. Wiping tables. Rinsing dishes. A different kind of hard work.

Opal and I rented Rollerblades, headgear, and pads near Chelsea Piers. I wasn't going to worry about fingers or hands or wrists today.

"You look like some macho hockey player." She laughed at me.

"And you look like a marshmallow on steroids." I laughed back at her.

We could barely move, but we made an attempt on a path lined with tall reeds. Slight gusts of wind came off the river, cooling our cheeks. When Opal took off her helmet to rest, she adjusted a rhinestone barrette holding back her braid. She had put in a few highlights, and they shimmered in the sunlight like Rapunzel's gold.

"How does it feel to have no real plans this weekend?" Opal asked me.

"It feels great and weird at the same time. Great to be free. And weird to be free."

"No one's forcing you not to be free, except yourself."

"You're making it sound easy, and it's not. It's complicated."

"What's easy? Anything you love doing is hard work. But if you make the effort, there's a feeling inside like nothing else in the world. I'm happiest while I'm making art."

I looked at Opal. Was I happiest making music?

That night her mom made lasagna with a huge salad, and she surprised me with a cupcake decorated like a sunflower. "It looks like a Van Gogh painting!" Opal said with glee as Mrs. Rich put a candle on the top. I blew it out and made my decision about the summer.

While she and Opal's dad got ready for the movies, Opal teased them, "Don't stay out late!" which meant, *Don't come home too early!* Then we slipped into some of her fancier duds and went to a comedy festival across town. She had bought tickets for the first show, at seven-thirty.

While we waited on line, she said, "Do you like your surprise party?"

"I see you invited my closest friends." I gestured toward the line of strangers behind us on the sidewalk. As I turned around, I noticed Brad coming up the street. "Oh, you!" I gave Opal a gentle poke in the ribs.

She poked me back as Brad joined us. "Come on, we're the Three Amigos. Or **Three** Men in a Tub." Then Opal began to laugh with a snort.

106

"The Three Little Pigs?" I said.

Brad put in his two cents. "The Three Billy Goats Gruff."

"Goldilocks and the Three Bears," I chimed in.

"I thought you were good in math." Opal scrunched up her face as the line began to move. "That's four!"

When we got settled in our seats in the black-box theater, Brad handed me a small package. "What's this?"

"Don't get all excited; it's nothing big."

"Brad." My shoulders slumped, embarrassed. "*Another* present?"

My eyes widened as I opened the box. It was a portable metronome that I could tuck in a pocket. "This is perfect. I can take it with me this summer."

When I nudged him with my elbow to say thanks, his face shifted from happy to sad as the lights went out, and I heard him whisper, "Don't go."

And I whispered back, "I have to."

"I know," he said.

After the show, Brad headed uptown and Opal and I went to an Italian ice cream place around the corner.

"Do you like him or the sax guy more?"

"Opal!" I nearly dropped my lemon ice on the ground. I looked at my Italian ice and her gelato and motioned with my pink plastic spoon toward our paper cups. "Is one better than the other?"

"Tonight's definitely a gelato night," she informed me.

"There you go. And for me it's an ice night."

"But tomorrow could be gelato for you?" she asked.

"Maybe." I smiled. "I do like them both."

At the end of the weekend, I walked into my parents' bedroom. "I've made up my mind."

Mom put down the novel she was reading and patted the edge of the bed for me to come and sit down. Dad looked up from a score spread out on the quilt; it was a piece a friend had written for his group to perform during their summer tour. He seemed distracted, flipping a page. "About what?"

My mother put her hand over his sheet music. "The decision we were talking about earlier—what Ally should do this summer."

That got his full attention. "What's the verdict?"

I hesitated. "Music."

Smiling, he glanced over at my mother. "Settled."

My mother had no expression, which really unnerved me. "Ma? You're not happy with my choice?"

"If you're happy, I'm happy." Her eyes shifted away.

"You sure?" I asked her.

"I want it to be a good experience," she answered.

"We both want that," Dad jumped in.

"I can't promise anything. I hope it is," I said.

Then she put her hand on my wrist. "We could find you a teacher at Peabody Institute at Johns Hopkins. They've got one of the best music programs in the country, too. Then you could do music *and* math over the summer in the same place."

"I told you, I don't want to start with someone else."

"Sometimes fresh eyes can be . . ." She searched for the words. "A new vision."

I shook my head.

My mother's lips formed a straight line of concern. I knew the look. Guilt.

Ruby once lectured Opal and me, "Parents think we don't know what's going on inside them, but we know without them having to say a word. A lifted eyebrow. A syllable that goes up at the end of a sentence. Even silence says a lot." At the time, neither of us knew what she was talking about. Now I knew. I knew my mother was as confused as I was. "It'll be okay, Ma. Don't worry."

Mr. Block had us do three more choir rehearsals before the spring concert. Between end-of-the-year testing and who happened to gain possession of the auditorium for which period, fights broke out between the debating team coach and the health teacher, who liked showing dumb PowerPoint presentations. I tried not to fall into a coma when the lights went out. We were studying, for the eightieth time since elementary school, the unit called "Your Body and You." She handed out pamphlets titled *Getting to Know the Opposite Sex*. Was this my grandmother's generation? Even my mother wasn't this lame.

Neither of my parents had set up any gigs for the night of the concert, even though I told them they could. "It's no big deal," I kept insisting, but they ignored me.

Grandma snapped photos as I came into the living room wearing a yellow dress.

"Grandma!" I shouted, looking at the camera shots. "Erase them! I look awful."

"Look at that *shana punim*." She gently squeezed my face. "I want one of the three of you." We stood close together. The second I looked up at my parents, instead of straight ahead smiling, she took the picture. *"That's what I wanted."*

It was a warm night as we walked to my school. You'd think no one in Manhattan cooked because restaurants were overflowing with people eating outside at tables lining the sidewalks. It seemed as if the entire Upper West Side smelled of garlic and olive oil.

The steps to our school were so crowded it was difficult to get inside the building. As I went toward the entrance, I saw Opal's parents wave me over. I introduced them to my grandmother, again, and then to Brad's father, Mr. Clark.

"We're so glad to meet you!" Opal's mother shook his hand. "Opal's thrilled to be working part-time at your place this summer. Cooking can be so artistic."

Brad's father agreed, smiling. "It's a culinary art. I could use the extra pair of hands. I'm so tired lately, and Opal works like a beaver."

"We didn't know that about Opal. Our older daughter, Ruby, yes . . . but Opal?" Mr. Rich grinned.

I smiled uncomfortably at all of them. "Gotta run."

I didn't know why, but I still felt weird about Opal working there. *Or jealous?*

The concert went off with the string section doing their normal screeching—like chalk across a blackboard—and the winds were off-key. The percussionist lagged behind a beat or two on the drums. Right after intermission was my solo, the prelude. Mr. Block also featured a tenor—one grade ahead—in a short song, and a violist who made me think of the joke we had at Juilliard—a viola's got a bigger surface than a violin to

110

drool on. I was overwhelmed by the applause as I slipped off the piano bench, bowing and staring at my shoes. My family was by the center aisle in the middle of the auditorium—not too close or too far—clapping. Dad and Mom beamed while Grandma snapped enough pictures to fill albums for the next twenty years.

I waited for Opal backstage. She seemed involved with the choir, hugging and saying good-bye, so I headed for the nearest exit by some scenery when someone put their hand on the small of my back. I jerked away in karate mode. It was Brad.

"You scared the—" I broke off, staring into his eyes, which sparkled like gorgeous glass marbles—the kind that have swirls of blue and hazel and gray.

"You knocked their socks off."

"Oh, come on." I waved my hand dismissively. "It was okay."

"More than okay." And he gave me a kiss on the lips. My first kiss.

I felt a rush and got goose bumps. Not the scary kind. The good kind. His touch was tingly. A warm glow spread over me, and without thinking I kissed him back. A spotlight streamed down onto us, almost like the moon, in the half darkness, as I leaned against a set of a merry-go-round from the spring show, *Carousel*. Silver stars made out of aluminum foil swung from strings high above our heads.

He wrote down the number at the restaurant on the corner of the concert program and handed it to me. "I'll be there mostly, helping out my dad."

"You and Opal," I said with a careful smile.

"You could, too, if you wanted. I can ask my dad."

"I can't. The music . . . ," I mumbled.

"I know. Where again?"

"Vermont."

"For how long?"

"Six weeks."

"Six weeks?" He gulped.

"Six weeks isn't so long."

"It isn't?"

But it really was.

"I guess this is good-bye for now." His eyes were no longer twinkling.

I nodded, not knowing quite what to make of all this.

If someone kisses you and you kiss them back, shouldn't it be a no-brainer?

But it wasn't. It just plain wasn't.

# Summer

## SUMMER

Under a hard season, fired up by the Sun,

Languishes man, languishes the flock and burns
the pine.

We hear the cuckoo's voice; then sweet songs of
the turtledove and finch are heard.

Soft breezes stir the air . . . but threatening north
wind sweeps them suddenly aside.

The shepherd trembles, fearing violent storms and
his fate.

*—From a sonnet by Vivaldi*

# July

A lesson has to be an affair of give and take for both parties;
never all the giving on one side and all the taking on the other.
—Nadia Boulanger, composition teacher

Mom and Dad packed up the van for the six-hour drive to
Vermont. Pre-college kids, college students, graduate students,
and assistant teachers were all heading in that direction
before the July Fourth weekend. Opal and I promised we
would stay in touch every day.

I spun around to take one last look at my bedroom and
noticed the few stuffed animals on my bed. I lifted a purple
moose I had named Julia—the one Mom had bought after
I made it into Juilliard—and snuggled my face in her still soft
and furry lavender stomach. My eyes got all watery as I turned
to go. "Good-bye, room."

On my way out I kissed Beethoven on the nose and gave Grandma a huge hug. "Be good to yourself. You hear me?" she told me, then she stuffed a bunch of dollar bills in my hand and closed my fingers around them. "Treat yourself to something sweet!" She waved and stood there smiling, holding Beethoven's paw in the air, making him wave, too, until their faces became two tiny dots on the front stoop as our van headed away.

Mom snapped herself cheerfully into the safety belt. "Isn't this an adventure!"

As we drove, it was all the unsaid things that began to work on me. Would I have a good time? Would I practice a lot? Or too little? Would I like the other kids? Would they like me? Had I packed too much stuff? What had I forgotten? But the real question was, why was I doing this? Was music my air? I looked out the car window, watching the skyline turn into shady suburbs, then countryside, and finally farmlands with fields that went on and on. Big old houses with porches and tractors in driveways by barns spotted the landscape. Everything became greener as we crossed the border from Massachusetts into Vermont. It reminded me of one of the colors in Opal's paint set. I was suddenly choked up. Then I thought of Brad. Our first kiss. My first kiss. How his breath had smelled slightly of garlic and mint mouthwash and how I didn't mind. If you like someone, it smells nice. If you don't, it's totally gross. A faint smile broke over my face, then faded. I missed home even more. I would have texted him if he had a cell phone, but he didn't. I sent one to Opal.

Miss u! It's not evn 24 hrs!
Miss u 2.
The rock group? Bono?
Ha. Ha. No u!
How's Brad?
OK. And u?
Homesick.
Already? Don't b.
Still BFs?
Forever.

After she made a smiley face, my cell went out of range. Was she dicing carrots with Brad? Dancing to salsa music as they chopped? Telling jokes? Sharing secrets? Was he going to become a substitute for Eric—her fantasy boyfriend, who was out of her league, like Alex was out of mine? Would Opal do that to me? Would Brad? I tried to put those thoughts out of my mind.

We stopped so that Dad could fill the car up with gas and Mom and I could stretch our legs. She put her arms around me. "I love you, Alley Cat." And she kissed me on the forehead. "I'm going to miss you so much."

"I'm going to miss you, too."

"We'll visit when you play in a recital. Like last year."

*Would they come if I played nothing at all?*

"I know it's not close by, but we're here if you need us."

"But isn't Dad traveling to Eastern Europe with his group?"

"Just for a few weeks. I'll be home. And some of the

parents of the younger kids are renting condos in the area if you need anything." She combed away my bangs with her hand. "It doesn't have to be an emergency to ask for help. I worry about you. Just remember, there are adults around."

"Eduardo will be coming up after the fourth if I need anything."

"In Miss Pringle's old wreck? Oh, that makes me feel a lot better. An old car on curvy country roads with you in it. Now I can sleep soundly at night."

"Ma-a!"

"Don't Ma me. Be smart, Ally. And safe. And healthy. Okay?"

"Okay."

We hugged again. Then Mom ripped open a bag of pretzels, handing me one.

The sprawling motel was on the side of a mountain dotted with tall spruce trees—a miniature alpine version of *The Sound of Music* minus the Von Trapp family singing "Do Re Mi." It overlooked a pond filled with swamp grass and cattails at the bottom of a hill by the main road. Wildflowers lined a long graveled driveway to the top. When we got out in the parking lot, instead of the pungent odors of the city, the air smelled of pine needles, honeysuckle, and freshly mown grass.

The steady rhythm of a tennis ball off in the distance beat like a metronome. I recognized two boys from other summers and waved. They waved back, then volleyed a chartreuse ball over the net, swiping their rackets effortlessly through the air, not caring if their arms got too tired to play piano.

We went through sliding glass doors and were greeted by an accompanist who played in concerts with many violinists. She had a clipboard like the coaches had in school and looked very official. Mom smiled. "Allegra Katz."

She moved her finger across a chart. "Room two twenty-one. With Emma Moore."

I smiled nervously as she handed me a keycard to the room. "Last year I had a space to myself."

"That was a different program," she said, looking past me to my parents.

Dad gave a sarcastic grin. "It was more like a boot camp than one for music."

Was he talking about the army-like cots, the mushy leftovers, or the routine of practicing six hours a day in a place the size of a sardine can?

"You're lucky it's just the two of you. If this was a regular sleep-away, you'd have twenty to a bunk," she said. "We're so crowded this summer we had to make many of the rooms into threes and fours. We even put kids of different ages together. Like Ally and Emma."

Was she older or younger than me? My stomach ached. Mom put her hand on my arm. "This'll be like having a sister."

"Like Ruby?" I muttered. "The pit bull."

"Oh, come on." Mom bumped her hip playfully against mine.

"I like being an only child. Opal told me that by the time

she could sit up without drooling she realized having a big sister was way overrated."

Mom threw her head back and laughed. "Tell her sibling rivalry is here to stay."

After Dad parked the van, we began carrying my things to the second floor. The staircase was near the pool, where the older teenagers seemed to have taken over, blasting rock music, singing karaoke, sipping soda, and eating chips. On the ground floor, we passed Timothy Young. He was already practicing on an out-of-tune upright piano in a motel room that had been set up as one of the rehearsal rooms. Mrs. Young and her two other children were listening while her husband practiced his golf swings on the sweeping lawn outside the wide picture window.

When we got to room 221, only one bed was made up. I was glad my roommate had chosen the one closest to the bathroom, leaving me with a bed where I could look out the window at night, just like at home.

Mascara, eyeliner, bronze concealer, lotions, tubes of gel, conditioners, bangles, and bracelets were scattered on the counter in the bathroom. I hadn't started wearing makeup yet, except for some blush at my concert, so I wondered, *How old is Emma? And who has nails to polish when you play any instrument?* Mine were always clipped and filed short.

I'd just picked up the Frosted Passion pink enamel from her wire basket brimming with colors when a voice from behind me sang out, "Ally?" I nearly jumped out of my skin, embarrassed she caught me in the act.

"It's okay." She tossed back the corkscrew curls of her

thick black hair, removing large movie-star sunglasses from her matching black eyes and then hooking them on her halter top. Her eyelashes were full like a zebra's. And her skin was the color of deep mocha.

My father smiled broadly as he came in with a duffel bag full of folded sheets, towels, and washcloths while Mom followed holding shopping bags of snack food and music. Julia's purple paw was sticking out of one, and I quickly grabbed her, tossing the moose on my bed. "Ally's dad," he said. "Otherwise known as Doug. Doug Katz."

"Emma Moore." She cocked her head to one side, pushing away the violin case strapped over her right shoulder. As she put out her hand to shake his, the developed muscles in her bowing arm bulged like an athlete's. "Douglas Katz the violinist?"

Dad smiled modestly. "In person."

"I have all your CDs of Bach's partitas."

"Then I guess you're the sale in my royalty statement."

Mom smiled and shook her head.

"No, there were two," Emma joked. "My teacher at Interlochen last summer was the other one."

"Do you come from Michigan?" Mom asked.

"Detroit."

Looking at the many things still unpacked, scattered on the floor and bed, the UPS box unopened, my mother asked cautiously, "Is your family here?"

"Just me." She gave an awkward shrug, putting her violin in her half of the closet next to a suitcase.

"Then come to dinner with us," Mom offered, Dad nodding in agreement.

Even though I knew it was the right thing to do, and I'd want some family to do that for me, I said, "If you're busy, we'll understand." I crossed my fingers behind my back and prayed, *Please say no.* I wanted to spend this last evening alone with my parents.

But she picked up a gray hooded sweatshirt from her bed and wrapped it around her waist. "Sure, why not?"

I bit my lower lip. We followed my parents toward the minivan and climbed into the back seat. As I sat there, I kept thinking, *She just had to say yes.* "How did you find out about this place?" I said finally.

"Through my teacher. She felt she had taken me as far as we could go, and she knew of a great teacher coming here who would work with me."

"That's generous of her."

Emma looked at me, confused. "Shouldn't a teacher do that for her pupil?"

I smiled to myself. *Yes.*

"Anyway, I wasn't going back to my summer program. You had to wear lame uniforms."

"Uniforms?" I guess Emma had been in a kind of boot camp, too.

"Blue corduroy knickers for the girls and light blue shirts. White on Sundays! With red socks. There are like a thousand people around the campus, and they have to be able to iden-tify all the campers by age groups."

"You're telling me everyone knew exactly how old you were by the color of the socks or shirt you wore?"

She grimaced. "You got it."

"Weird!" But that would have been very helpful with Alex.

She lifted the bottom of her pants and wiggled her toes in her hot pink flip-flops. "Guess you can't tell how old I am. No socks." She laughed. "Fifteen."

Two years older than me.

"And you?" she asked back.

*Should I fib and also say fifteen? But she'd find out. Why start a friendship on a lie?* Opal and I were best friends because we always told each other the truth.

"Thirteen."

"Oh." She sounded disappointed. "You seem old for your age."

"It's Manhattan. It does that to a person."

She laughed again, fingering the silver cross hanging from a strand of tiny jade-colored glass beads around her swan-like neck.

My father asked as we sat down to dinner, "How long have you been playing?"

"Since I was nine," revealed Emma.

"You began at nine? Late start," I said.

She nodded. "Everyone in our school had to pick an instrument by fourth grade. Someone donated a bunch of used ones, and I figured a violin would be easier to manage on the school bus than a cello."

"Or a tuba," I interjected.

She continued on. "My grandmother also pushed me the older I got. She said, 'I'd rather have you practicing than hanging out on the street with boys.' Little did she know I could do both. Anyway, I figured, it's free, why not? And you?" Emma turned slightly toward me.

"Since I was little."

"Well, your father . . ." She glanced over at him. He smiled, poking at his salad.

"And my mother." I looked over at her. "She's a vocalist."

"Oh. What type of music?" Emma asked her.

"I used to sing opera."

"At the Met," my father added.

Mom's expression tightened. "Now, all kinds. Mostly jazz."

"Not heavy metal," I said, turning toward Emma.

"I could try," my mother teased me.

"*Mom!*" I rolled my eyes, thinking of her going goth on me.

"Where do you study?" Emma asked as our cheeseburgers and fries arrived.

I hesitated, then said, "Juilliard."

A grin spread over her face. "Oh."

From that one little *oh* I knew what she was thinking: that my parents got me in. Because my dad was sort of famous. And my mom once was, too. Emma didn't know how hard *I'd* worked to get in. And to stay in.

"Do you like playing the violin?" I asked.

She looked at me oddly. "Why else would I be here?"

I took a sip of my iced tea, watching my parents' reaction.

"What are you studying now?" Mom asked, probably trying to figure out how advanced she was.

"The Paganini concerto. I just started to work on it before I came here."

126

"That's wonderful, trying such a difficult concerto," my father said, and grinned.

"There's an eleven-year-old pianist up here who accompanied a fourteen-year-old violinist on it at Juilliard," I put in.

"Goody. Then maybe that pianist can help me this summer," she replied.

I looked down and said nothing as the waitress took away my unfinished meal and brought a thick slice of lemon meringue pie, which I mostly shared.

On the route back to the motel, we were quiet as we traveled empty unlit roads with only stars and an occasional neon bar sign to light our way.

A lot of people had arrived by the time we returned to the motel, and they were milling around the lobby. A few older boys gave Emma the once-over when we entered. You just knew from those looks that if she had had a double bass or any other type of heavy instrument, they would have been all over themselves trying to help her carry it. It's strange being invisible while you stand next to someone who's *so* noticed.

Some teachers and students had gathered in the lodge by a large stone fireplace. There was a coffee table scattered with board games and discarded paperbacks. Two boys were playing checkers. A bunch of kids I knew were doing a puzzle of a masterpiece I had once seen in a museum with Opal. I picked up a piece, filling in a missing spot, and they smiled up at me. I did the puzzle for a little while as my mother and father spoke to some other parents and Emma went upstairs to unpack. Then I kissed my parents good night. They left for their motel

right down the road and I got ready for bed. I sent another
text message to Opal while Emma was brushing her teeth.

> Miss u. A lot. It's bucolic.
> Flash card word? Take a break. Meet nu
>     friends?
> My roommate. Emma Moore.
> Do u like her?
> Seems nice. From Michigan. Year older
>     than u.
> Cool.
> Gotta go.
> Gud nite. cu 18r.

Before Emma and I went to sleep, I cuddled Julia under the
blanket, taking a whiff of the laundry detergent Grandma
used, and whispered in the dark, "You still up?"

"Yeah," she whispered back, turning over so that I could see
her face in the moonlight. "First night in a strange place. With
*no* sounds. At home, I'm not used to the sound of nothing."

I listened to the bullfrogs and cicadas, which sounded like
something to me.

We suddenly heard a few kids running out in the hall
toward the candy and ice machines, giggling. "Is that why you
chose the bed furthest from the window?"

"No." She punched her pillow, puffing it up. "Fear. You
never know what or who's out there."

I guess we both lived in big cities, but in two different
worlds.

Sunday morning while Mom slept in, Dad and I walked to the foot of the gravel road, where there was a place to eat overlooking the pond. We sat on a cedar porch near the edge of the water, watching minnows as we feasted on stacks of blueberry pancakes oozing in puddles of maple syrup. For once it was just me and my father, and no one talked about practice or performances or competitions or juries. My only thought was how many pancakes we could gobble down. I never wanted this moment to end.

But it did.

After we finished setting up my half of the room, we all went to a general store to buy toiletries I had forgotten, along with a few bags of jelly beans with Grandma's money. I also got pale peach nail polish in a shade called Palm Beach. Mom and Dad wanted to leave Vermont in time to beat the Sunday traffic on I-95, so we headed back to my room. Dad whistled a tune the whole way, and no one spoke a word.

When they were ready to start the trip back to Manhattan, Mom hugged me. "I love you," she whispered. I could feel her warm breath on my scalp.

My lower lip trembled uncontrollably. "I love you, too."

"You'll call?" She kept holding me. "Not like last time, when you didn't."

"Yes, Mom, I'll call."

"Have fun and do well," Dad said, and he put his arms around both of us and held us in a tight circle.

All we could hear was the breeze rushing through the trees.

I waved to them until the car faded from sight. Then I went back to my room and began to cry out loud, dipping my head down into Julia like I used to do with my nooney, the flannel blanket I'd had when I was little.

Emma walked in. I wanted to die. "Couldn't be as bad as when my mother left." She took in a breath and let it out in a big sigh. "And I don't mean here in Vermont."

I tried to dry my eyes off with my fists. She walked to my side of the bed and grabbed at the box of Kleenex, handing me one. I blew my nose and said nothing at first, and then I pried.

"Your mother left you?"

She nodded.

"How old were you?"

"Around five."

I didn't know what else to say. I thought about asking, *Who took care of you?* But she answered, "My nana's raising me."

I wanted to say, *What about your father?* But I didn't.

She answered that for me as well. "I never knew my father."

I couldn't imagine not knowing my father. Or my mother leaving me.

We sat on the edge of our beds, facing each other. I mean, what do you say to someone after that? That maybe she was better off without them?

Her eyes welled with tears. "It's a funny thing how something that happened so long ago can stay with you, form who you become, or even define you. Of course, you can change who you are."

What defined me? Could I change who I was?

She smoothed her hand across the bedspread. "Every so

often the memory creeps up. It's raw. The nerve endings feel exposed." She sighed. "Sometimes I fantasize that I become famous. They come hear me play. And they're sorry that they ever left because I grew up to become this great person. In spite of them. It's just a dream I have."

"Maybe not." I smiled. "Is that really why you kept up with the violin?"

"No. It turns out I love it. I go somewhere else when I'm playing."

"I do, too, sometimes. Like my dad says, when I'm in the zone."

"You're okay," she said, looking at me.

"Even with the crying-like-a-baby part?"

"Yeah, even with that."

Which was better: to have parents who dreamed too much, or to have no parents, so your dreams had to be completely your own?

Emma's stomach rumbled. She grabbed me by my arm. "Let's grab some chow."

When we entered the crowded dining hall, I smiled at students I knew from home or last summer as Emma slid her tray along, getting silverware, a napkin, and dishes. "You're not hungry?" she asked, gazing at my empty dinner tray.

"Last July, I lost ten pounds. My parents kept sending care packages. This year Dad says he's going to FedEx my grandma if I don't eat."

"Then come on, girl. You'll need energy for practice." Emma piled some smelly mystery meat smothered in brown gravy onto my plate, then some soggy green beans.

I took a small bowl of salad with some dressing on the side. She added fresh corn to my tray.

On our way to find seats, I said hi to a number of people from Juilliard, and introduced Emma. We passed Miss Pringle sitting down with the Young family—Mrs. Young was cutting up Timothy's meat!—as well as a few other teachers with their pupils. I smiled at Miss Pringle, and she smiled back. "Have you thought about what you'd like to play this summer?" she asked.

I held my tray, the food getting cold. "I brought some music from home."

"So did I. We'll go over it at your lesson. Hope you're ready to work."

I turned to grab a glass of lemonade. Beneath the smile, I heard the firmness in her voice, clear as a bell.

After our meal, the program director, Mr. Bechman, clinked his water glass to get everyone's attention. "Howdy. Welcome to our first summer festival in Vermont. To start it off with a big bang, there's a trail that goes up the hill to where we can view the Fourth of July fireworks tonight. So cover up. It gets pretty darn chilly up there!"

Emma and I already had sweaters with us. "Let's see if the schedule of lesson times is posted yet," she suggested.

Curious, I followed her to the bulletin board by the main office.

"When's yours?" she asked, searching for her name while I searched for mine.

"Nine-thirty tomorrow after breakfast. Gives me about a minute to practice."

She moved her finger across the list. "At least mine's an hour later."

We drifted outside, waiting for the others on a bench by a path lined with black-eyed Susans. Emma picked one and put the flower behind her ear. "Race you to the top of the hill!" She took off. I ran alongside her. The lake below reflected the moon, lighting our way. I sat down on a rock when we got to the top, puffing, waiting for the others to follow. I drew in the dirt with a twig. She threw a pebble into the darkness, then another. "It's a real pretty spot," she breathed.

"Sure is." I gazed at the houses dotting the far shore of the lake, sparkling with lights as band music wafted through the air over them. "Maybe we could play together sometime?"

"Isn't that what we're doing?" she chuckled.

"I mean, like in a duet. I was in a trio last summer."

"Maybe. I have to see what my new teacher gives me."

"I understand." I made a circle in the dirt. "Maybe jazz?" I persisted.

"Jazz on the violin?"

"My mother said Bach would have written blues harmony if he'd lived in a different century. We could call it *bebach* instead of *bebop*."

She rolled her eyes.

"Or I could write something."

"You write music?"

"I started to compose for my chamber music group. I'm going to finish the piece over the summer and polish it up in the fall with my composition teacher."

"Huh," was all she said. Then she threw another pebble. "You like doing that?"

"I do. A lot."

As we were interrupted by groups of kids guided by flash-lights, Emma began to rate each boy. "Hottie," she said, motioning toward Santiago, whose arm was slung over the bony shoulder of Cheryl Kim, a cellist he dated off and on in the city.

"Wait till you see his roommate, Eduardo. He teaches me."

"Lucky you."

Her face got all animated when some boy with a foreign accent said hi, showing off his dimples.

"This could be a very interesting summer." She raised her eyebrows. But when two boys built like tree stumps sat in front of us, along with another one as tall as a beanpole who blocked our view, she added, "Or not."

"Geeks *avec* freaks?"

"More like two fire hydrants and a ladder," she joked back, continuing to comment on the male population as if they were candies on a conveyor belt, discarding the ones not delectable enough. I wondered what Emma would make of Brad, who wasn't out of a mold like a perfectly wrapped chocolate heart. Or Alex, who was.

The band music got louder as fireworks exploded in bursts of gold and silver alternating with red, white, and blue sparkles sprinkling over the lake. Our necks craned while we watched colors shoot across the smoky sky.

The dimpled guy moseyed over to Emma as we began to

leave with everyone else. "It's a good way to start the summer," he said.

She tossed her head back. The flower she had put behind her ear had remained perfectly in place, whereas mine had already fallen out. "Where are you from? You don't sound like a local boy."

He flashed that great toothpaste commercial smile again. "Hamburg. Germany."

"Definitely not a local boy," she flirted. "I'm from Detroit. Michigan."

A bunch of people rushing back down the hill pushed their way between Emma and the German guy, and we lost him in the confusion and the dark.

"He's kind of cute," she said when we got back to our room, flopping down on her bed and hugging her pillow. I smiled.

Before we went to sleep, I told her, "I'm thirsty. I need some ice water." But instead I slipped downstairs to the lobby and logged on to my e-mail to see if Brad had contacted me— he hadn't. I let my parents know I was still alive and kicking. Mom had sent an e-mail asking if I wanted anything, while Grandma had sent one telling me I was the most gorgeous, talented, and brilliant child in the world. Again. Then I IM'd Opal even though it was late.

Alley Cat: The boys here are OK.
(I knew that would be your first
question.)

Paint Gurl: I'm that predictable? Not!
Just OK?

Alley Cat: Emma thinks some of them
are hot. Well, one bona fide—he's
from Hamburg, Germany. And one
semi-hottie. (Santiago, who lives
with Miss Pringle, remember? Emma
might need glasses.) The food's OK.
So is the room.

Paint Gurl: This year sounds better
than that hellhole you went to the
year that crazy cellist lit a fire
outside your bunk. Totally
certifiable.

Alley Cat: His father beat him. He
wouldn't feed him if he didn't
practice.

Paint Gurl: He should have been locked
up for life—him and his dad.

Alley Cat: Talking about pyromaniacs,
we saw fireworks. Did you go up on
your roof to watch them?

Paint Gurl: Ruby invited friends,
including Eric, who continues to
ignore me unless he needs a refill
of Coke or something and is unable
to stretch the two inches. A crisis
like that calls for me to pass him
one ASAP.

Alley Cat: At least you're on his radar. I wish I were on Alex's.

Paint Gurl: If you could call it that! More like an alien spaceship intruding. I asked Brad to come. My parents invited his father since he closed his restaurant for the holiday. (My aunt made a play for him. The one from my birthday party who waddles like a duck.) Mr. Clark marinated some amazing kebabs. Brad and I pitched in with the prep. I've diced enough onions to fill an ocean with tears.

Alley Cat: So you're becoming a cook?

Paint Gurl: Don't hold your breath. I'm still a firm believer in take-out. When you come home, pool party in the baby pool on the roof! I squirted Brad with a hose. He got me back. Then Ruby. Then Eric. It got out of hand.

Alley Cat: I'm there! In six weeks. Still breathing. XO.

What was I doing here, away from everyone I cared about? It was only the end of the weekend and already I was a distant memory for Brad? Was Opal going to like him as more than a friend the more they hung out together? I wished I were in the kitchen with them, stirring steaming pots, licking coconut icing from a large mixing bowl, dancing to music the way we had the night of her birthday. I rushed back up to our room through quiet hallways.

Emma stared at me holding an empty ice bucket. "Where's the ice?"

Monday morning I walked down the hall of the first floor, where one of the rooms was assigned as Miss Pringle's studio. A big piano was in the center. She wasn't there yet, so I waited outside with music in my arms while some guy with his head in the piano plucked at strings, checking the hammers.

I wondered what she'd pick for my new repertoire as I noticed scores stacked sideways in cardboard boxes between the piano legs. There was the Beethoven G major theme and variations. It was flashier than his sonatas. I could show off with cross-handed passages. Audiences went for that. But it took more than putting one hand over the other to impress Miss Pringle. Some of the twenty-four études of Chopin? I wanted something different after the prelude. Scherzos, ballades, and impromptus? Too simple.

After the piano tuner ran a few scales, he looked up. "Would ya come over here and play something fer me so I can check out the sound?"

"Me?"

"Do you see anyone else here?"

I walked inside and fooled around on the keyboard, stretching my hands easily over an octave to nine notes, and then almost to ten, ending with a B minor scale.

He scratched his beard. "Maybe something with a little more oomph?"

I played a fluffy waltz, gliding my fingers across the keys.

"How does it seem?" he asked, putting his tuning fork and tools away.

Entering the room, Miss Pringle answered for me. "Come back in a few days. Let's see if it takes the humidity. These instruments are so temperamental."

I put my music on the shelf at the piano. *Not only the instruments.*

I smiled uncomfortably and began to sneeze from the sweet scent of phlox drifting in the half-open window.

"I hope you're not getting sick again—a repeat of last year."

I waved toward the garden, sniffling, "Allergies."

"Take care of yourself. There's a lot of music literature we need to cover if you're going to get anywhere this summer. And there's a big Beethoven competition this fall."

*A Beethoven competition.* Mozart was last year. I had practiced over vacations and weekends, skipping parties, movies, and extracurricular activities. And in the end, a girl a year younger, with nerves of steel, won.

"I brought a Beethoven sonata from home." I slid the music out to where she could see it: Sonate für Klavier und Violine no. 5 in F major, op. 24.

She shoved it aside and spread another Beethoven piece out on the piano shelf. "Your next piece should be a concerto for the competition. His Piano Concerto no. 4. Could you sight-read the beginning?"

As I began to read the notes and play them, she started to

hum and beat out the rhythm with her hand. If I brought Brad's pocket-size metronome to the next lesson, I thought, maybe she wouldn't clap or sing. She tapped her pencil lightly on a pile of music. "Is someone helping you before we meet again?"

"You mean Eduardo? I was going to sign up for him."

"He's not here yet. I have four assistants coming this summer. Santiago's already around . . . if he gets down to business." I guess she'd noticed Cheryl Kim, too.

"But what about Eduardo? I'm used to working with him. Besides you," I added.

"He's going to be busy studying pieces for our Sunday concerts with his chamber group. He's assisting me with a few of my students this year, but not all of them."

I looked at her blankly. *What am I, chopped liver?*

I had trouble focusing on the concerto, worrying that I might not get the help I wanted from Eduardo between the lessons I had with Miss Pringle. So our session didn't go well. When her next student arrived, Miss Pringle said as I was leaving, "Get someone before your next lesson. Santiago isn't too bad. He's beginning to teach."

I wanted her best assistant. Not second-best. Or third- or even fourth-best.

As I was walking down the hall, I overheard Emma's new teacher greeting her as she went into a room for her lesson. "Miss Moore, your violin teacher from home told me over the phone that you have perfect pitch. I look forward to our lessons together."

Emma said cheerfully, "Me too."

140

"So what would you like to accomplish this summer?" she asked.

No one asked me what I wanted or needed, or talked about *our* lessons *together*.

I went to a practice room and spread out the Beethoven concerto, foolishly hoping Miss Pringle would say I could do the sonata instead, but I knew she was dead set on this. I did some five-finger exercises. Then I started to work at it, playing notes over and over and over again, returning to the beginning, and then sometimes skipping a few measures, going on to an especially difficult passage to try to get it right. After putting in a couple of hours on only the first two pages, my wrists went weak and my fingers were numb, so I stopped and sauntered over to the office. "Has Eduardo arrived yet?"

"Tomorrow," the woman at reception told me.

"Do you know what room? I'd like to leave him a note."

"I'll see that he gets it."

"I'd rather do it myself."

She raised an eyebrow and grinned.

I stiffened, putting the note back in my pocket, and turned away.

I headed to the ice machine, and this time really picked up some ice, to reduce the swelling in my hands and shoulders from the tension of playing. Then I went back to my room and iced my hands while I watched Emma practice a difficult Kreutzer exercise. She bowed with such strength that one of the horsehairs on her bow broke and floated wildly above her head. She ripped it off with a quick yank, while she continued to play. Then she changed books, and I peeked at the music. "Paganini's caprices. Tricky fingering. Those are hard to learn."

"That's what I'm here for," she said.

I smiled awkwardly. She noticed the sonata laid out next to the concerto on my bed. She reached for the separate violin score that was inside the piano part and thumbed through the pages, examining the notes my father had scribbled throughout. "I played it this past year."

"You did?"

"All but the last movement." She looked up. "Did your lesson go well?"

"I'd like to prepare the sonata, but she's making me do this concerto for a competition in a few months."

"And I'm changing over to the Bruch Violin Concerto. My teacher prefers me to do that instead of the Paganini. She feels it is a better fit for me right now. A little easier."

"Maybe we could do the sonata?" I gave her a pleading look. "Just for fun."

She continued to pore over my dad's notes. "Maybe. Can I borrow this?"

I smiled to myself, feeling less homesick, as I nodded.

After lunch I changed into my bathing suit and called home. "Are you okay?" My mother sounded rushed but concerned. Last year I'd waited a whole week to call.

"Fine."

"Good. How's everything? The food? Sleeping? Your roommate?"

"I need a recording of the Beethoven number four. Do you or Dad have it?"

"Anyone in particular?"

"Everyone. Emanuel Ax. Lang Lang. Whoever did it is fine."

I saw Emma walk by the bathroom holding some beach towels, motioning to me that she was leaving.

"Gotta run, Ma."

Emma was already in a bikini sunning herself by the pool when I got downstairs. I squinted in the glare as she waved me over to a chaise longue she had saved. Tucking my towel more tightly around me, I made my way over to her, trying to avoid a bunch of boys squirting water pistols at some girls circling them and squealing. I lay down and slathered on sunblock. Then Emma did my back.

The guy from Hamburg pulled up a chair to read a book. Emma smiled at me mischievously, then at him. "What do you play when you're not reading?"

He glanced up, about to turn a page. "Violin."

She put out her hand. "Me too. I'm Emma."

"Erik," he answered, shaking it.

Trying to imitate Emma's boldness, I said, "I'm Ally," then added, "my friend from home knows an Eric. Eric with a c."

"I'm Erik with a k," he said politely.

*Why did I say something so dumb?*

"And your instrument?" he asked me.

"She's a pianist," Emma jumped in, cutting me off.

I placed my hands in my lap.

"What are you working on?" Emma asked him.

"The Mendelssohn."

"Veddy romantic," she replied flirtatiously.

"One of my father's favorites," I said, trying again to be part of things. But I was like an empty space between their bookends.

"Her father is Douglas Katz."

Erik's eyes widened. "The violinist? Who did that new CD of the partitas?"

"That one," Emma said before I had a chance.

"Wow." He was looking at me differently now.

Emma flipped onto her stomach and tugged at her bikini bottom, drawing his attention away from me. After a few minutes, she rolled back over like a rotisserie chicken. "Want to go for a dip?" she said.

Erik quickly closed his book, stood up, and followed as she strutted away and dove in a graceful line off the diving board. I tagged along while they raced each other, showing off their competitive spirit. I wondered what they'd do in a violin competition. Would they be as friendly?

On the way back to our room, alone and dripping, I checked near the office. The list under Eduardo's name seemed to have grown longer.

When he still hadn't arrived days later, I began to get really upset and asked around, but no one knew when he was coming. And I was afraid to ask Miss Pringle. Everyone was already into their daily routines, and I hadn't gotten any extra help while I was waiting for him. I saw Santiago in the dining hall one night and was tempted to ask him, but I trusted Eduardo—he was my teacher, too. I respected him and I hoped he respected me. I didn't want to train with just anyone.

Then, right before the weekend, Eduardo suddenly showed

144

up. As he unloaded Miss Pringle's old station wagon, he had a sour expression on his face, which was unlike him. I hoped he was just tired from the long drive and that nothing was wrong.

"Is *that* your other teacher?" Emma asked on our way out from dinner, watching him struggle with his luggage and some boxes sealed haphazardly with tape.

"I hope so." Flustered, I added, "Yes, in the city."

"He's pretty cute, but he looks totally wasted."

I gave him a wave, but realized it wasn't the best time to ask him my burning question: would he teach me this summer?

Over the weekend there was a fishing derby by the pond. The winner got a ten-dollar gift certificate for the general store. I caught a few minnows. Gloating, Timothy Young tilted his plastic bucket to reveal several catfish swimming in aimless circles at the bottom. Emma, holding an empty pole, nudged her elbow against mine. "Not too obnoxious, is he?" Emma let out a whoop when she finally caught a big one with her fishing rod, and seemed to take joy in Timothy's pouting as she proudly paraded it around.

Miss Pringle surprised me when she plopped down by us, dipping her toes in the water, making ripples. "This reminds me of my childhood in Georgia."

"You mean you weren't practicing every second?" I muttered under my breath.

As I was about to put more bait on the end of my hook, Bin-Yu came charging down the hill toward me. "Eduardo's looking for you."

I jumped up. "Where?"

"At the lodge. Something about a lesson. Did you miss it?"

I rushed up the gravel road, my heart thumping in anticipation.

The woman in the office was on the phone. When she saw me, she handed me an overnight package probably filled with CDs of the Beethoven concerto I had asked for from my mother. Before I could say anything, she went back to her call.

"Please." I began to pace the way I did before a concert. "I'm late for a lesson!"

She put the receiver down on the desk. "So what do you want from me?"

"I need the room number of Eduardo Cruz."

"Three forty-three," she said, annoyed, then returned to her conversation.

I raced upstairs and pounded on Eduardo's door.

He opened it, looking agitated. "Hey, you look worse than me."

"Did I miss a lesson?" I panted, out of breath.

"I want to talk to you about that."

I began to feel dizzy.

"There are a lot of people here this summer, and . . ."

His words became blurred in my ears.

"I discussed it with Miss Pringle," he continued.

My eyes watered.

"Only for the summer. In the fall, we'll return to our lessons."

"No!" I was shocked at the sound of that word coming out of my mouth—such a short word, only two letters, but it meant so much.

"Ally, there are many students here."

A squeaky voice came out from somewhere inside me. "And I'm one of them."

He let out a huge sigh.

"I don't care how many other people signed up. I want to take my additional lessons with you. When you criticize me, it never sounds mean. I feel you're trying to help me become my best. You understand me."

The unsaid words were, *Miss Pringle doesn't.*

Eduardo put his hand on my shoulder.

"You *have* to teach me." I began to bawl. "You just have to."

A clear stream of snot dribbled from my nose, and I wiped it away with my sleeve, not caring how disgusting I must have looked.

"Ally," he sighed again, "I don't even know if I'm staying."

I looked up. "What do you mean? You just got here."

"My *abuela*, my grandmother, is very sick, and my student visa's run out. So I'm illegal right now. If I return to Venezuela, I might never be able to come back to the States. I'm dealing with the school and an immigration lawyer in the city to renew it. I need to see her." He choked on his words. "But I also want to stay up here and rehearse the Rachmaninoff more. I'm auditioning for the doctoral program. I'm in a real bind."

Now it was Eduardo's turn to become sad. He was caught like the fish in Timothy's bucket. I'd never thought about his music, his studying with Miss Pringle. That she was his teacher, too—that even teachers had teachers.

It was my turn to understand him. "I'm sorry. I'm selfish."

"No." He shook his head. "You're not."

*No. Miss Pringle is. Why do I have to beg for something I deserve?*

"Somehow we'll work it out."

"If you stay."

"If I stay." He attempted a smile.

I exhaled, relieved. When I left, I headed to the lobby and went online, intending to tell Opal the news. When I logged on, I saw that Brad had finally e-mailed me. Excitedly I opened it.

```
Dear Ally—
Sorry I haven't been in touch. I fall into
bed, beat, and get up the same way. My
dad's wiped all the time, so Opal and I do
what we can. Some days I almost feel like
a real chef. I hope my little gift was put
to use. I still remember the night I gave
it to you. Is the summer going good? Bye
for now.
Brad
```

I e-mailed back.

```
I'm going to put your "little gift" to
good use. More than you know! Hopefully
it'll keep even better rhythm than my
teacher! Thanks for asking and thinking
of me. See you.
Ally
```

Should I have ended with *Miss you?* Because I did miss him, and Opal, too, even though I felt as if the world outside had stopped and my life was here, in this small corner of Vermont in the middle of nowhere.

That night my father called from the road. "How you doing, sweet pea?"

Out of the blue I said, "Remember when you and Mom were my first teachers? And you gave me that tiny one-fourth-size violin? And you stood by my side with your full-size one trying to show me how to hold the bow?"

"Yes, I remember."

"Once I put it under my chin I knew that instrument wasn't for me no matter how beautiful it sounded. I wanted Mom's piano. The black keys looked like sticks of licorice floating on ice cream. Sometimes I wish you and Ma were my teachers, like old times."

"Oh, honey, then you wouldn't be where you are."

"And where's that?" I asked, my voice evaporating into silence.

Sunday evening the teachers gathered in the lobby and held something like a master class without the pressure. Mr. Bechman asked, "Would anyone care to play?" After Erik and Timothy, Emma did the first movement of the Beethoven sonata, which she knew by heart. When she was done, she looked over at me and wiggled her eyebrows. I saw the expression on Miss Pringle's face and knew that Emma had done well.

"Can I ask her?" I said in a hushed tone when Emma returned to my side.

She understood that I meant Miss Pringle. "Let me run it by my teacher first. Okay?"

The following morning at my lesson, Miss Pringle parked herself in a chair. "Eduardo's staying. He convinced me that taking on an extra student won't overload him." That extra student was me!

At lunch Emma agreed to play the sonata. "My teacher okayed it."

Now I had to convince Miss Pringle. So I peeked in her studio between students, bursting to tell her. "Could I do the Beethoven sonata with my roommate? I have the violin part with me."

"We discussed this. I want you to do a concerto. It's *your* playing I am concerned with, not some violinist's." She brushed her hand dismissively in the air.

"It won't interfere with the concerto. I promise."

Miss Pringle shifted in her seat. "It won't qualify to be played with a full orchestra for the competition."

"Can't I study both?"

"After that jury this past May, I hope you know what you're doing."

*Gee, thanks a million.*


Days slipped into days full of practice, down time, and more practice. In the evenings, everyone took turns playing Scrabble or poker for M&M's. We did crossword puzzles and read trashy romance novels that had been left by winter guests.

Once I opened the book on music and math that my math teacher had lent me, but a few of the older boys tried to quiz me on fractals, vector spaces, and differential equations, so I quickly put it away. There were outdated DVDs lying around that we watched over and over again when we weren't doing nighttime master classes or performing for each other in chamber music groups. When I was alone, I also worked on my composition or listened to the CDs my mother had sent so I could play the Beethoven concerto the right way. During the late afternoon when we didn't practice, we swam, or sometimes we played concerts in libraries, community centers, churches or temples, rehabs and hospitals. For the moment, the hospitals made me realize how lucky I was.

Unlike me, Emma loved the idea of performing.

At our first practice together, I asked, "Do your palms get clammy in public?"

She shook her head as she rosined and then tightened her bow.

"Do your fingers freeze? What about your legs? Do they tremble?"

Again she shook her head as she lifted the violin.

"My rear end sometimes gets sweaty and sticks to the piano bench."

She laughed, adjusting the chin rest to a comfortable position.

Emma played notes and I answered, or I'd begin and she'd come in, forming our own dialogue, plunging ourselves equally into the piece, trying to understand what Beethoven wanted to communicate. The difference in our ages, where we went to school, and how we grew up all melted away—what counted was how we played the music together. Then we started taking risks, stretching ourselves, discovering new things every time we played the piece. I didn't care what she thought of me, and I think she felt the same way. It wasn't about getting approval or making progress or trying to impress anyone. It was all about the music—staying true to the sonata, how *we* wanted to interpret it. I loved, loved, loved rehearsing with Emma.

More than ever, it helped me understand why I also wanted to compose. The idea of making something out of nothing was gradually becoming more important to me than being a soloist. I could think up ideas for other players and other instruments besides piano. I could hear a flute in my head and write the part. Or maybe even something for a trumpet. Time, space, people—nothing in the entire world mattered. It was as if I disappeared to an ideal place far away, like that boy in an ancient Chinese fairy tale who went into a painting.

Whenever a practice room was free, I spent some time working on my new piece. Sometimes I'd cheat, using an hour or two at the piano to compose instead of doing scales, exercises, or the concerto. That's when I was happiest, when no one was judging me except myself. I was my own jury.

Then one afternoon Miss Pringle poked her head into my practice room on the way to her studio. I quickly gathered up stray sheets from the composition pad and slid the concerto into place along the piano shelf. Her eyes followed me. "What are you doing?"

"Nothing."

"Nothing?" She glared.

"The concerto. And the sonata. In my free time," I hastened to add.

"I'd like to hear you and your roommate—Emma? Is that her name?"

"Yes," I said, ruffled. "Emma Moore."

"Tomorrow. At two."

"I'll check to see if she's free."

"I already did, with her teacher. We'll both be there."

I smiled nervously. "Okay, then. Two o'clock it is."

"Before you know it, we'll be halfway through the summer. So you'd better get going. I only continue with people who put in the work."

"I've been practicing." *I pinky swear*, I wanted to add as she closed the door behind her.

When I reached our room, Emma was propped against the pillows on her bed. She was strumming a guitar, singing the Beatles classic "While My Guitar Gently Weeps."

"My teacher wants to hear the sonata."

"So play it."

"She wants to hear *us*."

"I'm not playing for anyone's teacher because *she* says so."

"Emma, come on. She checked with your teacher. She's going to hear it, too."

She continued to form chords, stopping on a fret. When she saw my wounded expression, she said, "Okay, I'll do it, for you. And *my* teacher."

I smiled. "Thanks."

"No problemo."

She went back to singing another soulful song. The battery on my cell needed to be charged, so I couldn't text Opal; instead I ran downstairs to IM her.

```
I'm going to be doing a duet with Emma!
```

Opal replied,

```
I'm very busy, too, you know, with Brad.
```

*Okay*, I thought. *I'm gonna leave that one alone.* But what was going on with her and Brad? Was there more to it?

Then Opal sent me another message.

```
I hope you're at least having fun this
summer, Ally.
```

```
I am, Opal. Are you?
```

```
Well, I'm challenging myself, too.
```

Opal sounded distant. Ordinarily it would have driven me crazy, but I didn't have the time to stew because after dinner Emma and I had to put in a couple of hours on the Beethoven.

"I think we nailed it." Emma closed the pages of the violin part.

"Hope so."

"Don't be such a worrywart. We did."

Just like Opal would have, Emma put on a mix CD and

turned the volume way up. We danced in the middle of our room to some old Motown tunes, doing Diana Ross's hand motions when she sang "Stop! In the Name of Love." The kids next door pounded on the wall. "Stop! In the name of people who want to sleep around here!"

We giggled, running into our bathroom, and took turns gargling lyrics with our mouths filled with tap water, trying to guess the titles of each other's songs. I did a mean rendition of Willie Nelson's "On the Road Again" in its entirety. It would have made my mother the opera singer and bar hound proud.

The next day we rehearsed separately, then together, using Brad's metronome like a lucky charm. Right after lunch, Emma went upstairs to get her violin, while I headed to Miss Pringle's room wearing a new blouse with tiny pleats in the front. Emma's teacher was waiting outside in the hall, the door closed. "Hello, dear," she said with a grin, her eyes twinkling. "I'm looking forward to hearing you." She put her hand out to take mine. "Sonia Moussekovsky. Call me Sonia. Or Sunny. Your hands are so cold. They say cold hands, warm heart." I smiled as she put her hands around mine to warm them.

Emma arrived promptly at two, just as Miss Pringle was opening the door. "You'll work on those passages we discussed," Miss Pringle said to Eduardo as he exited, looking wiped. He had the Rachmaninoff concerto marked up with Miss Pringle's handwriting, and looked like I often did when I left a lesson.

I whispered to him, "Get rid of those coins." He let out a low chuckle.

"Come in." Miss Pringle invited us into the studio.

Emma's teacher, Sonia—I had trouble calling her by her first name, let alone Sunny—gently patted Miss Pringle's arm as Emma and I followed her inside. I walked over to the piano while Emma opened her violin case, lifting a burgundy velvet cloth with its eggshell-colored silk underlining. She tweaked strings and turned pegs, tuning her instrument to the piano, while her teacher settled in on a spare folding chair. When Emma was satisfied, she spread the sonata out on the music stand next to the piano bench.

Miss Pringle raised her eyebrows. "You don't have it memorized? I wish you'd try."

"We're still working on some of it. We will," I said, avoiding her eyes.

"That's not necessary. They're not soloists," Sonia interrupted. "This is like chamber music. It's perfectly acceptable to play a duet with the score in a performance," she added with a wink. "And you can ask a friend to be a page turner."

I knew Dad's quintet used music all the time when they performed even though they didn't need to. I looked over at Miss Pringle. Her smile faded, but I guess she didn't want to make a scene. Both teachers folded their arms in front of them, waiting.

Emma raised her violin, gave me a glance, and nodded. Then she closed her eyes. My elbows went in and out as my body swayed along with Emma's, back and forth like waves. I pedaled softly, raised my hands off the keyboard, and ducked my head down, hunched over the keys. Suddenly I felt a theme so much I couldn't sit still, and lifted myself off the bench. The sonata made me want to dance, just like Emma and I did to "Baby Love" in our room.

Between movements, Emma wiped her palms on her cargo pants, then her T-shirt, readjusting the handkerchief between the chin rest and violin. Then she'd stare at her bow and begin again, examining her fingers skimming the fingerboard as she played. She shook her head with intensity, lifting her eyebrows, scrunching her nose, puckering her lips, or dipping her knees during a particular part that moved her. At the last downward bow, she gracefully lifted it off the violin, and silence resounded.

Sonia began to clap. "Bravo!" she said with enthusiasm. "Marvelous!"

Miss Pringle gave a slight smile. Emma and I exchanged nervous glances.

"I'd work on the last movement," Miss Pringle told us.

Emma came to my rescue. "Ally thought it needed it, too."

*I did?* I looked at her, and she gave me a devilish grin.

"We've decided to do informal weekly concerts in August in an outreach to the community. That way, everyone gets used to performing in public. The more you do, the easier it becomes," said Miss Pringle. Emma was all ears. "We're also having a fund-raiser for the program toward next year, so our students will be playing a series of mini Tanglewood-type concerts in the town square on the lawn. Every student is participating over the next couple of weeks. Maybe you two can play this at one of them."

Was this her way of letting us know we had played well, without actually saying it? Emma's teacher grinned like a proud parent while Emma packed up her violin and smiled wider than I had ever seen her do.

"A fine mess I got us into," I muttered when we got into the hall.

"Hey, it's fine. Really fine. We'll get noticed."

"Good save." I grabbed her hand as we escaped, running upstairs to our room. "About you saying how I thought we needed to work on the last movement, too."

"Anytime." She paused. "She's a piece of work, your teacher. Is she worth it?"

"You know her reputation. She's one of the best."

"That's not what I asked."

I had no answer.

Right after dinner Emma and I got ready for movie night. I couldn't help wondering if Opal had seen any good movies this summer with Brad.

"Should we ask Erik to be a page turner?" Emma called out as I showered.

"Will you be able to concentrate?" I teased her.

"Why not?" she replied as she applied silvery eye shadow.

"Should you do it or should I?" I coated my hair with Emma's creamy lavender conditioner, then rinsed.

"Whatever. Maybe you should. You're the pianist."

"I thought you liked him." I peered out of the shower stall.

"He's okay."

"Just okay? You could have fooled me. I can't imagine what you'd do if you liked someone."

"He's not my type."

"And what's that?" I stepped out of the stall, wrapped in a towel.

"I'll know when I see it. Someone less white-bread." Preoccupied, she pulled at one of my wet curls, and it sprang back into place. "Let me cut your hair."

"Have you done that before?"

"Hundreds of times."

"*Hundreds?*" I questioned her. "You run a beauty salon on the side?"

"Okay, thirty, forty. My grandmother, aunts, little cousins. And myself."

"Yourself?"

"And my neighbor's dog."

"What kind of dog?"

"A poodle."

"You had me at yourself, but if you can do a poodle, I trust you with mine."

As hair fell on the tiled floor around my bare feet, I glanced down, frightened. "Don't look yet!" she insisted, clipping the ends, checking to see if they were even. Then she stood back, like Opal did at her easel, and snipped a stray hair. "*Finis!*"

I looked at myself in the mirror. "You took off more than three inches!"

"It'll grow back."

"Not this summer!" I felt kind of annoyed. My bangs were skimpy.

"Do you like it? You can see your big blue eyes now."

"I'm used to shoulder length." I glanced down at the scattered locks.

"You look sophisticated with it short."

"I do?" I vamped. "Really?" I asked, the annoyance vanishing.

She turned on the blow dryer. "We could be almost the same age."

"Almost?" I gave Emma a nudge.

At this moment, I felt unfaithful to Opal.

So I texted her before we left: I miss u. Your BFF.

I wanted to believe no text came back because her cell phone was off.

Emma polished my toenails, and I did hers in the pale peach color I had bought at the start of the summer. "It's *so* Miami," she said, admiring her feet. Then she put on short silky pants and a slinky black V-neck sweater with a tiny gold necklace. Both of us wore sandals so we could show off our pedicures.

Before we left, she dabbed jasmine essence behind my ears, and then applied a touch to hers. "We're going to get eaten alive," I said.

"By whom?" She looked over at me with a mischievous grin.

"Not by whom, by what—mosquitoes! We just became dinner and a movie."

I grabbed bug spray just in case, throwing it in the pocket of my denim jacket.

It was twilight by the time we got to the lawn near the

two tennis courts. No one noticed my hair. I was expecting a comment or two and felt both disappointment that it hadn't made an impression and fear that it had and everyone was afraid to say anything. A king-size white sheet hung flat between two poles like a big screen, reminding me of Opal's labels dangling on the string in Central Park. A chorus of bullfrogs croaked along with chirping crickets, competing with the cartoon that was playing before the movie. Emma and I found a spot in the back not far from Erik, who appeared to have hooked up with Bin-Yu. Everyone was sprawled out on blankets. Some campers had brought their own pillows and snacks and were passing the food around. I took out what was left of my jelly beans and shared them with Emma. I had saved the red cinnamon ones for something special.

I could make out the silhouettes of Santiago and Cheryl holding hands, walking beside Eduardo, but there was a fourth figure I wasn't sure about until the projector stopped when the cartoon was over and the sheet filled with bright light. It was Alejandro. Alex. What was *he* doing here? He seemed to show up at the most unlikely moments. My heart began to race. I became fixated on the back of his neck as he sat several blankets in front of ours—how he moved his hand through his hair, a thick silver ring shining on his thumb. His hair had become long over the summer, and when he flicked it off his neck he looked gorgeous. Why had I cut my hair now, of all times? I wanted to disappear under my blanket.

"You okay?" Emma rubbed my sleeve when she saw I wasn't laughing at the funny parts.

"Yeah." I faked a little laugh.

"What?" She looked at me.

"Nothing. Let's just watch the movie."

When the movie stopped for the projectionist to change reels, Alex stretched out his arms—a halo of light glowing around him—and turned, gazing in our direction. He gave me a little wave. Then it happened. His eyes locked with Emma's. "You know my line about finding my type," she murmured, "'I'll know when I see it'? Well, I see it."

I got a pang inside my chest.

When the film was over, we got up to leave. Alex hung back and magically wound up next to Emma. You know how people walk in groups, and sometimes their hands touch for a second while they're walking? That's what happened with Alex and Emma. He flashed a smile at her. "Alejandro Sanchez. Alex."

"Emma Moore." She tilted her head to the side as if she were suddenly shy. At least she didn't stoop so low as to bat her long, thick eyelashes at him.

It was like I wasn't even there. Like *no one* was there. Just him and Emma. I wanted to curl up and hide, even more than I did when I hit a wrong note.

"Surprised to see me?" he asked as we all walked back to the lobby.

"You could say that," I replied. "How come you're here?"

"I met a conductor near Mexico City at that family wedding. She heard me play. She's touring Vermont in August with a Latin American orchestra near Rutland and they need a brass section for certain pieces."

"He's their go-to guy." Eduardo slung his arm around his

friend, overhearing him. "I said he could bunk with me to save money on room and board."

"Uh-huh. For how long?"

"The next two weeks." Alex looked over at Emma.

She looked down and smiled to herself.

*Two weeks!* Any other time, maybe, but now . . . ?

Emma and I were supposed to perform in two and a half weeks! I needed her to be into our music, not him. And I wanted him to leave her alone. Nothing could have prepared me for this.

# August

Music is one of the ways we can achieve a shorthand to understand each other.
—Yo-Yo Ma, cellist

Emma and Alejandro became an item that night. That's what she called him—Alejandro. Not Alex.

"The name Alex isn't ethnic enough," she exclaimed when she returned to our room way after midnight. And she wouldn't shut up about him. "He's so cute. He's so great on the sax. His arm muscles rippled when he was jamming with some of the guys in the lobby."

I'd never thought I would say this, but I yearned for Miss Tippytoes—the ballerina Alex liked and had waved to on the plaza—to be back on the scene. This was *way* too close to home. I turned my back to her, trying to sleep, and stared at the moon out the window as she went on and on: Alejandro this, Alejandro that. I put on my headphones and listened to the Beethoven concerto to block her out. Tears pooled on my pillow. I held on to one of Julia's purple antlers. *When will that be me? And with whom? Brad? Someone else?* I felt so alone and left out. Under the covers, I texted Opal. I need u. Luv, A. No smiley face. No answer.

I had bad dreams all night and kept waking up in a sweat. I was being chased.

The next morning, Emma checked herself out in the bathroom mirror for the longest time, wiping gloss off her front teeth, then pressing her full lips together. As she adjusted her bikini top under a tight-fitting tangerine-colored T-shirt, she said to my reflection in the mirror, "Could we put off practice for a few hours?"

"How come?"

"I've got to work on my concerto with an accompanist my teacher assigned me to, since that's the real piece that I'm being judged on this summer, like you. Then Alejandro and I are going for a boat ride. So can we do the sonata later on in the afternoon?"

She didn't ask me to come with them. My head understood that. My heart didn't.

"You're like a mushroom in the rain, Alex," I told him as we got on line for breakfast. I decided to keep calling him that instead of using his full name, like Emma.

"What did you mean by that?" he asked, finally sitting down with a group of us.

"You seem to show up everywhere. Master class. Here."

"Hey." He gently knocked my arm, nearly causing me to lose my grip on the bowl of blueberries.

"I'm glad he showed up." Emma took a sip from her cup of coffee.

I swirled the milk in my cereal with my spoon until the whole thing became a soggy mess, watching the two of them playfully steal forkfuls of food from each other's plate.

When we went upstairs to brush our teeth, I asked, "What time will you be back?"

She took out her violin and set up her concerto on a music stand. "I'm going to run through my piece here, and then with that accompanist in a practice room. Alejandro and I are skipping out on lunch. So threeish?"

"See you then." I should have said, *Have fun*, but I didn't.

After practicing all morning and then another hour after lunch, I waited for her in the lobby. Every time the door opened, I looked to see if it was Emma, and when it wasn't, my shoulders slumped as anger built.

At half past three, Opal called. "Got your nine-one-one."

I walked outside with the phone, where the reception was better. "Alex is up here. He likes Emma. Emma likes him." I let all my frustration spill over. "Now I wish Eduardo had left, because even though I want lessons with him, then Alex wouldn't have been here. And Emma and I are supposed to perform together in a few weeks, and I'm here waiting for her to go over the piece, and she's late. And is there anything up with you and Brad? And why haven't you answered my texts or called me?"

"Whoa, hold on a minute. I just did."

I began to cry into the phone.

"You're not making sense," she said.

I cried even more.

"Al," she said softly, "nothing's going on with me and Brad. The only things heating up are sauces and soufflés. His dad has been so tired lately we're putting in more hours than ever. Yeah, we're having a great time. Like friends. Like you and Emma. You sounded tied up with her, you know, and your work. Okay?"

"Okay." I took a breath.

"One thing solved. I can't do anything about those other things."

"I know."

"Look at me and Eric," she said. "To guys like that, you and I are just kids."

"I know, but I can't help what I feel."

"I thought you liked Brad."

"I do."

"He's more your age, Ally."

I sighed. "I know. But weren't you the one who told me to date older?"

"Yes, but Brad's different. And he's cute."

"I know."

"If you know so much, why do you sound nuts?"

"I guess I don't know."

We both began to laugh.

"You'll let me know you're okay?"

"Yes, Mom," I teased Opal. "Still best friends?"

"I was wondering the same thing lately," she said. "Forever."

We hung up and I went inside. I waited some more, but Emma never showed up.

After dinner I cornered her. "What about now?"

"I'm beat," Emma told me. "Can I have a rain check?"

"Do you want to do this sonata or not?"

"You know I do."

"Then we need to go over it so we can do it perfectly onstage."

"It's just . . . I didn't know this was going to happen."

*Neither did I.*

But I played dumb. "What's 'this'?"

"Ally," she said, rolling her eyes, "you know. Alex."

"Yeah," I said with a hint of bitterness, "who would have ever expected that?"

We vegged in the lobby with a whole bunch of kids. Erik was flipping through the TV channels. Emma was curled up in a ball with her head resting on a throw pillow, her eyes half closed, when Alex returned from his rehearsal two hours later. She perked right up and somehow had enough energy to go out dancing at a bar up the road with a bunch of assistants and him. And again no one asked me. I didn't have a fake ID like her, and even if I'd had one, I looked too young. I hung out playing cards until the director told us it was time to go to sleep.

The next day I passed by a practice room and found Alex

and Emma playing together along with a CD. I overheard Alex telling her, "It's Django Reinhardt—a great jazz guitarist. Listen to him go at it." They saw me and motioned for me to come in, but I stood in the hall, trying not to enjoy the music, which was next to impossible.

I went back to our room, plopped on my bed, and tucked my arms around Julia with an enormous frown plastered on my face. I tried not to sound bitchy when Emma got back. "What about the sonata?"

"What about it?" she replied, putting her violin case in the bottom of the closet.

"We need to practice, too."

"We will," she said impatiently, as if I were some annoying little kid.

"When? We're supposed to perform soon."

"I'm aware of that."

"So?" I said petulantly.

"So what?" she answered.

"So maybe Erik won't need to be a page turner."

"So maybe he won't. You're too much." She blew me off and left in a huff.

My mother called the very next second. Her timing was amazing. I answered the phone with "What?"

"That's a nice hello. Are you in the middle of something?"

"Yes."

"I can call another time, then, honey."

"What do you want?"

"To find out how my daughter is doing."

"I'm fine."

"Was it something with Miss Pringle? Are the lessons going okay?"

I let out an impatient sigh.

"Eduardo? You've never had a problem there."

"Still don't."

"Anyone else?"

"Can we change the subject?"

"I sent you a care package. Grandma baked cookies and her famous rugelach. I threw in a salami. And some deli mustard. Are you eating?"

"I'm pigging out." I sounded snarky.

"You're not gaining too much weight, are you?"

"I've gotta go, Mom. If I can fit through the door."

"You'll call me? I'm here if you need to talk."

"Sure."

"I hope whatever is bothering you ends."

A while later Emma returned and threw a stick of red licorice on my bed. "Truce."

"I don't want to fight. I want to play," I said with relief.

She grabbed her violin and the music. "Then let's play."

I smiled as we went to a practice room and put in over an hour.

"That didn't go so bad," Emma said.

"I agree. Do you think we need a little more?"

She glanced down at her watch. "I can't. I'm meeting Alejandro soon. He's coming back from Killington. They were playing for a bunch of senior citizens."

She headed upstairs, while I went to dinner alone and sat with some of the other campers. When I got up to get a piece of layer cake, Eduardo sidled up to me. "Ally."

I looked up.

"I've got to run down to New York to straighten out this visa mess."

"When will you be back?"

"As soon as it's taken care of. But I have to cancel our lesson this week."

*Oh, great. What next?* I thought.

"Don't worry." He patted my arm. "Your concerto's coming along. This'll give you a chance to surprise me when I return. I'm hoping it's only a few nights."

"Me too."

"By the way, how's that sonata going? Since I've heard no bad press"—he smiled, and I knew he was referring to Miss Pringle—"I'm assuming well."

I shrugged.

"If there's time, maybe I can hear that, too, when I return?"

I shrugged again.

When dinner was over, Bin-Yu, Erik, and some friends were about to start a Ping-Pong tournament. "You want in?" Bin-Yu asked. I didn't answer. She pulled me by the arm to the game room next to the cement patio by the swimming pool.

In the middle of the third round, I noticed Emma and Alex walking into the shadows at the edge of the pool. They

171

stopped, and Alex smoothed his hand through his hair. Some strands fell on her face as he leaned in to kiss her. She put her arms around his neck, leaning her head on his chest. I imagined what that might feel like. But that was like imagining a piece without actually playing it.

I felt awful and couldn't fall asleep. The hours ticked by, and Emma didn't come back. I wondered if she was okay. Nighttime had faded into the grayness of the in-between morning light when I finally heard her tiptoeing in. I whispered, "Where were you all night?"

"Out."

"I know you were out. Out where?" Opal and I would have told each other.

"What are you, my mother?" She got into bed.

I didn't say anything nasty, although I wanted to say, *You don't have one.*

After that, she worked on her concerto every day, and I worked on mine.

And she made less and less time for our practice.

A couple of days later, I caught her and Alex making out in the tall grass behind the music shed before the first of the barn recitals. That same day, Miss Pringle said to me, "I wonder if it was such a good idea to collaborate. Your friends are giving Santiago and Cheryl a run for their money."

"What do you mean?" I pretended to be clueless.

"Your duet friend and that saxophone player," she said indignantly. "She's not getting down to business. At least not music business."

What could I say? This was the one time I totally agreed with Miss Pringle.

And if I agreed with Miss Pringle, then things were *really* bad.

They went from bad to worse when Emma and I finally met to rehearse. Alex walked her to the door of our practice room and smiled at me. I made an attempt to smile back. Emma gave him a peck on the cheek. He said, "I'll see you when you're through." She began the piece the minute he left.

"You started to play without me!" I shouted.

"You don't know when you're supposed to begin by now?"

"You're supposed to nod or glance, so we come in exactly on time, in sync."

"We're not in sync! About anything!"

"I'm saying let's work together like we used to."

"Telling me when to come in," she grumbled. "Asking when we can practice. It was *your* idea. Not mine!"

"What?" I dropped my hands to my side. "We're partners in this, I thought."

"Partners? Ever since Alejandro arrived, you've been acting weird."

"His name is Alex," I stated. "At least that's what *he* told me."

"Okay, Alex," she said sarcastically.

"I guess he's your partner now."

She shook her head. "What is Alex to you?"

I didn't answer her.

"I thought you liked that kid Brad."

*"Kid?"* My eyes narrowed.

"Guy. Boy. What's the difference? Isn't he more your speed?"

I looked into her eyes, fuming.

"Are you jealous?" she asked.

I glared at her.

"You are, aren't you?" She stood with one hand on her hip. "You're jealous."

I wished she would stop saying that word. I felt humiliated, and gathered up the piano part so quickly I knocked some of the pages off the shelf onto the floor. I bent to catch them, creasing the edges of my father's sonata music in my haste.

She shut her music, too. "I can't do this anymore. It was a nice concept, but it's not fun anymore."

"You've gotta be joking." In a rage, I slammed the wood cover shut over the keyboard, and the strings vibrated from the force of my fury. "So that's it?"

"That's it."

"I don't believe this," I muttered to myself. Then I looked right into her eyes. "I guess it just wasn't as important to you as I thought! You said we'd get noticed if we did this together at one of the concerts. So now how's that going to happen?"

"I've still got my concerto! And you've got yours!"

"Yeah, right!" I ran from the room, ashamed of my anger.

She poked her head out of the door and yelled after me, "What did I do that was so terrible? Like someone? He just turned eighteen. Don't you think he's a bit old for you?"

I didn't want to admit that she hadn't done anything so terrible; it just felt terrible. And I couldn't make that feeling go away. It grew and grew like a balloon filling with air until it was ready to burst. I stopped, turned, and shouted, "You totally screwed me with my teacher. How am I going to do the sonata and make it right with her? It's going to make me look really bad!"

She hollered back, "You should have thought of that sooner!"

Bin-Yu stuck her head out of a practice room. "What's going on?"

"Mind your own business!" I shrieked.

She meekly went back into the room, closing the door.

"You're out of control, Ally. It's just one concert," Emma said, sounding exasperated. "You can still play your concerto. And I can play mine. We don't have to do the sonata!"

"You can't do one concert? Are you *that* selfish? This is my life!"

"And mine."

"By the way," I said snidely, "I hate the haircut you gave me! It's too short."

"Big deal. I told you already, it'll grow. It's hair!"

"It's *my* hair. Stick to poodles!"

She gave me a piercing look.

I ran back to our room and sat on my bed. I missed dinner. I sat there some more, not moving until it began to get dark. When Emma showed up—she had practiced elsewhere—she put her violin in the closet and left as quickly as she'd come, without looking at me or saying a word. I waited for her to come back. When she didn't, I went to her side of the closet, picked up her case, placed it on my lap, and remained with it there in total darkness for almost an hour. I wanted to smash her violin to pieces. I considered prying open the case, but

I thought of my father and how he'd feel if someone ruined his violin. So I put it back in the closet.

When it got very late, I switched on the light above my bed, took out a pad, and began to write, pouring the emotions swirling around in me into the music.

Emma returned the next morning and began to pack up her stuff.

"What are you doing?"

She remained silent.

"Emma, where are you going?"

She continued to stuff her clothes in her suitcase.

"Emma, come on."

She ignored me.

"There's no room anywhere else."

"I already found a place. Last night."

"You'll be crowded if you bunk with other girls."

"Maybe I'm not bunking with other girls."

I looked at her. "I don't want to argue."

"You started it."

"What are you, three?"

She got quiet again and continued to gather her things, leaving the nail polish I'd bought on the countertop, taking all the others that were hers.

"Emma? Please don't do this. My teacher's going to be furious at me."

"Is that all you care about? Not my problem."

"Emma," I begged. "Don't go. You know what it's like to be left."

I was sorry those words came out of my mouth. She shot me a look.

"I don't need this. It's gotten way too heavy for me." And she shut the door.

I sat alone on the bathroom floor and cried and cried until my eyes burned. Then I got angry again.

What was I supposed to do now? Tell Miss Pringle I was dropping the sonata after I had pleaded with her to let me do it? Or do the concerto—but only the first two movements, because I hadn't concentrated on the third? She'd look at me like, *I told you so.*

I searched and found out where Emma was staying—with three other girls who were older than her, at the very end of the first floor. When they all went to sun themselves in the garden by their room, I slipped in and found a sleeping bag spread out with Emma's nightie on top of it. I crumpled up the photo of Alex I'd been carrying around for months and left it on her pillow. Then I did something awful. I took the Palm Beach nail polish and painted on her violin case Fugue You! instead of what I really wanted to write. Then I ran. I kept running until I got to the general store down the road, where I bought a bottle of nail polish remover. When I got back to my room, consumed with guilt and fear, I found a note slipped under my door:

*Don't talk to me.*
*Don't e-mail me.*
*Don't say good-bye.*

*You're dead to me.*
*P.S. Have a nice life.*

I held it in my hands and stared at it until the words were etched in my brain.

Eduardo came back from Manhattan in the late afternoon, but I couldn't go for my lesson. Instead, I left the nail polish remover in a paper bag in front of Emma's door, but I knew the polish would never totally come off her black cloth violin case.

Alex left the next day before dawn. The orchestra tour was *now* over. I never got a chance to say to him, "See you next fall" or "Good luck." I wondered what Emma had told him . . . or hadn't told him. Could I face him again?

At my lesson with Miss Pringle I lied. "I don't think the sonata will be ready."

"Then get it ready," she ordered. "Time is getting tight."

"W-well," I stammered, "I can't."

"Why can't you? You're almost there, aren't you?"

I couldn't tell her Emma and I had had a major falling-out.

"You were right. The concerto's more challenging. I'm going to focus on that."

She put down her pad and pencil. "You decide to buckle down now and do a solo? You certainly won't have the entire piece ready for our final summer recital. And I'm not so sure about it for the Beethoven competition, either. You extended yourself in too many directions. I initially advised you *not* to do the sonata."

I looked down, twisting a tissue in my hand, afraid to tell her the truth.

"You might have to make other plans in the fall. I don't know if you're taking the piano seriously enough. These aren't some little weekly lessons you're doing with a local teacher, you know. This is a career being formed. Or not."

*Other plans?*

I stood there frozen, unable to move.

In that moment, it hit me: I was going to drop her before she dropped me. It wasn't going to happen twice, first with Emma and now with her. But how was I going to tell my parents?

If Emma had still been my friend, I would have told her what Miss Pringle said to me, and she would have made me feel better, saying I was better off without her. And she'd have understood the pressure I was under even more than Opal or Brad because she had experienced it herself. Emma knew what it was all about. But instead, I saw Emma and her new friends eating together and joking around. It was also odd how no one seemed to realize that she had moved out, except for the girls she was now shacking up with. But then, we were all pretty much on our own and no one checked up on us. Too many egos into their own thing. It wasn't like this was camp, with a counselor who might say, *How come Ally didn't show up for swim?* So when I remained mostly in bed, no one seemed to notice, because all that mattered was *their* practice and *their* upcoming concerts and *their* success. Whether we practiced or not was up to us, and the only way anyone would know that we hadn't was at the lesson—or worse, a concert. And ours was coming up.

So I stopped eating with everyone else and started sneaking fruit and snacks or sodas in my room. I came out only for a lesson with Eduardo. I passed his studio, where he was practicing his Rachmaninoff, and when he saw me, he beckoned me in. "Where've you been?"

"Around."

"You missed a lesson."

"Sorry."

"Is everything okay?" He looked straight at me, searching my face.

After a long pause I said, "I don't think I'm going to play in the community concert."

"But you've been preparing all summer."

"I don't know. The sonata . . ."

"I didn't get a chance to hear it, but I heard it was okay. What about Emma?" Eduardo asked.

"She's concentrating on the Bruch now. Maybe a caprice."

"I see." He took in a breath. "So work on your concerto."

"Miss Pringle thinks the last movement isn't ready."

"Sometimes that's her way of pushing a student harder."

"I think she *really* doesn't."

He moved off the piano bench. "Let's hear it."

I played the first movement, then the second. On the third, I couldn't do it by heart. "You see what she means?"

"The first two are very good, but the last needs work. I know you can do it. What else do you have on your mind up here except music?" He smiled.

*If only you knew.*

In the evenings I heard students running back and forth

in the halls, laughing, staying up late, and I felt even more alone. Sometimes I would stay up all night and compose. When I didn't feel like doing that, I tossed and turned in my bed until it was almost light outside. So I'd basically stopped sleeping. And I couldn't play the piano. My heart wasn't in it.

I began to hang out in my room even more, playing CDs I had brought up, scribbling notes on my music pad for hours in bed, or watching DVDs if no one was around, except for the one night when I dragged myself out to see some Judd Apatow comedy that Erik had rented from the video section in the general store and I saw Miss Pringle with some of the other teachers by the office, ready to go out. She had a white cardigan draped over her shoulders and pearls around her neck, and she seemed festive and bubbly. Eduardo was dressed in a suit. He was performing at a local church. We weren't required to attend, but I felt bad I didn't want to go.

I decided then and there that I wasn't going to play at *any* concert. I'd act like I was going to do everything, and then I would say I was sick. Who could fault me for that?

Miss Pringle noticed me going down the hall for ice. "What's this I hear? You're definitely not playing the sonata?"

"Who said that?"

"Eduardo. Sonia. And Emma."

I froze. "Emma?"

"Yes, Emma. I saw her at dinner and asked how it was going, and she told me you two decided to focus on your own pieces."

I was too embarrassed to say anything after I had fought so hard for it. I also couldn't believe Emma told her that.

"A collaboration is when two people struggle to produce something. You two seemed to be pulling it off. Now you're not?"

I looked down.

"Whatever is going on, get it together, Ally."

I nodded then, and she let me go.

Days before xeroxed flyers of the performance schedule went up at local restaurants, farm stands, the firehouse, the diner, the elementary school where summer activities were held, and places of worship, I told Miss Pringle, "I haven't been feeling so well."

"The show must go on. You played with a high fever in the third grade, I remember."

She couldn't force me. "Please take my name off the program this year."

She turned around without saying a word and walked away.

Parents were making their usual trek up for the final recital of the summer. This time I wasn't looking forward to my parents' visit. When they showed up, I was waiting for them downstairs so they wouldn't see I was living alone. I ran into their arms.

"How's it going?" asked Mom. "You look very pale." She turned to my father. "Does Ally look under the weather to you?"

"I guess she wasn't in the sun a lot." He winked at me.

"We're so excited to hear you play!" Mom stroked the side of my hair.

My stomach began to churn.

"You cut your bangs so short."

I thought of the locks left scattered on the floor when Emma cut my hair.

"It looks . . ." She paused, cupping my head in her hand. "A little uneven."

I touched my bangs, remembering how Emma said she could see my blue eyes.

"We'll straighten it out at home." She smiled tentatively.

I began to get more and more worried as it got closer to dusk. Dad went to park the car in the parking lot near the barn, where the concert was going to be, and as my mother and I waited for him I saw many other parents and students walking together toward its entrance, bending over to pick up the programs from a cardboard box. I started to weep uncontrollably.

My mother threw her arms around me. "Is it what I said about your haircut earlier? You'll look fine when you play."

I couldn't stop crying.

"Sweetheart, what's wrong? You can tell me."

In my head I said, *No, I can't.*

"Are you working too hard? That's it, isn't it? You're overtired. I think Ally's working too hard." She looked over at my father as he walked up.

He squeezed my shoulder gently. "Come on, let's go for a quick bite."

I forced myself to go to the snack bar next to the barn, even though I wanted to disappear into my room. As I sipped some lemonade, I saw Emma off in the distance through the window, holding some music. I pushed the rest of my food aside and made an excuse: "I really can't eat before a concert."

We walked along the path to the barn and took three seats near the back. Mom scanned the concert program. "Where's your name?"

I couldn't avoid it anymore.

"Ally?" She looked at me, confused.

"I got bumped," I lied.

"You what?" Her voice got kind of loud.

I put my hand over her mouth. "Shh."

"Did you hear that, Doug? Ally's not playing tonight. Why didn't you tell us?" My mother's eyes were focused on me.

Dad looked puzzled. "How come?"

"See all the kids?" I gestured. "There's a packed house this year."

Mom said, "Weren't there many concerts over the past weeks? I thought you were in this one also. The last recital of the summer. This is what we paid hard-earned dollars for? To hear *other* kids?"

"Ma." I looked in her eyes and spoke a half-truth. "My piece wasn't ready."

How could I tell her that the sonata was ready—totally—but the concerto wasn't?

"Oh," she said softly, looking down. But her sigh said it all.

I couldn't tell her the whole truth: that this was the worst summer of my life. Even worse than the one with the pyromaniac cellist at Auschwitz in the Adirondacks.

While Timothy and his brother played during the recital, I saw my mother's lips press tightly together. Then Erik, Bin-Yu, and Emma performed in turn. She didn't do the Bruch. She probably didn't have it ready, either, because we had worked so hard on the sonata. So she did one of her Paganini caprices, which showed off some fancy fingering. When she was done, she seemed satisfied as she bowed and looked straight into the audience at Sonia, her teacher, who was clapping the longest and loudest. She handed Emma one red rose, as she did to each of her students. I glanced over at my father's face as we sat through what felt like the longest recital ever played. He looked almost as unhappy as Mom. I guess I had let him down, too.

On the way back to my room, I asked my parents, "Can I sleep with you guys tonight?"

Dad glanced at me in the rearview mirror. "Of course." Then he exchanged a momentary look with my mother. I stared out the window at the winding road.

"Don't you want to be with your friends? It's the last night," said Mom.

I didn't answer her question. "I'll just pick up a change of clothes, my retainer, and my toothbrush," I said as we pulled into the parking lot near my room.

"Need any help?" Mom asked as she waited in the car.

"I'll be fine." I ran upstairs to quiet halls.

Everyone would be celebrating the end of the summer after they returned from the barn concert. I knew the partying would go on until dawn. I was happy to be on a rollaway bed at the foot of my parents' mattress in the motel up the road. Away.

"I'm sorry," I whispered when Dad shut out the lights, "about not playing."

"As long as you tried your hardest," he whispered back.

Mom was silent in the dark. I could hear her breathing. Her disappointment was filling the room.

The following day, one of the most painful things was leaving without saying good-bye to Emma, and not telling her that I was sorry for the way things had turned out and how we'd both let each other down. My parents even asked, "Would you like to take Emma for breakfast? A farewell meal." And when we packed up my room, they grilled me, realizing her half of the closet was empty: "Did Emma leave already? We wanted to at least say good luck. We didn't get a chance to last night."

I couldn't find Emma anywhere. I asked around. I went to her new room. All her stuff was gone. She had left without saying anything. I wasn't surprised, but it still ached. I knew we'd probably never see each other again. Or maybe if we did meet somewhere by accident—at some concert or program—there'd be that moment where we couldn't look at each other, but we'd both know the other was there. It was even more painful than realizing there had never been beginnings or endings or any in-betweens with Alex and never would be. The kiss I'd had with Brad was real; everything else was a dream, imagined.

We left in a summer storm with fierce thunder and lightning, rain beating against the windshield. "Heard Miss Pringle's staying on up until Labor Day. Too bad we couldn't find her to say good-bye also," said Mom.

*Thank God*, I thought. I knew she'd have blown my cover. Miss Pringle wasn't pleased that I hadn't performed. It scared me to death to even think of how she had looked at me when I told her to take my name off the program.

I texted Opal on the way back to Manhattan.

> I need u!
> She texted me back: We're on vacation until
> Labor Day.
> By the way, I wrote her, how's Brad? Haven't
> heard from him.
> U didn't know? His dad's sick. Brad's with
> his aunt.
> Is it bad?
> Yeah. He's got the big C. Cancer.

I telephoned Brad at the number he'd given me for the restaurant and left a message on the voice mail because I didn't have his aunt's number and I wanted him to hear in my voice how sorry I was: "Call me. Just heard the news."

Grandma was waiting for me with Beethoven, standing exactly where they'd been when I left: on the front stoop, waving. Only this time it wasn't good-bye.

"*Shana punim,*" she said with a smile, stroking my cheek.

Her apron smelled of carrots, celery, dill, parsnips, and boiled chicken.

I was home.

# Autumn

# AUTUMN

Everyone is made to forget their cares and to sing
    and dance
By the air which is tempered with pleasure
And [by] the season that invites so many, many
Out of their sweetest slumber to fine enjoyment.

The hunters emerge at the new dawn
And with horns and dogs and guns depart upon
    their hunting.
The beast flees and they follow its trail;
Terrified and tired of the great noise
Of guns and dogs, the beast, wounded, threatens
Languidly to flee but, harried, dies.

*—From a sonnet by Vivaldi*

# September

Show me a really fine talent that succeeds, and I'll show you an ambitious parent.
—Ruth Slenczynska, child prodigy, concert pianist, and teacher

A grace note is a musical ornament—a note written smaller that isn't important to the melody or harmony. It's an extra-fast beat in the time signature of a musical measure. That was what I felt like—a grace note. A note not fully played or heard, and sometimes even silent.

I was in limbo. I couldn't lie forever about giving up. To them. Or to myself.

Opal was on vacation. Gone.

Brad was away. Gone.

Eduardo left for Caracas after he came back from Vermont.

He admitted, "I'd never forgive myself if I didn't see my grand-mother again. I have to return to my country."

"Now?" I said. "What about your visa? And your master's?" *And me?*

"I'll work it out. Somehow. There's a program called El Sistema that enrolls poor kids in music school. They lend each of them an instrument and put them in a youth orchestra as a way of getting them out of poverty and drugs. I'm going to get involved with them. Miss Pringle helped me when she first came to Venezuela. Now I should give back."

He put a dime on my hand, but this time in my palm instead of on the back like he had done at my lesson months ago. I tucked my fingers around the coin as if it were gold. "Your future students are lucky."

I cried the night of his flight. How could I continue the piano without him?

After Labor Day, Opal rang me. "We're ba-a-ack! Pool's open."

"What pool?"

"The wading pool on my roof! Get your lifetime pass out."

"Let me put on a bathing suit and shoot down to you. Half hour okay?"

"See you in thirty."

"Where are you going?" Mom asked when she saw me wearing my tank top and shorts and carrying a canvas bag holding a beach towel.

"Downtown to Opal's. To sun ourselves on her roof."

"No practice? Pre-College is starting soon."

"I know." I couldn't help sounding irritated.

"Okay." She backed off. "I was just reminding you."

"Like I could ever forget."

"Someone's real touchy."

"Yeah, someone is." Under my breath I muttered, "Control freak."

"I heard that."

"So?"

"So be nice."

"I am," I muttered again. "If you want to direct, go to film school." Then I left.

The first thing Opal said when she saw me was, "You got a trim."

I smiled awkwardly, remembering the day of my haircut. "Emma did it."

"Cool," said Opal. "You have a kind of shaggy thing going on there." She touched my uneven bangs.

We sat in a baby pool with purple dragons on it, drinking Virgin Mary's. I told Opal what had happened with Emma, also gone from my life. At least I had Opal.

"That's rough," she said. "And mean. I didn't know you had it in you."

"Hey," I said defensively, "what about the time you poured turpentine on Ruby's good sweaters? She smelled like an art studio for weeks!"

Opal smiled sheepishly. "You got me there. Although Ruby used it as an excuse for a wardrobe upgrade."

"I feel horrible. Should I send Emma money to replace her violin case?"

"Would she accept it?"

"Probably not. She's got a lot of pride." After a moment I said, "Emma got my teacher more pissed at me than she already was." I knew I was just trying to justify my behavior, which made me feel even worse.

Opal looked up from swirling the stalk of celery in her drink. "Seems like she's on your case even without Emma."

Should I have kept everything to myself?

Opal wiggled her toes—each one painted a different color—in the water and changed the subject. "Eric left in mid-August for college. We brought Ruby up over the weekend. Her freshman dorm's on the fifth floor, where servants used to store students' trunks during the early nineteen hundreds. *I* had to help carry her stuff up the stairwell. No elevators. She's such a pain in the neck." Opal sucked on a lime wedge, puckering her lips. "But I miss her."

"*You do?* You hate Ruby's snoring." I sipped on my plastic straw.

"I got used to it."

I thought of Emma—how we'd whispered in the dark, how I'd fall asleep to her rhythmic breaths. I looked over at Opal's dog napping in the sun, dreaming whatever dogs dream of. "So sleep with Sapphire."

"I do," she confessed. "Sapphire's been sleeping in Ruby's bed under the covers with her head on a pillow."

"I'm coming back in my next life as your dog."

Opal playfully petted my head and said, "Stay."

I splashed her and sipped some more tomato juice. "Tell me about Brad."

"It was fun . . . until his dad . . . got . . . cancer."

"Why didn't Brad tell me?" I tried to hide that I was hurt.

"You'll have to ask him. But I think he was in a state of shock. When you have one parent left, it's even harder to take. I don't even want to go there."

I furrowed my eyebrows. "Is he going to live?"

"They hope so. He needs chemotherapy. And radiation."

"Is Brad coming back?" My voice broke.

"The plan is to see how the first round of chemo goes. His aunt and uncle—the pacifist and the hunter—are taking in Brad until Mr. Clark's back on his feet."

"The Boise relatives?"

She nodded. "Bambi meets the Terminator."

"What about the restaurant?"

"Closed down."

"Oh. That's why I haven't heard from him. I left a message on their machine. Brad loves that place."

"So does Mr. Clark," Opal sighed. "So did I."

I closed my eyes, allowing the sun to beat down on me.

"Should we do this again next weekend?"

"I can't. It all starts again," I said.

"It?"

"The whole routine. School. Practice."

"See you next June." Opal gave me a major eye roll.

"Very funny." I gave her one back. "Not."

After we dried off, she showed me a sketch she'd done of Brad while he was cooking, his head turned to the viewer. Or was he looking at the artist—Opal?

When I came home, I passed by the half-open door of the studio. My mother glanced up, closing an old Cole Porter songbook. "School starts tomorrow."

"My pencil case is packed," I said.

"The Beethoven competition is coming up this fall."

"Thanks for bringing it up in case I wasn't freaked out enough."

"You'll be performing without a net. It *has* to be perfect."

"Even circus performers don't do that!"

My mother took in a deep breath. She ran her long, graceful fingers through her hair, her tarnished earrings—the ones Dad had given her for her forty-fifth birthday last year—brushing against her neck. "You need to get started. I don't want to upset you."

"You just did."

She looked distressed. "If you're going to become a really, *really* good musician, then do it now. Stop wasting time."

"Wasting time? You've got to be kidding. What have all the years of practicing been about?" I thought I would explode listening to her.

She kept going as if she didn't hear me. "You've got a window of opportunity left to become a great talent. Don't blow it!"

"I'm thirteen!"

She put her arms out, like, *So?*

"What more do I have to do?" I asked her.

"The creative process is an endless journey to reach higher, push further. Always having to do better than better. Nowadays, everyone's running faster and faster."

Dad walked in on us to grab a score. "What's up?"

We both screamed, "Nothing!" and I turned on my heel.

"Sorry I asked," he said facetiously. But I heard him say to Mom as I ran out, "Is she okay?"

My mother answered, "Sometimes she drives me up a wall."

And I thought, *Look in the mirror.*

When school started, I fractured my pinky playing Ultimate Frisbee during gym. The school nurse said, "There's nothing you can do other than splint it, wrap adhesive tape around it, and wait until it heals."

The first thing Mom asked me when I called her from the nurse's office was, "Which hand?"

I understood exactly where she was coming from, because I was coming from the same place. "The left one," I answered.

The nurse shook her head and looked at me as if I'd been hit in the head instead.

"At least you can practice the melody in the upper staves with your right hand," my mother replied.

"I don't know. Maybe I should put off lessons for a while."

There was silence at the other end of the phone. Then she said, "We'll talk about it later."

When I got home, I didn't bring up the subject and neither did Mom, but you could just feel it floating in the air, hanging over us like a giant blimp. She was scraping green fuzzy leftovers into the garbage pail. "They look as if they've seen better days." I picked up a container, sounding casual, trying to rinse.

She looked at my bandaged pinky. "Don't get that wet!" She grabbed at the container, stacking it in the drainer.

"Can't I help?"

"You could have helped by being more careful."

"What are you saying?"

She slammed another container in the drainer, soapy water still swishing off its side. "Sometimes we create situations to get out of things."

"I was in gym. Give me a break!"

"I just wonder if the Frisbee thing was an accident."

I put down the sponge, in slow-boiling rage. "What does *that* mean?"

She continued to scrub a pot as if it were the most important thing in the world.

"That I made it happen?" My voice elevated.

"Well, you got out of playing at the end of the summer, and now this. I don't think there'll be much practicing going on."

"Thanks a lot for caring about me."

"I'm disappointed." She slammed the pot in the sink.

"Oh, like I'm not."

She gave me a look that said, *Maybe you're not.*

I stormed past the piano and pushed my cat off the bench onto the floor with a thump. He meowed. Then I bent over to scratch behind his ears. "It's not your fault, Beethoven," I whispered.

My mother headed into the studio without saying a word.

I went upstairs and began to sulk. *I hate her. Hate hate hate her,* I thought.

She came upstairs to see me before I went to sleep. I didn't answer when she knocked at my door and tiptoed in. I pretended I was out, but she must have seen my eyelids fluttering. "Ally?" I remained still and tried not to breathe. "I know you're awake." I finally let out a breath. "I realize things this summer must have turned out . . ." She paused. "Not so well for you. And you're probably anxious about lessons again."

That was an understatement, because (a) I didn't know if I wanted to continue, and (b) I didn't know if Miss Pringle wanted to. The last time I'd seen Miss Pringle she had said, *You might have to make other plans in the fall.*

"Don't worry, I'll try to have the Beethoven ready in time for the competition," I said with my eyes remaining closed. "Even if I have to play with one hand."

"You think that's all I care about?" She smoothed her hand across the sleeve of my upper arm.

I didn't answer her.

"Isn't our aim the same?"

I continued to be silent. Then I blurted out, "And what's that?"

"Your happiness."

I opened my eyes. "Sometimes I wonder."

My mother looked hurt.

"I don't know after this summer if Miss Pringle will even have me as a student," I admitted grudgingly. And I didn't know if I'd have her even if she did.

"I bumped into Hannah's mother in the supermarket recently. She mentioned Hannah switched studios."

"That's nice for Hannah."

"There's more than one highly qualified teacher."

"Oh, don't start in on that again. I know there are."

"So?"

"So if everyone knows Miss Pringle's the best, then everyone thinks her students are, too. They win the competitions and get to do the solos in the Juilliard Theater."

"At what cost, Ally?"

"I've never heard you talk like this, Mom."

"Me neither."

"Just yesterday you gave me the you're-thirteen-already-don't-blow-it speech."

She looked ashamed.

Here was my chance to say, *Enough!* but instead I said without looking at her, "I'll think about it."

"Okay." She swallowed. "No one has to be stuck."

Was she talking about herself or me?

"Maybe you'll be luckier than me. It's a rough road your father and I took. And yet there was no choice. Music was something we *had* to do. It's our passion."

"Then why are you encouraging me?"

"Because I see it's who you are, too. You're gifted."

I stared at her, taken aback. It wasn't something she or Dad often said. Or maybe I just never heard it.

"You're surprised? You begged me at four to have lessons. Imagine that. You said, 'Mommy, teach me to play.' To say something like that when you're so young and to want it with such certainty. And it's not like you banged on the keys like some kids. You picked out the notes. Separately. Carefully."

"Maybe I just wanted to sit next to you on the bench as you played?"

Then I turned over in bed, realizing I had blown my chance to tell her the truth.

Miss Pringle nearly killed me when I told her over the phone about my pinky. She said with her slow southern drawl, "Now why were you playing sports when you know you have a competition in a few months? Why weren't you playing the Beethoven? We'll talk about it at your lesson."

So she still wanted to have me as a student. Maybe.

I looked into her steel-blue eyes when I showed up. "I'm sorry."

"Why couldn't you do homeschooling?" She let out a long sigh. "I wonder if you're really dedicated."

*Anyone who practices four hours a day at least—wouldn't you call that really dedicated?*

"Well." She shot me one of her looks—the kind that says so much without saying anything. "What are we going to do for the next hour?"

*Fifty minutes left to the lesson. Then forty-nine.*

I tried to play notes with one hand, without the bass. It sounded like Schroeder hunched over his toy piano in the *Peanuts* cartoons. So I dipped in my backpack and slipped out a CD—the piece I had been working on when she caught me writing instead of practicing. "I did this over the summer. Would you like to hear it?"

Miss Pringle glanced at the CD noncommittally. Then

she said, "It would have been nicer to have heard a recording of a Beethoven concerto from this past summer."

*Forty-five minutes. Three-quarters of an hour left.*

The room fell silent except for her heavy black leather orthopedic shoes tapping against each other as she rested her feet on the tattered ottoman in front of her faded upholstered chair. She kept the beat like a metronome, although nothing was being played. The CD remained on the edge of the piano, untouched. And that's when I wondered if she would take the time to listen to *me*.

"I'd better be going." I left the CD on top of the piano.

"See me when you're healed. Although master class begins next week. Listen to the Beethoven concerto in between."

On the elevator down, the doors opened at the fourth floor and Alex got on. I felt trapped, but he ruffled the top of my hair the way an older brother might. I was annoyed, but also relieved that Emma evidently had not told him about our fight. He looked down at my hand. "What happened?"

"You should see the other guy," I teased him.

"Should I be scared?" he teased back.

"Frisbee. I broke my pinky."

"Yikes. How long will you be out of commission?"

"As long as it takes."

There was an awkward pause.

"Have you heard from her?" I asked him finally.

"Her?"

"Emma."

"Oh, Emma." He gave me a crooked grin. "We exchanged a few e-mails."

"I thought you two were . . . an item."

"A summer thing. You know how those things are."

*I do? No, I don't. I wish I did.*

When I got out of the elevator in the lobby, Hannah was standing near the guard desk talking to a bunch of other pianists. When she saw my hand, she did a double take and mouthed, "What happened?"

"I should just wear a sign for the rest of the day: *Freak Fris-bee Attack*," I told her as we went down the steep wooden steps and passed the glass doors of the student lounge.

"I never do sports. But then, I'm homeschooled—it's not like my mom's going to face off against me in a game of Ultimate."

I laughed, thinking of Hannah doing team sports with her mother. Then I thought of me and Mom, who often seemed to be on opposing teams.

"I switched studios, you know," Hannah told me.

"I heard," I said.

She smiled. "I'm trying."

*Was I trying or standing still?*

I wondered how Hannah would do—and how Miss Pringle was taking it. It was okay if she cut a student loose, but never the other way around. *Never.*

My father rushed in that evening excited. "I was invited to fill in at the New Wave Festival at the Venice Biennale in the last two weeks of September!"

My mother looked as though she were going to burst. "Oh, Doug!"

"Why don't you go with Dad?" I said.

"Because I'll miss you. You've got school. And the semester just started."

"I'm in the eighth grade. Grandma's here. I can take care of Grandma."

Grandma smirked.

"It's Italy, Ma. Opera! Venice! Home of Vivaldi!"

She sat down at the kitchen table, looking like she was struggling with the idea.

"When was the last time we went away together?" my father asked her.

"Vermont."

I thought of that sad weekend not so long ago when they'd come to take me home.

Dad looked at her. "I mean *really* away. Just us."

She thought for a moment. "Before Ally was born?"

He nodded.

She turned toward me, still uncertain. "You'll be okay?"

I rolled my eyes. "Will you?"

"You'll practice?"

"Yes," I said convincingly, even to myself.

She looked at my bandage. "You'll try?"

"Ally said she'd try," Dad said to Mom.

Grandma gave me a wink.

*Get real.* How could I go out for a competition in this shape?

Mom got busy buying airline tickets, booking a hotel room, packing, buying cat litter, and food shopping for Grandma

206

and me. She'd check off each item on her list as she'd accomplish the task, and talk to herself. "Did I forget anything? Water the plants." And she'd go to the sink to fill a jar with fertilizer and water.

"Ma, I think I can water plants while you're away."

"You're right. You're not a baby."

I got busy with school. Regular school. Opal wanted to sign my pinky.

"Opal, it's not a cast," I insisted.

"Yeah, but you can still play the sympathy card."

And she initialed her name in a tiny heart with a purple felt-tip pen.

"I wish Brad were here," I said.

"Me too."

"Have you heard from him?" I asked.

"No. Have you?"

I shook my head, relieved she hadn't, although I wished I had.

Thinking about his father got me scared. What if something happened to my parents and they didn't come back from Venice? How could I be glad they were going away, yet scared at the same time?

The night before they left, we ate dinner together. Grandma thought the three of us should be alone, so she went out with a friend. Dad was sitting down at the table holding plates and napkins when he turned to my mother. "Maybe you can visit your mentor? Didn't she move to Milan? Or was it Rome?"

"Rome," said my mother, tensing up.

"Was she the opera teacher who trained you at Juilliard?" I asked.

She nodded. "In the young artist program."

"Your mother was a finalist for the Met auditions." My father smiled proudly. "And she made it." He rubbed her back lovingly.

"You should see her," I said. "It would be a missed opportunity if you didn't."

My mother looked up from her meatballs, realizing I'd used one of her usual lines.

"Not this trip."

"Why not? Isn't she really old? You might not get a second chance."

"We're going straight to Venice. And that's that. Don't talk to me about second chances."

The look on her face was one I'd never seen before. After a moment, Dad cleared his throat. Mom put down her fork and made as if to rise, but Dad put his hand on top of hers. "It's okay, honey," he said softly.

I looked from Dad to Mom. After a long silence, she finally said in a low voice, "I didn't get a second chance."

"At what?" I asked.

"Life."

I looked at her, confused.

Her eyes brimmed in red with tears. Quietly she said, "I bombed opening night of *La Bohème*."

I didn't quite understand. "It was all over after that? From that *one* time?"

She nodded. "Yes, from that one time. All the big critics were there. The Met pulled me from the role of Mimi after the reviews came out, and I was put in the choir. A minor part. That wasn't enough for me."

"You still sing."

"There's singing, and then there's singing. Where do I sing?"

"I thought you liked singing in all those clubs." I was quiet for a while as I digested all this. Finally I looked at Mom. "You never told me that." I put my arms around her as if she were the child.

"Parents don't always tell their children everything," she said with a wan smile.

"We learned in school that Einstein had many chances after many failures. Can't a person learn from their mistakes? Can't you get a second chance?" *Can't I?*

"It's too late."

"Is that why you're so ambitious for me?"

Mom looked over at Dad, then back at me, and sighed. "I want you to do all the things in the world that I never did."

"I'm not so sure I can."

She and Dad both looked at me like, *Why not?*

It was strange. I felt sorry for her—for what had happened to her, and because she'd felt she had to keep this secret hidden for so long—but I was also angry. I wanted to say, *How can you push me if you can't get over it? Why should I try harder if you won't? What kind of mother are you?*

If I had been stronger, I might have said those things, but

I backed off and remained at a distance that felt longer than the length of Opal's ball of string.

When I put my head down on my pillow that night, I couldn't fall asleep. I heard so many voices in my head: my grandmother's, my mother's, my father's, Eduardo's, Miss Pringle's. *When do I get to listen to my own voice? And the rhythm of my heart?*

As the taxi waited by the curb the following day, Mom said, "I love you! Practice!"

I glanced at my pinky.

So did Dad. "Whatever you can do." And he gave me a big hug. Then they got in and headed to the airport.

While they were gone, I scratched out notes here and there. Grandma asked absentmindedly at dinner one night, "Did you try and practice? I remember when I broke my baby toe it was impossible to drive. I just couldn't press down on the gas pedal. I guess it's the same thing playing the keys on the piano."

I'd nod as I poked at the meal.

"Have you written anything new?" she asked me.

"No."

"You can still compose."

"I could."

But I was on vacation, too. We watched DVDs together, cuddled up on the couch with Beethoven purring up at my feet. And during the week, while Grandma went to her book group, water aerobics, volunteer work, and new yoga class, I played hooky while she was away.

* * *

I sat and had a Coke at Ray's—the pizza place where I had gone with Brad.

I went to the library, got a book out, and read it on a park bench for hours.

I took a walk in Central Park and saw the leaves turning red and orange.

I bought a large salted pretzel dipped in mustard and fed the geese.

I watched a woman sketch animals at the zoo.

I saw kids playing soccer, tumbling and pushing.

I gave every street musician I saw my spare change.

Listening to them play, I wondered: wasn't there more to being a musician than only making music? Wasn't it seeing and hearing and feeling and touching, and sometimes even being quiet and doing what seemed like nothing at all? Because nothing at all is sometimes a lot, and that September it was just what I needed to do. Nothing had become my grace note.

It threw me into a panic because I knew the time would come soon when everyone would expect me to start the whole routine all over again. But now I'd seen what it was like to stop.

The first Saturday of full classes at Juilliard, Grandma had to wake me up. I was late. And I didn't like to be late to anything. I dragged myself out of bed to shower and felt as if I were slogging through mud. I decided to ham it up—like Mimi in *La Bohème* with a case of tuberculosis.

"You'd better stay home," Grandma insisted, putting her lips to my forehead—her way of taking my temperature without a thermometer. "You feel feverish to me."

"Oh?" I said. The warmth of my hot shower must have lingered. I felt guilty lying to my grandmother.

She made a beeline for the freezer, not wasting a second, and plopped a chicken into a big pot of boiling water. "You want dill?" she asked.

"Sure!" I said, adding a cough or two.

Two hours later, Grandma laid a dish towel on my lap, brought me a bowl of soup, and tucked me in front of the TV under an afghan. "Is it hot enough, darling?"

I slurped noodles off a large soup spoon and said, "Mmm," as she ladled a matzoh ball the size of a small planet, with bits of diced carrots and celery alongside chunks of chicken, into the bowl.

One noodle fell on the blanket. I quickly scooped it off. This was an afghan that Grandma had knitted before I was born. It had covered me after Grandpa died. I'd hidden under it with my hands over my ears when my parents fought. It had been a safe bed for Beethoven when we took him in off the street as a stray kitten. Opal and I had peeked through its fringes during the scary parts in movies.

I extended my "cold" into time off from school—missing classes and not making up homework.

"Are you really sick?" Opal asked when she came to the house later that week after Grandma informed the secretary in school. I didn't exactly look as if I were ready to croak right there on the spot. "Is that blush you have on, or have I never noticed that your cheeks are naturally hot pink? Are you scamming me, Allegra Katz?"

I didn't answer.

"You are, aren't you? Did you ever think of trying a new gig, like acting? Doesn't Juilliard have a drama school?"

I gave her a smirk.

"Ally? You seem off."

"I haven't been sleeping." That wasn't a total *lie*.

"That can get you crazy," she said. "When I don't get enough sleep, I get zonked—like I'm pudding."

"Tell me about it."

When Opal left, I tossed the homework assignments she'd brought off to the side.

Philip Glass, the most famous modern composer alive, said in a documentary I had seen with Grandma earlier in the week that music is like an underground river. It's always there. All you have to do is listen.

So I listened to my voice inside—my underground river.

And it told me to stop.

With my parents away, I did just that. I was tired of being so perfect, doing everything that was expected of me.

I stopped school.

I stopped lessons.

I stopped everything.

Because when was the pressure of doing and not stopping ever going to end?

Like Mom had said, it was endless.

I thought maybe stopping would be a huge relief, but strangely it wasn't. Well, at first it was. But then it felt like a big empty hole filling with guilt. It gave me a chance to think. What if I really told my parents I was never going to play again? With all these hours of thinking and not practicing,

213

I started to wonder, *Who am I without the piano? Who is Ally?* And that terrified me.

So the next Saturday, while my parents were still off in Europe and my grandmother was out at some lecture and a dinner date, I did something very un-Saturday-like—I crawled back into bed. When I woke up hours later, I did something I couldn't undo. I went into my closet, took out all my scrapbooks going back to first grade, and ripped up all the photos that my family and other people had taken of me at concerts. Then I threw out every single program I had, from the first recital I ever played when I was four until now.

Then I took the silver and turquoise bracelet that Mom had given me on my birthday and I tossed it on my parents' bedspread. It landed right near Mom's pillow.

And on that Saturday, as our answering machine picked up a call from the Pre-College office stating that I was absent for a second week in a row, I took a couple of Mom's pills from the medicine cabinet. Just a few, to help me go back to sleep, and stop everything from swirling around constantly in my head. Or maybe a bunch.

Grandma nudged me awake when she got home, touching my cheek. I gazed at her, drowsy. Torn photos were scattered on the carpet around my bed. She bent down to gather the pieces, trying to put them together again like Humpty Dumpty.

"You're throwing out your entire past," she said, sounding close to tears. "Why?"

I didn't have a one-sentence answer for her—or for me.

Later I found out that Grandma called a friend from her book group—a psychologist—and she rushed over. All I knew was that two blurry figures came into my room, and Grandma's friend asked, "Can you sit up for me?" I gazed through half-closed lids and struggled to prop myself against my pillows. "Good, Ally," she said encouragingly.

Grandma gave me a sip of water. My throat was so parched that I gagged.

I looked at her friend, dazed, then at Grandma, like Why is she here?

"Do you think you might hurt yourself?" she asked me outright, and I answered without thinking, "I don't know"— because how could you know what you're going to do in the future? So she said, "Your granddaughter should be seen. Immediately."

Grandma took me to the emergency room. She wouldn't let go of my good hand.

The doctor asked me the same thing.

And I answered the same way: "I don't know."

I wasn't sure of anything anymore except that I wanted to disappear.

So the doctor there did what he had to do, and admitted me.

Grandma had already called my parents, and they came home on the next plane. They arrived in twelve hours.

Twelve hours during which I was alone in a special wing of the hospital.

Without Grandma. Or them.

# October

After silence, that which comes nearest to expressing
the inexpressible is music.
—Aldous Huxley, writer

Mom and Dad waited behind a double glass door as a guard checked them like criminals or like in the airport when you go through security. Mom emptied her purse and Dad his pockets.

*No guns, knives, scissors, tweezers, nail clippers, or forks—even plastic ones.*

*No bottles of water or soda cans with aluminum pop tops with sharp edges.*

*No pills or outside food.*

*No cell phones. In case someone took a picture? Or to ensure no contact?*

216

I gazed up at a spider plant hanging from a hook on the ceiling near the nurses' station and said to an aide, "Someone could hang themselves from that."

She looked at me, then up at the plant, and smiled. "We could use you for quality control."

When they got buzzed in, they hugged me, unwilling to let go.

And I didn't pull away.

"Nice shirt." Dad rubbed at the worn collar of the flannel shirt I was wearing, a brown-and-purple plaid that was his favorite to practice in. His eyes were filled with regret and pain. He leaned over to kiss me and I felt the bristly stubble on his unshaven face.

"You're not wearing socks," I said to Mom as I glanced at her bare ankles in her ballet flats. The temperature had dropped the night I came into the emergency room.

"We packed and ran when we . . . heard." She looked over at Dad, her knees almost buckling under her as she sat down on the hard metal and plastic chair next to me. "Is it cold in here, or is it me?" she asked, hugging herself. "Feels like it's freezing." She was trembling.

I wiped the back of my neck. The room felt hot and stuffy to me.

A young doctor came in, wearing a starched white coat. "Ally, do you want your parents to leave so we can talk?"

I shook my head. I wanted them to stay with me and *never* leave.

"Can we take Ally home now?" Mom tried to sound casual, as if I had come in for my annual checkup before school.

The doctor folded his arms. "We'd like to keep an eye on her."

"I'd like to take her home," my mother repeated softly.

"I don't think that's a good idea."

She looked at the doctor pleadingly. "I'd *really* like to get her . . . home." I knew she'd been about to say, "out of here."

"Ms. Marduvian, without any disrespect, this is serious."

"We realize that," my father said, rubbing Mom's arm as she slumped back into the seat.

The doctor looked at me, then over at them. "When Ally was asked in an interview if she might hurt herself, she didn't assure us that she wouldn't. We don't take that lightly. And neither should you," the doctor said politely but assertively.

The room got very quiet.

Mom blinked, inching to the edge of her seat.

"Let's see how it goes for the next week. One step at a time." The doctor put his hand gently but firmly on her shoulder. "That's what I'm recommending."

At first, Mom and Dad took turns staying with me. We heard wails from a nearby room and noise from the staff in the brightly lit corridor. Mom curled up in bed with me, head to toe, holding on to my foot as if we were tethered to each other.

Adults always say lame things like *You learn from your mistakes.* What would I learn from this? That I was surrounded by crazy people.

There was a boy who watched TV with one leg of his pants pushed up over his knee while the other pant leg was down, like normal. He had a sneaker and tube sock on that leg; the other one was bare. Was that a metaphor for something?

In group therapy, there was this scrawny anorexic girl—I'll call her Willow—who made Miss Tippytoes look like a Mack truck. If she thought she had gained an ounce, she circled the ward continuously like she was doing track. Another girl who wouldn't get dressed—I called her PJ—wore a rumpled hospital gown open in the back. A pretty seventeen-year-old, Latisha, reminded me of Emma. She smiled but kept to herself, curled up in an armchair, reading constantly. She never had a visitor and her wrists and thighs showed traces of cuts. And then there was my roommate, Vampire, who slept all day, doped up on something, and was up all night pacing.

"She's like a lox," my grandmother said of Vampire when she came to visit one afternoon and peeked in our room. "There isn't enough chicken soup in the world to get that girl going." Grandma had brought me a towering thermos filled with hers, but it was tucked in a cubby on the other side of the locked glass door by her PBS umbrella, its metal spikes poking out.

The umbrella was obvious. But why no soup?

"I brought you a hot corned beef sandwich, but they wouldn't let me bring that in, either. You could have shared it with that one." She motioned to Willow. "Looks like she could use a little meat on those bones."

"Grandma," I said under my breath, hoping no one had heard her.

"Is there anywhere we can talk?"

I walked her to a large open space in the back, away from

the TV room by the nurses' station, where mostly everyone hung out. We passed Latisha in a lounge. She studied us carefully, then gazed down at a blank page in a book as we turned into an alcove around the corner and sat under a window with metal grating.

"Oh, darling," Grandma sighed. "What are we going to do with you?"

I shrugged as we sank into the cushions on the long couch.

"Love you," she breathed in, holding my hand. "That's what we'll do."

She didn't ask what was wrong. She just held my hand and loved me for being who I am. Ally. And that was enough for her.

The next time my parents came, Mom brought two books and handed one to Latisha. She looked up, seemed grateful, and began to read without checking the title—as if it were an oasis in the desert of dated, dog-eared paperbacks lying around. Hers was *Jane Eyre*, which I had read in sixth grade. The other was for me: poems by Robert Frost with a quote of his on the front jacket: *The best way out is always through.*

Mom and Dad stayed from when visitors were allowed in until they had to leave before dinner. We stretched it out as long as we could, holed up in a conference room, closing the door. The staff mostly let us alone, except for a nurse who would pop her head in with a cheerful grin to check on us. We talked about nothing special because there was too much to say.

The psychiatrist called it "the elephant in the room." More like a gorilla.

I told him, "I can't make my mind stop. I want to feel nothing because I feel too much all the time."

He looked up from the notes he was taking. "Ally, if you didn't feel as much as you do, then how could you make the kind of music you do?"

"I never thought of that."

"Being a sensitive person isn't a bad thing. Some of us just feel more than others. Don't beat yourself up because you feel. Think of the people who go through their entire lives without being in touch with their emotions. You think that's a good thing?"

I stared at my hands in my lap. "They don't get hurt as much."

"Maybe they don't experience as much, either. Maybe they walk through life."

His phone rang. It jolted me. I looked up at him. Then it suddenly stopped.

"We learn all throughout our lives from the choices we make. That's the journey—the growing and learning. Toward happiness. What makes you happy?" he asked me.

I thought of doing yoga with Grandma. Being with Opal. Cooking with Brad.

"I used to think I knew, but I'm not so sure anymore. I get it in tiny spurts."

"That's better than nothing." He smiled.

"I miss my friends Brad and Opal." I hadn't thought of them a lot lately.

"That's good."

And I began to cry.

He pushed a box of Kleenex toward me, and I took one and blew my nose. "What's wrong? Crying means you touched on something. Deep inside."

"The piano doesn't make me happy," I said, wiping my eyes, "anymore."

"Then take a break."

"I did."

"And are you happier?"

My mind went to my mother. My father. If they only knew.

"No. Yes. No. I don't know. That's why I'm here, I guess. I need help."

"Saying it is the first step. Maybe I can help you sort it out."

I began to cry again. "I can't tell my parents that I want to . . ." I choked. "Quit."

"Think of it like this. There's no right or wrong. No perfect decisions. And these decisions can change. Get altered. And reinvented."

I liked that. It felt a lot like math. And composing.

He leaned forward, adding, "And you're not in this alone. Okay?"

I nodded. I liked that even more.

"Happiness is like the icing on the cake," I said on the way out of his office.

The therapist gave me a wide smile as he held the doorknob. "So let's get you to a place where you're enjoying the icing again."

When I saw my parents the next time, I asked them, "Are you happy?"

Mom was unpacking the bag of toiletries she'd brought

me. She looked at me like, *What's this now?* as she slid a bar of fancy milled bath soap onto my dresser, and answered, "It's the small moments that make me happy."

"Not the big ones?" I asked. "Like starring in an opera?"

She smiled wistfully, but answered in a way that I didn't expect:

"I am happy sipping hot tea with lemon and honey," she said, "sitting in the kitchen, the light streaming through onto a pitcher filled with purple irises, reading. Slipping under a thick fluffy quilt, the sheets cool. Watching a fire in a fireplace during an ice storm, hearing the wood crackle, the embers fall. Taking a long hot bath. With candles. And lavender. Of course, Billie Holiday. That goes without saying. Cuddling with Dad. Laughing with him till my stomach hurts. And you. Your hug. Your smell. Even your pizza breath. I'm happiest when you're happy," she told me. "What can I say? I'm a mother." And she put her arms around me. "I'm your mother, Ally."

"So I guess you're not so happy right now," I said, and she gave me a sad look.

And my father, his only answer was, "Living. Just living each day." Dad is more of an in-the-moment kind of guy.

During the week, Opal came, her braid tinted bright purple. They made her leave her backpack outside. She pulled some papers from it before she entered. "Do you want the homework I brought so you don't fall behind? I told them you had mono."

"Fall behind whom? I'm sick of competing. Toss them. And how did I get mono?"

"Not from kissing. Brad's away," she teased. "You could have sipped someone else's soda and caught it."

I rolled my eyes.

"I thought you might . . ." Her voice trailed off. "You usually like to keep up."

I pulled the assignments from her hands. "That's the old me. Thanks."

"Okay." Her forehead wrinkled. "I have to go," she said to me, wiggling.

"You just got here."

"I mean I drank too much Snapple at lunch."

"Oh. Over there." I pointed to the bathroom in the hall. "I'll wait outside."

I wondered whom she was eating with now that Brad and I were gone.

She stuck her head around the door. "There are no locks!"

"Do I look like a locksmith? I'm standing here—go!"

"Totally gross! Anyone could walk in. How are you doing this?"

"Do I have a choice?"

When she came out, she said, "There's a shower inside. You also bathe with an unlocked door?"

"An aide stands by."

"This is like prison." Opal glanced around, fidgeting with a rubber band from her pocket.

"Don't let them see that!" I widened my eyes.

She looked puzzled. "Huh? It keeps my drawings together."

"Strangulation." I made choking sounds like my throat was closing up.

"O-kay, Ally, you're weirding me out now." She tucked her hands in the pockets of her jeans, putting the rubber band away, and looked over as the assorted group of patients lined up by the nurses' station, waiting for their meds. "What's with the kid whose pants look like half of him's in Florida and the other half's in Alaska?" she asked.

"Maybe he's bicoastal?"

"Very funny. You're still my Ally." She put her hand next to mine, almost touching it, but not quite. "Why didn't you tell me?"

I looked away.

"I could have been there for you. On the outside, Ally, no one could tell. I knew you were pulling away, but then you'd always do that when you were getting ready for a competition or performance."

"Don't feel bad, Opal. It's not your fault."

"I know, but still . . ." She put her forefinger on top of mine and left it there. "Still BFFs?"

"Always."

As art therapy was about to start, Opal decided to blend in with the group. Nobody seemed to realize she wasn't a patient.

"I don't know if fitting in around here is a good thing or a bad thing," Opal whispered.

"Put your name on the bottom of your painting," instructed the art therapist.

Opal wrote *Sapphire Rich* underneath a bunch of random squirts at her easel.

"Looks like something your dog actually did," I said.

"Excuse me? I'll have you know Sapphire's a canine of many talents—like that cat who paints."

The art therapist paused behind us, picked up Opal's work, and push-pinned it to the corkboard. "This is promising."

"It's rad," the boy with the pants corrected her as he did finishing strokes on some skeletons gushing with blood.

"O-kay," Opal murmured to me, looking over at his drawing. "This might be a good time to exit. Goth boy over there is giving me the eye."

When the class ended, the art therapist said to Opal, "Sapphire, you have real talent. Does this painting represent anything to you?"

"The chaos of the universe."

It was the first time I'd actually smiled in here.

Opal and I giggled all the way to the door and waved to each other as she left me "bonding" with this new group of "friends."

As Grandma would say, you make do.

I needed to get out of here. Enough was enough. I had learned my lesson.

Toward the end of the week, I sat with my parents in an interior courtyard filled with a patch of grass and copper-colored fall mums. It was the first time I'd been outside in almost a week, and the setting sun was glaring. Seeing an airplane go by, actually hearing it, reminded me of my parents telling me that when I was almost a year old I'd pointed toward the clouds and said, "Bird."

As I remained on the bench between them, a tall cinder-block wall covered in ivy surrounding us, Mom inched closer. "The doctors told us that you can go to your school for a few classes tomorrow. Would you like that?"

I wanted to leave, but I wasn't sure if I wanted to face anyone.

"But they want you to come back here in the evening," she added.

"Sleep *here*? I want to go home, Ma."

"I know." She stroked my hand. "For only another night or two. Slowly work your way back into the world." She smoothed her hand up and down the arm of my soft baby-blue turtleneck sweater, trying to reassure me and reassure herself, too.

My father sounded like a coach in a movie, wanting to inspire his star player before a big game. "You can do it, kid. Show 'em your stuff." He put his arm around my neck in a mock headlock, and a tear dripped down his cheek.

I wanted to take care of them, and do it for the team— Mom, Grandma, and him. "I'll go."

When I left the hospital on a day pass, I felt the way I had after Grandpa died—out of place. Back then I'd seen people doing everyday things: shopping for groceries, walking their dogs, mailing letters, laughing, eating, and going to sleep at night in their own beds. But for me everything had been hazy.

I'd known I would never again see Grandpa wearing his eye-glasses or slippers, or play checkers with him, or smell his aftershave.

It was the same with the kids at school. They were slamming their lockers, getting ready for lunch, wondering if their hair looked okay, and talking about the pop quiz the period before. Life went on as before. For me it always would be after. And it would never be the same as before.

Ms. Johansen-Williams was my math teacher again this year. She stopped me in the hall between periods. "Are you okay?"

*Did she know?*

My eyes got glassy. She must have noticed, because she pulled me into the teachers' lounge, away from the dizzying, almost overwhelming hustle. When we were alone, she filled her mug with coffee and handed me a paper cup filled with ice water.

"I-I've been . . . ," I stammered, not looking her in the eye.

She rested her hand firmly on my forearm.

I hesitated. "I needed some time off."

"Everyone needs some." She hugged me. "Even grown-ups."

I thought of my dad and how he'd been on overload after his Asia tour.

"I'll make up what I missed," I said, feeling ashamed.

"Don't worry about that. Take care of yourself first."

I paused. "I might do some homeschooling."

"I'm here if you need me. Even to come tutor you."

It was as if a huge weight had been lifted off my shoulders. "Thanks."

"Anytime. You're my most brilliant math student."

I felt pure happiness—something I hadn't felt in a long time.

And when I saw Opal in the hall, she screamed like she had seen a ghost. "What are you doing here?" She did a little happy dance, jumping up and down in place.

A few kids turned around, saw it was just Opal, and went back to whatever they'd been doing.

Opal threw her arms around me.

"Testing the waters," I whispered into her ear.

"How are they? Warm enough?"

"Not yet."

"I'll be your swim buddy," she whispered back, squeezing my hand.

After I left school, my parents were waiting outside for me with a coffee ice cream soda. I was sick of hospital food. Maybe my mother was right: it was the small things, not the big ones that counted.

I left the psychiatric wing after ten days—the longest ten days of my life. But for everyone else who was staying, it was as if time stood still: Vampire was out of it and wouldn't know when someone else took my spot. Pants Boy continued to watch TV, doodling dripping skeletons. Razor Girl's cuts began to heal, but faint traces remained etched in her skin. Latisha showed me that she'd put her name on *Jane Eyre*. It made me feel sad about Emma again. I wished I could make it up to her for what I had done. Instead I gave Latisha my book of Robert Frost poems. Willow wandered in endless circles.

PJ slipped a note under the glass door as I stood on the

other side in freedom: *Let's stay in touch.* I ached inside, waving good-bye, hoping and praying I'd never see any of them again.

When we got home, I found that Grandma had left out a covered plate of her apple strudel with a Post-it on it: *See you tomorrow, darling. Tonight's for the three of you.*

We ordered in a load of Chinese food and ate right out of the containers. My mother raced over to the shelf where Dad kept the DVDs and old videos and grabbed one. It was me on my first birthday surrounded by gift-wrapping paper on the living room floor. I looked over at Mom, her feet tucked under her on the couch. Her face got contorted, the way it gets when she's about to have a good cry.

"Ma, what's wrong?" I asked as the three of us watched me bang on a xylophone like a rock star. I was wearing a Peter Rabbit terry-cloth onesie.

"If only I knew then what I know now and could go back and start all over again—smarter this time."

Dad put his arm around her, and she snuggled in closer to him. Sounding like my therapist in the hospital, he told her, "No rewinds. This is what we get. So go forward. Just let it happen. Try to go with it." Mom let out a deep breath.

I opened up my fortune cookie: *Confucius says: It does not matter how slowly you go, so long as you do not stop.*

I handed Mom a tissue, since hers was damp and shredded. Mom began to laugh out loud when she saw me bopping up and down on the video. She was singing "Little Rabbit Foo

Foo" to me while she fed me applesauce, the food smeared on my cheeks. Then the video shifted a few years later to me on a shiny tricycle riding in circles on the slate patio in the back of the brownstone—or should I say trying to ride? The wheels of the bike were squeaking at a decibel level that would have sent dogs howling. On my fifth birthday—my parents weren't great at dating these things—I was reciting "Jabberwocky," a poem from *Through the Looking-Glass*. I repeated the nonsense words without any prompting from my parents in the peanut gallery. Squinting into the camera lens, looking happy but intense, I said in a high scratchy voice, "I love you, Mommy. I love you, Daddy."

On the couch next to me, Mom whisked a tear away and leaned her head against mine. "I love you, Alley Cat."

"How much?" I asked, the way I had when I was little.

"*This* much." She put her arms out as wide as she could.

"Wider than the whole world?" I asked.

"Wider than the whole world," she answered.

Dad imitated her, his arms stretching out even wider.

The following morning when we went for our first family session, I settled down in a comfortable leather chair and my parents sat side by side on a couch. I looked at the doctor seated opposite to me, the sunlight flickering through the blinds behind her. "Call me Lyn." She put a loose-leaf binder on her lap and nodded for me to start.

I placed a plump throw pillow on my lap, almost as a fence between us, and looked anxiously over at my parents. *Don't cry. Don't lose it. Stick to the script.* I gulped, sucked in my breath, and said to Lyn, "I'm having a lot of trouble."

She smiled. "You can say anything you want in here."

She made me feel safe.

"I'm giving up the piano."

My mother blanched and sat up straight. I couldn't read my father's face, which meant he was gathering himself together, keeping whatever he felt inside.

"What do you mean?" Mom said.

"I'm quitting." I looked over at the shrink for approval.

Her eyes showed sympathy. Mom looked at her, too, and then back at me. "I don't understand." Her lower lip started quivering. She was trying, I think, with all her might not to cry in front of me, but she couldn't hold back the tears. Her eyes filled. Then a few tears dripped down her cheeks onto her blouse and she grabbed a wad of tissues, trying to blot them. She turned to the doctor and repeated to her, "I don't understand."

"It's making me sick." I looked away and put my head in my hands.

"What's making you sick?" Mom asked.

"Playing the piano."

"Playing the piano's making you sick?" repeated Dad.

"Composition doesn't."

"Oh." He glanced over at my mother.

She looked at Lyn, then at Dad, and finally at me. "Let's switch teachers when you go back."

"There's no *us*, Ma. It's my choice."

"You're not returning to Pre-College?" Her voice went up.

"Are you hearing what I'm saying?" I began to get more agitated.

"I'm listening," she said, trying to stay calm.

"Then listen," I repeated slowly, in staccato. "I'm not taking lessons anymore. I need to see what it feels like to be separate from the piano. I don't know what that feels like."

"So take some time off to see what it feels like."

"I did already." Then I couldn't hold it anymore. I shouted at the top of my lungs, "You quit opera! I can't quit the piano? What makes it okay for you and not me? Just 'cause you've blown it with your life, don't live it through me!"

My mother got up. She said nothing. My heart felt like an egg cracking in half. So when Mom walked into the powder room outside the office and I heard vomiting, the toilet flushing, twice, and then water running in the sink, I was sorry I had said anything. When she came out and returned to the room, her eyes were red, her cheeks were flushed, and strands of her hair were tangled and wet, clinging together in clumps. She saw that Dad had gotten up from the couch and had his arms around me.

As Mom sat back down, Lyn asked, "Are you okay, Elana?"

Mom answered, "If that's what Ally wants, it's her life."

"Tell *her*," Lyn said to my mother, motioning to me.

But I blurted out without waiting, "Now all of a sudden it's *my* life?"

Dad sat down again next to Mom. "I'd be lying if I didn't

say that I'm sorry you feel this way. But we're not going to force you." He folded his arms in front of his chest as if he were protecting himself. Maybe he was.

I turned away from them. "I guess that's it, then."

After a moment Lyn said, "We've got a few minutes left to the session and we can't leave it like this."

"I understand. I don't want to understand, but I do," my mother replied, looking over at her. "Life doesn't always get tied up with pretty silk ribbons, does it?" she said with a bite to her tone.

"That doesn't mean we can't try to listen to each other," Lyn said.

My mother heaved a loud sigh.

So did my father.

As we all got up, mine was the deepest of all.

I said as we left her office, "Will you still love me if I don't play?"

Both my parents began to cry.


Grandma walked in the moment we got home, holding her yoga mat. She looked at the three of us. "What did I miss?" Everyone's eyes were swollen and red. "A land mine?"

"I'm quitting the piano."

Grandma dropped her mat right there on the floor and rushed over to me. "Darling. Oh, darling." She repeated those words a few more times.

"I thought you wanted me to bathe in the sun and be free on Saturdays."

She kind of smiled. "I did. I do. But I never knew until

now that I want you to be able to do all those things, including nurturing the gift you have."

And that's when I began to cry and left the room.

Everyone gave me my space.

The next few days, we all danced around each other, avoiding the truth. There were moments it was so tense I wondered, *Should I take it back?* But I didn't. And couldn't. My biggest fear, telling my mother, was finally over. Or was it? I had to tell my teachers, too: Eduardo, and eventually Miss Pringle.

# November

Music is the language of spirit. It's the thing that wakes it up.
—Bono, songwriter and activist

Nothing much happened. Or so it seemed. Dad started rehearsing more at home. And so did Mom. Sometimes with an accompanist on the piano. My piano. It was nice hearing them, and yet it often made me feel guilty that I wasn't practicing. And when they didn't practice, we played cards or Chinese checkers. But I knew by the way Mom looked as she'd pass by the piano, the lid shut tight over the keys, that she was sad—like when she was in mourning after Grandpa died. There are three legs to a grand piano. In a way, each one represented one of us in our family. Now that I had stopped, it was as if one leg had been chopped off. Naturally, the piano would tip over and fall down. So my mother hung around watching me not playing the piano and doing just enough schoolwork to keep up.

My math teacher, Ms. Johansen-Williams, came over to tutor me, but she said, "You're so way ahead, I wouldn't worry about catching up." She smiled at my mother, placing her hand on Mom's arm. "You've got a very special daughter there."

Mom said, looking down modestly, "I know."

One afternoon Mom and I went to see Miss Pringle at her home. She hadn't called or come to visit. Her apartment door was unlocked, as it often was when she was waiting for her students to arrive, so we let ourselves in. She was finishing up teaching a new one, so we softly tiptoed by the living room to wait at her kitchen table. The clock over the sink was ticking, creating a counterpoint to the metronome in the living room. When I heard the front door shut, I got up. My mother stood up, too. "Are you okay?"

"I can do this."

"You're sure?"

"I'm sure."

"If you need me, I'm right here. Okay?"

"Okay."

She sat back down. I felt the weight of her anchor in this unknowing sea.

Miss Pringle smiled the biggest smile I had ever seen on her. There was a split second when I considered, *Am I making a major mistake?* Then she said, "Someone had a nice long vacation. I hope it was good and you're ready to work."

I looked away uncomfortably.

"Beethoven's still waiting, you know."

"I came to say"—I cleared my throat—"I need a break."

"You had a break." Her smile gradually dwindled.

"I need a longer one." I tried not to feel disgrace.

Miss Pringle uncrossed her ankles, putting those clunky black shoes of hers on the carpet in front of her. "With Eduardo still away in Venezuela, I'm busier than ever. You could lose your lesson time permanently." Then she flashed a swift smile. "I can't hold your spot open forever."

"I'm not asking you to," I confessed, my legs trembling as I stood by her piano.

"Then what are you telling me?"

"I'm not coming back." I finally came out with it.

She gave me a blank look.

"With me gone, as well as Hannah, it should make things easier." I couldn't resist the dig about Hannah and searched her eyes for her reaction, but found none.

Miss Pringle didn't say, *I'm sorry about your decision*, or *I'll miss you*, or *I hope things turn out well for you*, or even *I hope you reconsider and come back soon*. All she said was, "Well, good luck, then." She walked me to the door, and then, as my mother followed, she added, "I hope your daughter knows what she's doing. To squander a spot in Juilliard is such a waste of her future."

Even though I knew my mother agreed deep down inside, she still looked shocked as Miss Pringle locked the door behind us. I realized the next student would have to ring the bell. Maybe she was upset after all? But she didn't even say my name after all these years, like, *Good luck, Ally*. Nothing personal like that.

"What did she say?" Mom asked when we got out on the street.

"Not much," I said with a shrug. "It was my decision. What could she say?"

"A lot. She could have said a lot."

I gazed up miserably at the fourth floor of her building, hoping maybe she was gazing down at me, but it was foolish. When would I ever learn?

"She is who she is. It's like asking a dog to be a cat. It's hard for people to change. Should we go back? I could let her have it." Mom's voice was raised.

"Oh, Ma, for what?"

"For not saying all those things that someone should say who has had a relationship as long as she had with you." She clenched her jaw. "I could tell her no one knows what any-one's future is going to bring. Especially my daughter's." Mom zipped up my hooded ski jacket. "Now do you want to go for hot chocolate?" She locked her arm in mine.

"With the works?" I cocked my head to one side like Opal's dog when you called out her name.

"What would hot chocolate be without marshmallows and whipped cream?"

"Dull. Like a violin without vibrato."

My mother gave me a look. "Guess you can't take the music out of the girl."

"It's part of my bone marrow."

She smiled. "I guess so."

The wind swept up from the river onto Riverside Drive as we walked over to a coffee shop on Broadway. We sat at a

239

table in the glass storefront away from the draft that came in with each new customer. Mom told me, "It was tough seeing you brainwashed into thinking you weren't a good musician in order to make you into a better one."

"What do you mean?" *Did Miss Pringle do that?*

"It's an Old World style many teachers have. I saw that kind of teaching when I studied opera—that all my accomplishments were never going to be enough."

"Is that why you didn't want to visit your opera teacher in Italy?"

She nodded. "Probably."

"That's the way I've felt, too."

"I'm so sorry." She inched her hand toward mine. "Look, honey, criticism can be constructive. It can make you grow, become your best, and want to do more. There are people who know how to do it seamlessly and build you up."

I thought of Eduardo.

"There are others who do it in a way that can destroy."

And I thought of Miss Pringle tearing me down.

"It's a fine balance. A truly great *teacher* knows how to inspire. That's not necessarily true of a great *musician*. I learned it's not always about hitting each note flawlessly because sometimes you sacrifice emotion when you're striving for all that perfection. No one can teach that. And it's who you are, Ally, my sweet Ally."

I thought way back to that day in master class in March, messing up the Chopin.

"Can't you have both? Perfection *and* emotion."

"That's the recipe for a great artist."

"Like Dad?"

Mom repeated, "Like Dad."

"And you."

"Ah, me." She smiled wistfully. "Not sure about the per-fection part."

The waitress came with our hot chocolates and we stopped talking. When she turned to another customer, Mom picked up where we'd left off. "Technique can be taught." She stretched her arm across the table. "Feelings cannot be taught. I want you to know, and so does your father, we both think you're terrific, as a human being and musically. In a strange way, you gave us a gift—you brought us all together. Your father and I weren't smart enough to see the real gift you were trying to give us—you. I couldn't live without you." Her voice cracked. "Your entire life is ahead of you. You're making your own way. Maybe Miss Pringle didn't appreciate that sense of independence." She hesi-tated. "Or me." She stirred her drink. "Certainly she didn't take the time to see who you are. That you don't fit the standard mold." She took a sip of water. "You forced me to see it. I feel awful that you think I was living through you. Maybe I was."

I looked at her, then out the window. My eyes watered. "Sorry, Ma."

"Don't be." My mother choked up. "I'm sorry. And so is Dad." She touched her chest with her palm, lowering her voice to a barely audible whisper. "I miss hearing you practice while I'm doing the dishes or reading or lying on the couch or whatever. The sound of you playing has been such great joy. I don't think I ever realized how much until now, now that I no longer hear it."

I gave her a look. "Guilt trip."

"I can't help it. I'm being honest. And I love to see you perform."

"I think you get more nervous than me!"

"We might have a tie on that one."

"This isn't a competition, is it?" I let out a smile.

"You've got so much talent. I don't know where it all comes from."

"Look in the mirror."

"No, Ally. It comes from you. That's what she could have said. You're talented, Ally Katz, and I wish you the best."

I watched my mother. "You okay, Ma?"

"No." She wiped her eyes. "But I will be."

"So will I."

She reached out and put her hand on mine. It was warm. And comforting. "I should have taken better care of you, Ally. I'm angry. At her. But most of all at myself. For allowing it to happen."

"Oh, Ma." I put my other hand on hers.

"I would have told her, 'Ally has many things yet to be discovered.'"

That night, when everything seemed to be better and out in the open—all the moments I had feared the most in the past—I overheard my mother sobbing in my father's arms as I was going to my room. Neither of them knew I was listening.

"Let it out," he said. "It's a release."

"She told Pringle." Mom left the *Miss* out of her name.

"How did it go?" my father asked.

"How do you think? You know her."

"What did you expect? Move on. It's history."

"I wish I could put Ally in the car seat, buckle her in, and protect her," she wept.

"You can't do that anymore. You can't protect her from the world."

"But I'm her mother. I'm supposed to."

"Being a parent is helping her to walk and allowing her to fall down. All we can do is try to be there when she does. And we can't always be there. Now we have to let her run . . . and fly."

"Why couldn't Ally simply have told us?"

"In her own way—hers, not ours—she did let us know."

They got quiet.

"Why didn't we see it, Doug? I mean *really* see it? She seemed okay. Overworked, overscheduled—but okay. Were we too busy?"

"I saw it coming less than you. I was away a lot. And Ally isn't like most kids. She's complex. She has music. And not just the piano. She has school—an intense one. She loves math. Is at the top of her grade. Maybe she was telling us that she's all of those things? You tell me how many kids her age feel that if they don't make it by thirteen their career is over."

"I told her time was running out."

"You did?" Dad sounded taken aback.

"Yes," she admitted. "You played internationally at twelve."

"Exactly. I knew about the pressure."

"So did I," admitted Mom.

"We both should have known better."

"This has been a nightmare."

"And a blessing. We're getting closer as a family."

I overheard her sniffling and Dad kissing her. I tried to sneak into my room, unnoticed. My mother paused when she heard a creak of the floorboards outside in the hall. "Ally?" she said. I went into their room and walked over to her. She put her arms around me. Dad continued to hold her as he wiped his eyes, then hers.

It seemed strange that now that I had left Juilliard and was homeschooled I had more time than ever to practice for the Beethoven competition and I didn't. Weird, how life sometimes turns out. The big black piano loomed in our living room like a presence that never went away, staring me in the face, making me feel free at first to be rid of it, and then lonely—like I had lost a best friend and now we had become strangers. Could I live without this friend? Like I had without Emma. And sometimes I felt even worse, like the piano was a limb—could I exist without it? I still refused to sit down and give in. There was a hole in my heart that I was going to try to fill without music . . . if that was possible.

Opal came over. We sat on the floor inside my walk-in closet, closing the door, just like old times, and painted each other's toenails black. She added teeny stars on our big toenails. I thought of Emma. "Let's write down all the things you missed out on," she said as we waited for the polish to dry. "You have to make up for lost time."

"Opal, you'd think I was a hermit living in the woods."

"You spent most of your childhood rehearsing for recitals, competitions, and juries."

"My work's play, too," I stated matter-of-factly.

"Oh, yeah?" she said, taking out a pad. "That's not the way I heard it."

### Things to Do Like Normal People

1. Sleepovers
2. Parties
3. TV
4. Comic books
5. Hanging out
6. Sports
7. Movie matinées—on Saturdays
8. Twitter, Facebook, MySpace, major texting
9. Walking Opal's dog with her
10. Shopping

"Off-limits are concerts. Anything with music," Opal said bossily.

"Rock concerts aren't okay?"

"Pop culture is fine."

"Get rid of number ten. Shopping makes me dizzy. And number six—most sports."

I spent the weekend at her place. The first night Sapphire's snoring woke me up. After I tried to go back to sleep and couldn't, I wandered their loft. Opal's mom was making a quilt, and the patches were spread all over the rug on the living room floor, waiting for her to piece them together.

Sapphire waddled out of the bedroom and lay down on the fabric. I nudged her off. We curled up on their soft cushiony couch, falling asleep together. When Opal found us in the morning, she accused me of being "a traitor" and "liking Sapphire more."

"Have you transferred your sibling rivalry with Ruby to your dog?"

Opal scrunched her mouth and took out pancake mix. It was raining, and instead of getting dressed we stayed in our pajamas and watched a horror flick while we ate breakfast.

In the afternoon as we were walking Sapphire, Opal saw a film poster at a bus stop and screamed, "I'm dying to see that!" After we dropped her dog off upstairs, we went to the cine-plex, shared a bucket of popcorn, and bought two drinks that would have quenched the thirst of a family of eight. We snuck into a second movie halfway through.

On our way out I teased, "So does that take care of numbers one, two, three, five, seven, and nine on the list? More than half!"

"Tell me you're kidding. Two people don't count as a party. And you can't gang everything together. You have to spread out the list. You're too used to doing everything on a schedule, with a goal."

"And you're not?" I responded. "What are those art shows about?"

She jabbed me lightly. "They're about exploration."

I still ticked off all those numbers in my head, feeling I'd accomplished something.

That night we ordered in Vietnamese food, then went

online to watch TV. This klutzy kid in a tutu began dancing. There was the usual blank stare from the judges—I'd seen that before, in person—until she suddenly belted out the song "I Could Have Danced All Night" from My *Fair Lady*, knocking their socks off. "What's this program?"

"You're a space alien!" Opal shouted at me. "You've never seen a reality show? What rock have you been under?"

"Rachmaninoff."

She groaned.

"It's not as if I've never seen a reality show, just not an entire episode." I dipped into her container of noodles with my chopsticks. "I thought of a new show."

"What's that?" She took some vegetables from my container.

"*So You Think You're a Prodigy*."

Opal let out a snicker. "And the parents pay the producer how much?"

I laughed. "Still, here's this girl"—I gestured toward the screen of her laptop with one of my chopsticks poised in the air, a noodle dangling—"who never took a lesson in her entire life, and she bursts on the scene with this amazing voice."

"I've got goose bumps," Opal said.

"Me too."

When we were done, we e-mailed Brad just to say hi. I wondered if he'd reply.

Later in the week Opal said with real attitude, "Too bad you scratched shopping off your list. You're coming. End of discussion. I need advice on new outfits for winter."

"Sure you do," I answered.

She patted into place three small bows attached to her braid. "I do."

Days later, her parents drove us through the tunnel to a mall somewhere in New Jersey, and Opal and I wandered around while they looked for a new bed on another level. As we both tried on clothes and beaded bracelets that Opal insisted we could make ourselves in an afternoon, I said, "So this is what people do on the weekend? Shop?"

Opal looked at me. "Duh."

"Part of me feels like it's a real waste of time."

"And the other part?" she asked, eyeing a fake diamond barrette.

"We actually are having fun, aren't we?"

She put her arm around me.

"I'm not making this a habit," I warned her.

"Oh, Ally." She gave me a puppy-dog look. "Pretty please?"

"I love you, Opal Rich, but it's not happening."

Later I went back over Opal's list. The things I did with her were fun because they were with her, but I wouldn't do those things if I were alone. So I made a new list. Mine.

Ally's Things to Do

1. Concerts—nothing off-limits
2. Writing music
3. Mathematics
4. Gardening with my father
5. Singing stupid funny songs with my mother

6. Baking with Grandma (and Brad)
7. Kissing Brad
8. Reading for hours
9. Doing anything near water—picnics, shell hunting, etc.
10. Going to ballets, operas, theater—all that stuff

Opal started doing some of the things that I liked because that's what best friends do for each other—they meet each other halfway. Then we created a list that was ours. We bundled up and read side by side near Bethesda Fountain: Opal a dark romance novel, and me a biography of Einstein (who loved the violin too). We spent the day at an art museum and went out to see the sculptures on a rooftop terrace overlooking Central Park. "I hear a bird singing," I said, and she looked at me. "It's November."

"Miracles can happen."

"Or maybe it's a stupid bird who forgot to fly south."

"Maybe it just lost its way," I replied.

Opal looked into my eyes. We locked our arms around each other's waist. Then we went downstairs, saw the collection of medieval instruments, and heard a chamber music group playing on a balcony surrounded by glass-enclosed cases exhibiting porcelain vases and artifacts.

When we came home, Opal taught me how to tweeze my eyebrows and how to find the right shaving cream and pink razor for under my armpits so the stubble didn't feel like I was carrying around two Brillo pads. She showed me how to apply mascara, eyeliner, and eye shadow, and how to use blush to make my cheekbones look high and sculptured—although I had an idea how to get that look after hours of observing Emma. "You're a supermodel!" Opal crowed.

"I look like the bride of Dracula." I washed my face.

We watched tango tapes from Argentina. I grabbed a long-stemmed red rose from one of my father's concert bouquets and popped it between my teeth, and Opal dipped me to the floor without dumping me on the rug on top of my cat. "Now that's real trust," I told her. That's when she dropped me. Beethoven screeched. We both tumbled onto the rug, laughing hysterically "Thanks a lot," I told her. "So much for trust."

I still let her streak my hair with silvery blond highlights.

"So uptown," she said in a hoity-toity accent.

"I want to be downtown, like you!" She redid some strands to green.

My mother flipped out. "You look like a frog!"

Grandma added, "It's not even St. Patrick's Day. And you're Jewish!"

But from all of this, I was trying to learn to just be and not do.

I started to write music again. Not a lot. Just a little. Not at the piano. Not toward anything. Not for the chamber group or for an assignment. I didn't play it. I put it away and let the sounds settle in my head.

One night when I was alone and had time to think, I sent an e-mail to Emma with a quote from a famous composer who died in the sixties, Paul Hindemith:

People who make music together cannot be
enemies, at least while the music lasts.

I wasn't expecting to hear back from her, so I was surprised
when she IM'd me.

Time heals all wounds. Another saying.
Clichéd, huh?
Heard through the grapevine you gave
up the piano.
Hope it wasn't because of the summer.

Not really. Who told you that?

Alejandro.

I thought you and Alex weren't in
touch.

Here and there. Maybe Eduardo told
him?

He's away.

Santiago? I don't know. I'm still mad
at you, but not angry, if you get that.

I'm sorry. Can I make it up to you?

Stay away from nail polish. For
eternity.

We both hurt each other.

I wasn't out to hurt you.
Maybe our paths will cross?
If I ever play again.
Even if I don't, that would be nice.

I'm sorry you're not doing the
Beethoven competition.

Don't be. I would have rather done the
sonata with you.

Was it Miss Pringle who'd told Eduardo, and he'd told Alex?
Would she even consider it important to mention that I was
giving up the piano? Just like I had said to my mother, I knew
in my gut that everyone gossiped. And the music world was a
very, very small circle.

Emma's message reminded me that the competition was
coming up. Most of the time I put it out of my mind. Then I
received the *Juilliard Journal* in the mail. There was an article
about the competition, noting that the results would be
announced in the December issue. They profiled a few of
the pianists who'd be competing; many of Miss Pringle's students were among them. Bin-Yu was quoted briefly: "I'm totally
stressed out. I'm trying to compete with myself, to push myself,

but it's hard to ignore the talent around me. Everyone's practicing until one, two in the morning. You forget real life. But then, this is my real life." Boy, did I know where she was coming from.

A week before Thanksgiving, while Grandma and I were baking a pumpkin pie, Hannah's mother called. "How are you? I heard you left Miss Pringle's studio. We weren't sure whose you went to because we haven't seen you anywhere."

"I'm on break," I lied as I put the jar of ground nutmeg on the counter.

"Oh." Her voice went down as if I had told her I had an incurable disease. "I was going to talk to your mother, but since I got you, I'll put Hannah on to tell you the news."

I waited for Hannah to stop playing in the background and come to the phone.

"Hi. What's up?" I asked the minute she got on.

"You won't believe this. I won the Beethoven competition!"

"That's great, Hannah! That's *really* great!"

"It was insane. The judges kept stopping us anytime they wanted us to go on to another section in the piece. It was so disconcerting not to play the whole thing through. I thought Bin-Yu was going to collapse."

"She's okay?"

"Yes. She made it to the semifinal round and then was eliminated. She's pretty disgusted since she worked so hard and blew off a lot of her schoolwork toward the end."

"Sounds like it was tough, but you survived."

"Now I'll get to play the concerto with the entire orchestra in a huge concert hall!"

253

"That's so exciting! I'm so happy for you," I said.

"We showed her, right?" I didn't need to ask whom she was referring to—I knew it was Miss Pringle.

"Yes, *you* did. Did she congratulate you?"

"No. I haven't seen her around."

I remained quiet.

"I'm happier," she went on, "and feeling more challenged—in a good way—since I changed teachers. I thought you should know that—that there's life after her."

"Thank you," I said. And I meant it.

When I got off and told my parents, "Hannah won," I saw a glimmer of envy in my mother's eyes before she tamped it down.

"I'm glad the whole thing's over, aren't you?" she asked.

"It wasn't on my mind. Not anymore." That was a definite lie.

"Oh," she said, in a tone that let me know it had always been on hers.

"By the way, I'm not going to her performance. In case you were thinking of getting tickets."

"No," she agreed. "I don't want to, either."

Later that day the phone rang again. "Ally?" the voice at the other end said.

"Brad?" I said breathlessly. "Is that you?"

"It's me."

"You're back?"

"I'm coming home for the holidays. To be with my dad."

"For good?"

"For good."

*This is better than winning any competition,* I thought.

"I'm glad you'll be home soon."

"So am I," he said. "See you after Thanksgiving."

I hung up and wandered into the living room, where Grandma and my parents had just started watching my grandmother's favorite old film, *It's a Wonderful Life.* The main character learns in the end that the life he has is wonderful. He just never saw it was in front of him all along until he discovered it was gone.

The following morning Mom decided to clean the apartment for the holiday. I took a bite of a bagel while Mom put on an aria from *La Bohème*—the part where Mimi, the lead, is dying. I was almost dying along with her from the smell of the ammonia my mother was using on the kitchen floor. But the voice coming from the CD player . . . "That's you?" I asked.

"It's me." She took in a deep breath. Then she grabbed a mop, suds slopping the floor, and sang along. When she was done, I shouted, "Brava!" and Mom threw pretend kisses to the audience. On impulse I ran into the other room and grabbed the vase of flowers sitting on the coffee table. I came back into the kitchen and handed her the flowers.

"My public," she said with a small smile.

As she gazed at the ivory tea roses, their petals rimmed in burgundy, I knew she missed it: the applause, the adoring fans, the flowers. My mother missed singing opera. My mother had quit, too.

I turned off the opera and put on Kermit the Frog. This time Mom and I sang along together with him. I too sounded like a frog—solfège had taught me nothing. The silly song brought us to tears even more than Mimi dying because it was my favorite when I was little. She'd played it for me on my white plastic record player with the red plastic turntable—the one I could also use all by myself—and we'd listened to the lyrics over and over again: *Someday we'll find it, the rainbow connection, the lovers, the dreamers, and me.*

At four o'clock on the day before Thanksgiving, Dad poked his head in my room as I lay sprawled out on my bed staring at the ceiling.

"I thought it would be fun if we went to see the balloons being inflated for the Macy's Thanksgiving Day Parade. Like old times. Just you and me, while Mom and Grandma cook. We'll pitch in later tonight and tomorrow."

I sat straight up, throwing my feet over the edge of the bed. "Sounds good."

We could see the billowing giants rising from their late autumn slumber as we walked over to the open plaza near the Museum of Natural History. Canvas drop cloths were laid out everywhere on Eighty-first Street while a crew of technicians carefully unrolled yet more cartoon characters, as they waited their turn to come to life. They were anchored by netting and sandbags so they wouldn't take off and flatten a bunch of two- and three-year-olds like a tortilla.

I rubbed my mittens together as the temperature began to drop. "Are you playing any concerts over the holidays?"

Dad watched the crowd filling in while we stood in rows

like sardines. "A few. It's usually busier for us now through Christmas." He looked away.

"What?"

"Nothing."

"What, Dad?"

He took in a breath and his jaw tightened. "Our group's splitting up after the end of this year."

"What? Did you guys have a fight?"

He began to laugh, and I realized they hadn't.

"I'm going solo. I've wanted this for a long time. It seems like forever that I've been playing with other people. I want to record more, like I did with those partitas. I need something different."

*Tell me about it,* I thought.

We were quiet for a few minutes. Then Dad said, "You know, you're a lot like your mother."

I rolled my eyes.

He chuckled. "I guess no thirteen-year-old wants to hear that."

"You mean we quit things?" I said, a little more acidly than I'd wanted.

"No. I meant that you're both thoughtful. Loving. I could go on."

"And crazy," I added.

"We're all crazy. You know who's nuts? People who don't admit it. *They* make me nervous. We all have things in life that we have to deal with." He tugged at the long woolen scarf around my neck. "I'd have you no other way than who you are."

I glanced up as the balloon characters filled the sky. "I wonder if I was put on this earth to make music or if there's something else I can do. Like math, or whatever."

"I remember when you were little and you said to me that if you didn't grow up to become a musician, you'd be a poet. I joked that's a good profession to fall back on." He let out a deep sigh. "I don't want you to feel like a failure if you never return to music. I know you're still struggling. If you do decide to go back to it, if it's going to be your life, you have to get to a point where you do it for you. Stop trying to please everyone else. Especially Mom and me." He squeezed my shoulder. "Can you do that?"

"I'll try."

"You'll figure it out. Hey, I'm still trying, too."

When he said that, I realized that I had spent so much time worrying about telling my mother and him that I wanted to stop, and now I was worrying if I would ever play again.

In our next session I told Lyn this. She said to me, "You're putting yourself in a double bind."

"So how long should I wait to see what my life is like without it?"

"For as long as you want. Maybe forever."

"If I ever go back—and that's a big if—I know it has to be for me."

Like Dad had said.

# Winter

# WINTER

To tremble from cold in the icy snow,
In the harsh breath of a horrid wind;
To run, stamping one's feet every moment,
Our teeth chattering in the extreme cold;

Before the fire to pass peaceful,
Contented days while the rain outside pours down.

We tread the icy path slowly and cautiously, for
    fear of tripping and falling.
Then turn abruptly, slip, crash on the ground and,
    rising, hasten on across the ice lest it crack up.

*—From a sonnet by Vivaldi*

# December

Without music life itself would be an error.
—Friedrich Nietzsche, philosopher

At the end of Thanksgiving vacation, I said, "I'm going back to school."

Mom looked up from her book, surprised. Dad kissed me on the top of my head.

And Grandma said, "I missed packing lunches."

"Grams, cool it on the meat products," I begged as she popped one of her exquisite miniature Swedish meatballs into my mouth. The next day, I was off to school with leftover turkey on rye in my backpack. So much for reducing meat products.

In homeroom, I handed Ms. Johansen-Williams back the

book she had loaned me on math and music. "Please keep it," she urged, pushing it back toward me. "It's yours."

At the bell, I paused in the doorway before I left for first period. She glanced up from papers she was marking. "I'm thinking I might do a math program this summer."

"Trying something different?"

"Something like that."

She smiled. "Whatever you decide."

It felt beyond weird being in the halls again: the sounds of locker doors slamming, the smell of tuna fish salad and lentil soup in the cafeteria. When I saw Opal in the hallway—her braid dyed orange, a lighter tint of her natural auburn—with Brad close behind her, I finally breathed a sigh of relief.

"Feels strange being here," I told Brad as we walked.

"Yeah," he said. "I know. But you weren't away for so long."

Then I realized he *didn't* know—because I hadn't told him.

After school, we tried to think of a place where we could be alone and talk.

"There's a taqueria up the block from our apartment," Brad suggested. "My dad's been cooking there part-time between his medical treatments."

We sat at a corner table and ordered an enchilada and two tacos with a side of rice and red beans. I looked past him to see his father working in the open kitchen, his head wrapped in a paisley bandanna. Brad had told me he'd lost all his hair. He waved when he saw me, and I waved back. A busboy plunked down a cup of salsa, a basket of blue corn chips, and two glasses of water.

As I scooped up the salsa with a chip, some dripped down my chin, and Brad went to wipe it off with a napkin.

"How is he?" I asked.

Brad shrugged. "Everyone seems hopeful."

I gave him a sympathetic smile. "Were you okay out in Idaho?"

"Okay? Being in a house with a lawn to mow and leaves to rake? Riding a bus to school past nothing but open land? And no subways to get around?" Brad paused. "Nice scenery. Thermal hot springs up in the mountains. But I missed my dad. And being here." He leaned over the table closer toward me. "How come *you're* here?" he said, changing the subject. "Don't you have to practice after school?"

"It's okay." I played with the salt and pepper shakers on the table.

"It's okay? That doesn't sound like your routine."

"I've been out of school for a while, too."

"You have?"

"Doing homeschooling."

"So your piano teacher finally won."

"No."

"What, then?" He ate another chip, not rushing me.

I paused and took in a deep breath. "I was in the hospital."

He put the chip down on his napkin. "You were where?"

"In a hospital."

"And you didn't tell me?"

"It wasn't as if you were sending me e-mails."

"I was caught up with my dad. I wasn't sending any to anyone."

I nodded, understanding.

"What was wrong? Are you okay?" He touched his forefinger to mine.

I looked into those hazel eyes of his and knew that Brad was one of those good people in the world, caring and kind. We sat there looking at each other, and it was as if all the months he had been gone melted away.

I shook my head slightly. "It's easy when you say, 'It was appendicitis.' Or 'I had to have my tonsils out.' Or even something more serious . . ."

"Like cancer." He got pale.

*Cancer gets sympathy. So do a million other diseases. What does falling apart get? Is there a get-well-soon or thinking-of-you card for that?*

"Just say it," he told me.

"I had a breakdown."

He looked stunned. Then he said softly, "Why? Did it have anything to do with what we talked about, you wanting to stop playing piano but not knowing how to tell your parents?"

A server deposited our food in front of us. We let it just sit there.

Finally I said, "I saw everyone at school and at Juilliard racing around trying to outdo the next person, and it made me wonder, when is it ever going to end? Also, it got to me to be surrounded by nine-year-old prodigies who perform all over the world. Maybe I could be like them if I tried harder, but did I even want that? Practicing till my hands hurt so I could win a competition and play with the Juilliard orchestra? And then

it'd be something else after that. There would always be something else. More. More. More."

He stroked the tips of my fingers. "I have to admit when
I was with my aunt and uncle, I felt like I was on a break.
I wasn't working after school or taking advanced this or
advanced that. The kids here are already talking about where
they want to go to college and what AP courses they're going
to take. In our grade—can you believe that? So I get it." Brad
lifted a taco toward my mouth.

At first I couldn't take a bite. I had lost my appetite. He
insisted. Then I did—a teeny one. I lifted my soda, clinking
my can to his. "L'chayim."

"L' what 'em?"

"To life. My mother told me not to take life for granted,
and not to waste it—to do whatever I was going to do now."
I looked over at Brad's father, still working.

"My mother told me the same thing. She said it goes by in
a flash."

"And we should enjoy it along the way. Right?"

He clinked his Coke can to mine. "Okay, to life, then."

Mr. Clark sent over some dessert. "Flan," Brad said. Under
the golden top layer was a smooth velvety custard. Slightly
harder on the outside, softer inside—like me. I let the custard
slide on my tongue, the caramelized sugar coating the roof of
my mouth. I understood in this moment why Brad loved to
cook and why it was moments like these—the small ones—
that made me think that maybe the world was okay.

We left the taqueria stuffed and held on to each other as

light flakes of snow began to flurry down, coating our eye-lashes. I knew all the hurt he was holding inside, because I knew what that was like. I brushed my lips across his cheek. When I kissed him, I knew the sparks had returned.

The next day we did our homework in the library after school, then went for pizza. Once we traveled downtown with Opal and had dim sum and lotus cakes in Chinatown. On Friday Brad e-mailed me:

```
Want to go ice-skating?

In Central Park?

Can we meet over at Bryant Park? It's
free.

Can Opal come? She loves anything with
blades.

Better watch out for my cooking knives,
then.
```

We all met by the skate rental area.
"So much for cutting sports from your list," declared Opal.
"Be quiet, you." I poked her gently in the side.
The three of us held hands with me in the middle as we skated together. Then Opal took off on her own, dancing in the center of the rink to some loud, fast rock music. She swooped over to Brad and me, pulling us in her direction.

I resisted, holding on to the rail, my ankles wobbling. When I let go, I fell. Brad helped me up. "Guess I won't qualify for the Winter Olympics."

Opal rolled her eyes. "Can't you just skate because it's fun?"

"But I'm a real klutz."

"Big deal. No one cares or is looking. Get up and twirl, girl."

"You're a pest," I said to Opal.

"So are you," she said, pulling me to the center.

Then she threw her hands in the air over her head and shimmied to the song.

When we were done, we walked around holiday booths set up near the rink. Tiny Christmas lights strung between white tents twinkled in the cool crisp air. "Shopping and skating in one fell swoop," Opal teased. She rushed on ahead to a booth filled with funky socks and mittens and began to try on polka-dot gloves.

As Brad and I followed her, holding hands, a bunch of girls from Juilliard were heading in our direction. I tried to duck into a booth, but one of them—a pianist who studied with someone else—called, "Ally!" I forced a smile, unable to avoid them. "Did you hear about Hannah! You're friends with her, right? She had the same teacher as you." I nodded. "I didn't see you in the competition this year. What happened?"

"I passed on it this year."

"Oh," said the pianist. Her friends sort of gave each other sideways glances.

They started giggling as they walked away, and I thought, *Is it about me?*

Brad squeezed my hand. "You okay?"

I shrugged and nodded as Opal ran toward us, shoving a pair of mittens that were covered with musical notes into my free hand. "To always keep them warm!" I looked at her and gave her a huge smile. It wasn't often you got a friend like Opal. Or Brad.

Before we left the booth, I bought a greeting card engraved with some music in a collage of gold with parts of a violin. Inside, I wrote:

> Happy holidays, Emma. Have a good year. I hope you always get what you want.
> Your friend, Ally Katz

The night of Hannah's concert, she texted me:

> I wonder if Miss Pringle will show up.
> U coming?

> I'm sorry. Something important came up.

I couldn't tell her I didn't want to go. I figured Miss Pringle would go when the polar ice caps melted and palm trees grew in Greenland.

My parents and I went sledding in the park instead. My father asked as we walked up a snowy hill, dragging our sleds, "Would you like to practice the Beethoven sonata with me? The one you were doing over the summer?" I hesitated, looking at the silvery moonlight washing over him. "You don't have to answer me now. Just an idea."

Mom slipped her hand in his and gave us a smile.

I sat cross-legged on my sled and flew down the hill, with them following on their own sled a distance behind me. The wind whipped through my hair, and my cheeks stung from the cold.

"I'd like to try the sonata with you, Dad," I said on our way home. "The last time we played together, I think, was when you tried to teach me the violin."

"And you know how that went over." He smiled.

"Yeah, I took up the piano. But it was my calling."

He put his arm on my shoulder. "No rush. You hear me?"

"Don't expect much," I said to him, knowing Mom was listening, too.

He pressed my hand with his large one.

I teased, "Watch the fingers!"

"Your pinky's feeling better?" he asked with concern.

"It's all healed."

A few nights later my father was in his small studio. He had his good violin out, and I paused, listening to its sweet high-pitched tone. "Dad," I said, poking my head in, "when do you think we should start the sonata?"

"When you're ready. Why don't you run through it a couple of times first, so you feel comfortable on your own?"

"Thanks, Dad."

"Thank *you*. It will be a treat."

I let a few days go by, waiting for my thoughts to settle.

When I told my therapist, she asked me, "How do you feel about playing again?"

"I'm not sure." Then my eyes filled with tears. "Scared."

"You're facing your fears, and that's good."

"Lyn," I said, "my dad is going to be holding my hand this time."

"So you won't be alone."

I smiled nervously.

She leaned over from her chair and looked me straight in the eye. "And if you want to stop at any time, no one will judge you. No jury. No parent. No friend. Not me."

"But I judge myself. All the time."

"Then maybe you need to ease off on that."

"I'll work on it," I said.

"Don't be so hard on yourself. Can you do that for me?"

"I'll try. Habits are hard to change."

"I know." She smiled. "That's why I have such a thriving practice."

The next day, I came directly home after school. I stared at the piano, then lifted the lid covering its keys. I poked at a note. Then another. The sound went through me as though a bell were chiming loudly in a church. Clear and distinct. Beckoning. I opened the piano bench and searched for the sonata. It had been months. When I found it, I slipped out the violin part. There were Dad's and Emma's fingering scribbles. Should I put it back? *Just playing a few bars doesn't mean I'm committing myself or returning to the way things were.* I looked at the bench. I sat down and got comfortable. A few measures came out of me. Then a few more, until it became a whole

272

page. People always say when they want you to do something that you haven't done for a really long time that it's like riding a bike—you never forget how. But when I took my old bicycle to the park after a long period in which I hadn't ridden it, I wobbled and nearly crashed into a tree. That's exactly what happened with the sonata: I didn't remember, and I had to work at it.

I skipped a day to study for a math quiz, but the day after, I practiced some more. It sounded a little better, but not much. So I spent another day avoiding it. Then, after my homework was done, I knew I wanted to face it again, and I put in two hours. It felt good. When I glanced up to turn a page, I noticed my mother lingering at the threshold of the living room. "Mom?"

She waved me away with her hand.

"Are you okay?"

"I'm okay," she said, all choked up.

My mother walked over to me, put her arms around my waist from the back, and hugged me so tight I said, "Ma, I can't breathe!"

"Oh, Ally," she sighed, "it's delicious to hear this in the house again."

"Don't start," I said with intensity.

"I won't."

"You'd better not! It sounds pretty bad."

"Not to me." She gave me another hug. "It sounds pretty wonderful. How does it feel?"

"I don't know." I wanted to leave it at that. No hopes raised.

I waited a day in between, then gave it another go. I wanted to play alone, without anyone listening. Somehow, my mother must have realized this, because she went into the kitchen immediately. Later I joined her, and I helped her dice onions.

"Would you like to go to the opera with me?" she asked as we chopped.

"The opera?" I said with surprise, pausing with the knife on the cutting board. "Which one?"

"*La Bohème*."

I smiled at my mother. I should have known. "I'd love to."

"I'll get us good seats for the holidays. When you're off from school."

We both pretended it wasn't big, but we both knew it was.

As big as me starting to play again.

Some days were better than others. The next time I saw my mother lingering in the doorway, watching me practice, I swiftly closed the music book. "I need to be alone!" I shouted at her. "I wish I had taken up the violin, so I could go in a room and shut a door like Dad!"

She picked up Beethoven, brought him over, and sat next to me. "I was only listening. To something beautiful."

I patted Beethoven's head. Then Beethoven put one paw on the keys and played a discordant chord, and we both began to laugh.

"He's got potential," I teased.

"I think I'll refrain from signing him up for lessons. Wait and see if he develops some real skills first."

"I'm sorry, Ma," I apologized. "I don't know what got into me."

"That's okay. We all get like that."

Then we were quiet again for a moment. She touched my hand, picked Beethoven up, and left so I could be alone and do my thing in my own head. Being an artist, she understood what that was like, and I realized that I was lucky she was my mother.

After I felt more proficient, I told my father, "I think I'm ready to give it a go."

He followed me into the living room. I had already set up a music stand to the right of the piano with his part spread out on it. It's amazing how professional musicians can sit down with ease and play a piece without having seen it for a while, or even do it cold. For them, it really is like riding a bike.

"Dad, you zoomed through it like you've been practicing every day."

He gave me a crooked grin. "This is the language I speak."

"You speak music?" I ribbed him.

"Not every dialect, but most."

"How about heavy metal?"

"Not yet." He played a few screechy measures, piercing my eardrums.

"Maybe never."

We chuckled.

He was patient and steady. He'd say, "Can we focus on this measure?" or "Maybe try this instead. What do you think?" He'd show me as many times as I needed to be shown until it felt right. Hours seemed like minutes. With Miss Pringle, it had always been the other way around.

When we were finished, I went into the kitchen to get a drink of water. My mother was standing by the sink with her back toward me, but I could see her reflection in the window. And I will never forget how her face looked: content. Dad came in after putting away his violin. "You did good, hon," she said, and briskly wiped the corner of her eye with a dish towel.

"Thanks, Ma."

"I was actually speaking to your father." She turned as he put his hand on her shoulder. "And it wasn't about the sonata."

"What was it about, then?" I asked tentatively.

"Both of you. Together," Mom said.

My father plucked the towel from her hand and tossed it onto the counter. "Scrabble, anyone?"

"Monopoly?" I suggested instead. "I need to branch out into real estate development. I'm buying Park Place."

"In your dreams! I'm getting the blue properties and putting up hotels!" he called out as I went to my bedroom closet to get the game.

Grandma came home to find her only grandchild with stacks of pastel-colored cash in front of her. She eyed the game board, where I had houses and hotels on my properties. "A land baroness! Maybe you could get me a nice little condo on the beach so I could be off on my own without bothering any of you."

I threw my arms around my grandmother's neck. "Bothering us? Grandma!"

"You never know, I might shack up with some cute lifeguard. Or as they say, hook up."

"Grandma!"

"You think I'm not hip. I'm hip," she said. "I met a friend."

"A friend?" My father looked over at his mother with raised eyebrows.

"Anthony DiMaggio. I'm not sure how long it's going to last because let's face it, I don't know any Italian, and he knows about one Yiddish word: *bagel*. Although we discovered ravioli and kreplach have a lot in common." She gave a mischievous glance.

"When are we going to meet your new beau?" my mother asked her.

"Parents." I rolled my eyes.

"I know," Grandma said back. "I guess we'll just have to tolerate them."

Winter vacation began, and Mom and I got ready for the opera. I wore a black velvet button-down jacket with my black jeans, red leather ankle boots, and black glittery socks I borrowed from Opal. Before we left, Mom handed me the silver and turquoise bracelet Dad had given to her on her opening night in *La Bohème*—the one she in turn had given to me on my birthday, and which I'd eventually thrown back on her bed. I stared at it in my palm. "I want you to have it. I want it to bring you good luck, Ally."

"But it didn't bring you any."

"It did. I had you. A daughter I could hand it down to." She put it on my wrist, fastening the delicate clasp.

Neither of us said, "I'm sorry" because too many had already been said.

We went out for dinner at a Japanese restaurant on Amsterdam Avenue. As I sipped green tea from a small celadon cup, I couldn't help staring at the bracelet, its silver threads entwined like patterns of lace on my wrist.

Mom and I sat in first row center of the grand tier, quietly reading the program about the opera, set in nineteenth-century Paris during Christmas. Many of the artists in this performance had taken the same route Mom had: same school, same debuts, same operas. When the chandeliers dimmed and the curtain went up, Mom gripped my hand with excitement as the singers began the first act of the libretto.

"Do you love it?" I asked during intermission.

She smiled as we waited on the long line curling out of the women's bathroom. "I like it. Because I'm with you, I love it. This is a great evening."

I admired her lucky bracelet. "It is."

On Christmas Eve, which turned out to be the same night as the first night of Chanukah, my father was playing one of his final gigs with his chamber group at an interfaith concert. They were doing Handel's *Messiah* with a chorus, some Bach, and klezmer. Grandma, Mom, and I sat in a pew. We were close enough for me to see my father's face and how it changed with each measure as he played. It was sad to think of his quintet

278

breaking up because they were powerful together, grabbing my heart as their different musical voices became one. During the klezmer, they departed from the score, improvising as people clapped or danced in the aisles. Grandma got up and started to move toward a man who'd come in late. They hooked arms in a swirl like a square dance, and I figured that it might be her new "friend." When she returned to her seat, he sat down beside her, and she introduced him. "This is Tony."

Between Christmas and New Year's I continued to practice by myself, or with my father, who had the patience of a Zen master. When I made mistakes, he calmly said, "Let's go over it again if you want to." I always seemed to want to. And when I didn't, that was okay, too. He'd say, "I needed a break anyway." So when we didn't practice, we'd watch TV or I'd go off with Opal when she wasn't hanging out with Ruby, who'd come home from Yale for the holidays.

On New Year's Eve Mom and Dad threw a party, and Opal was sleeping over. Her hair had tinsel braided in with her own red-and-green-highlighted locks. Silver sparkles glittered on her cheeks. Around her wrists she had bracelets made of purple, magenta, and turquoise threads that she had dyed and woven with her mother, and she gave me and my mother each one. As she was passing around tiny egg rolls, she whispered forcefully, "Why don't you play something?" I shook my head, feeling awkward, hanging back.

"Come on," she insisted, "they're not going to boo you in your home!"

I threw my head back and let out a laugh. "That's what

you think. Most of these people are in the music business in some form or another. Trust me, they know how to boo. Professionally."

She handed me the tray of hors d'oeuvres and opened the lid to the piano. "I bet they know how to applaud, too."

One of my mother's accompanists took that as an invitation to play some Muddy Waters. When he got up, another friend sat down.

"You think you're off the hook?" Opal motioned to me. "Well, you're not." She grabbed my arm when the bench became empty again. "Let's give this puppy a shot."

"I don't think this is a Chopin crowd tonight."

"So cool it on the Chopin." Opal pushed me down onto the piano bench.

I rolled my eyes toward the ceiling. Then I looked back at her and grumbled like a three-year-old whose parent pushes her to perform for the relatives. My father noticed what was happening and extricated himself from a conversation, pulling my mother away from hers, too. She grabbed some sheet music, plopped it on the shelf in front of me, and sat down beside me. Dad took out his violin and tuned it up, and when he was ready Mom began to sing Billie Holiday's "All of Me." I followed her voice as we bopped to the beat shoulder to shoulder. Then I started to improvise. Dad went along with me, and so did Mom. There was lots of applause and some whistles and hoots when the three of us were done.

Opal put her hands on her hips. "I thought you said I wasn't ever allowed to hoot when you played. But they did!"

"Then I guess I was wrong," I said with a smile.

Some of the guests insisted that we do a few holiday favorites, which I attempted to do by ear while they sang. My father came in and saved me when I made mistakes. And so did Mom. It wasn't perfection—far from it—but that was okay. A man I didn't know leaned over and said, "You sound good." The thrill of that simple remark ran through me like an electric current, and I knew it was going to last for days. I also knew that Miss Pringle's spell had almost been broken. Almost, because while I didn't have to be perfect, in my heart I still wanted to be. But I could play in public and not feel as though I should dig a hole and hide after I hit a bad note or two, and I knew I wouldn't agonize over it for hours or even days after it happened.

Before midnight, my cell began to vibrate. It was Brad. "Happy new year!"

"Happy new year, Mr. Clark!" I joked with him.

"You want me to put my father on?" he teased back.

"No! See you next year, Brad," I said. "Which is in less than a minute."

While most of my parents' friends were counting along with the TV as the ball descended high above Times Square, Opal and I were counting with Brad and his father in the background, over the speakerphone. At midnight, Opal and I jumped up and down. My parents came over and enfolded us in a group hug.

"I wish you the world," my mother whispered in my ear.

"And a good year," my father added. I noticed he hadn't said "better."

Grandma came over to me carrying a present. I tore at the

281

wrapping paper and looked down at a burgundy leather cover. "A scrapbook?"

"For new beginnings. Maybe this time you'll save your music programs."

I gave her one of my famous looks.

"Darling, I need something to enjoy in my old age while I'm in a rocking chair."

I looked at her. "Yeah, right, your old age. Don't make me laugh."

"You're right. Isn't seventy the new sixty?" She went off to do the lindy with Tony DiMaggio.

I heard the fireworks over Central Park off in the distance, booming like an orchestra over the darkened sky. Opal and I ran up to the roof, full of expectation, looking ahead to whatever came our way.

# January

To play music is a state of grace and ecstasy.
—Leon Fleisher, pianist, conductor, teacher

It's sometimes fantastic to start fresh. To practice with no one looking over your shoulder, correcting, taping, breathing down your neck on each and every move. Then, after a while, it was also scary to look ahead alone, with only me to judge or analyze. "I need help," I said to Brad in the lunchroom.

"With what?"

"Music. I might want to take lessons again."

"Piano?"

"What else?"

"I don't know . . . guitar? Maybe you want to start a band."

"If I started a band, I'd be a keyboardist."

He knocked me gently on the head. "Hello. You do need help."

I peered at him. "I said I'm *thinking* about it."

"So find another teacher, then."

"Easy for you to say."

"You're right. But if you don't try, it won't happen."

This time, instead of holding everything inside, I went to my parents. "I'm thinking of taking lessons again," I blurted out while my father was practicing and my mother lay on the couch reading a magazine. She raised a single eyebrow, glancing over at him. This time I couldn't read her. My father rested his violin bow in his case.

"I love playing with you, Dad, and I want to continue, but I need . . ."

"You don't have to spell it out. I understand," he said.

"It shouldn't be like before," said my mother, sitting up.

"I know," I answered her. "If it ever gets like that, hit me on the head with a hammer to remind me."

Mom made a call to Hannah's mother, and then to Hannah's new teacher.

Then she, Dad, and I went to see the head of the Pre-College Division.

"There's another teacher," Mom informed him, "that's willing to hear Ally and possibly take her on."

The director sat stiffly behind his large desk and opened my file. "Ally missed a whole term. There are students clamoring to come here."

"There were circumstances," my mother said.

"She's ready to return," my father put in.

"I see." He gazed over my records as if they might change.

"What are we to do?" asked Mom. "Can we set up an informal audition with another teacher?"

"You can, but who's her teacher again?"

"Miss Pringle," she answered.

*Former teacher. Miss Pringle is not my teacher.*

"Ah, Miss Pringle. She"—he smiled to himself as if it were an inside joke—"can be feisty. Certainly our entire faculty is excellent, but I'd give it some thought before you set anything else up."

"Why?" my mother asked, instead of saying, *We have given it a lot of thought.*

He looked at her as if it was obvious that she and Dad should know the answer to that, which they sort of did, but Mom wanted to hear him say it.

"She's been here longer than anyone and has such enormous experience." He spread his hands. "She studied with the greats, but I imagine you already know that."

"I'm sure all your teachers are very experienced," Dad countered.

He nodded, fiddling with the paperweight in the shape of a treble clef. "True. We try."

My mother leaned slightly toward his green felt desk blotter. "You know how some marriages work and others, after a while, don't? Well, this marriage between teacher and student is no longer working. My daughter needs a change. She needs to switch teachers."

He nodded politely and formally.

My father gave one of his charming smiles. Then everyone

stood up and shook hands. "Thanks for your input," Dad said. "We'll give everything you said careful consideration. We just wanted to clear channels with the school before forging ahead."

The director turned to me. "Ally, let me know how it turns out."

I smiled uncomfortably and looked down.

Out in the hall my mother jabbed the button for the elevator. "Why did we even go?"

"We had to," said Dad. "Now it's out in the open."

"He was so discouraging. Couldn't he have been more helpful?" she said agitatedly.

"No, he couldn't," said my father. "He can't favor one teacher over another."

"He sort of did. Wasn't he telling us, without saying it, that Ally should stay with Miss Pringle? This time I'm putting my foot down."

"You don't have to," I answered, "because I am putting down mine."

The three of us went for muffins near our place before heading home.

"You okay being there again?" asked Mom.

I shrugged. "I guess."

"That would be a no? Or a yes?" she prodded.

"That would be an 'I don't know,'" I said.

"Fair enough," said Dad as he paid for the muffins.

After practicing for a week like I used to, there were moments when I considered myself totally nuts. But I went on the audition anyway. And it did feel weird being in the halls of Juilliard again, even weirder than when I'd returned to school. Miss Tanaka's studio was spare, with one orchid plant on a low teak table. The black piano looked stark and much larger against the tatami mat underneath it, which unnerved me instead of having a calming effect. She spoke very little English, smiled a lot, and was real friendly, but I didn't know how to speak Japanese like most of her other students and their parents. I was surprised Hannah was doing so well with her. During the audition Miss Tanaka was less intrusive than Miss Pringle, and at the end of our time, without words she showed me how to play a phrase another way and position my hands at a slightly different angle, which I appreciated. "I have time, teach you Friday nights, eight. Yes?" she said in broken English. I couldn't figure out if I'd be awake enough to play after a full day of school, or if I'd be too exhausted to get up the following morning and then put in a full day at Pre-College. Plus various rehearsals were often on Friday nights. So it wasn't a good match.

I tilted my head toward her. "Thank you for taking the time to see me."

She bowed slightly.

I was disappointed, but my parents said, "There are other fish in the sea."

In a moment of weakness, I said, "Should I stay with what I had?"

My mother gave me a fierce look. "No!"

Hannah called the next day. "How did it go?"

"Good. But she has very little time."

"I know. Could she fit you in?"

"Friday. A late lesson. I wouldn't be done until after nine."

"If you're lucky. She always runs late. So it might even be ten when you were really done. We tried," she said.

"Thanks. And I'm sorry I couldn't make your concert, Hannah."

"Next time," she said.

"By the way, did Miss Pringle show up?"

Hannah became quiet. "No."

"Her loss."


Dad and I continued to practice the sonata around his rehearsal schedule, but with a new Pre-College term beginning the second week of January, I needed a formal teacher. I was also frightened about Miss Pringle finding out.

Then Hannah called again. "Did you find someone yet? If not, Eduardo's coming back."

"*He is?*" I said ecstatically.

"Heard his grandmother died and Pringle got his student visa extended."

"Guess she's there for some of her students."

Hannah exhaled into the receiver.

I knew it might put him in a pickle, but I wanted to study with him. Would he?

During the weekend, I signed up for classes and made sure I got the same chamber coach as last year, even though I didn't have my main piano teacher yet. Dr. Rashad was passing by in the hall, and he stopped when he saw me. "Why, hello. How are you?"

"Fine," I answered.

"Still writing music?"

"Yes."

"Wonderful. Wonderful." He smiled brightly.

I took a deep breath. "Could I study privately with you this coming semester?"

"Of course."

"Really?"

"Go to the office, fill out a form, and I'll sign off on it."

As I was running down the stairwell I spotted Alex coming up.

"Hey." Alex looked surprised.

"Hey," I panted, pausing.

"How's it going?"

"It's going." I was bursting to tell someone, but I kept it inside.

Miss Tippytoes floated down from nowhere and put her arm around his waist, smiling widely. "Hi," she said to me.

"Hi," I said back.

"This is Tanya," said Alex. "Tanya, this is Ally."

She no longer was Miss Tippytoes. She became a person with a name and a smile.

As I turned to go, I looked up at him. "Have you heard from Eduardo?"

"His visa fell through."

My heart sank. "Are you one hundred percent sure? I heard the opposite."

"Ninety-nine-point-nine percent sure."

One minute I was flying, the next I had come down to earth. *Now what was I going to do?*

After I went to the office, I wandered into a half-filled

Morse Hall and sat down in a daze. It was an informal setting, but the young woman next to me seemed intense, listening. I smiled. She didn't smile back. *Cold fish*, I thought. A girl a bit older than me was playing the violin with a pianist several years younger. When I looked at the name on the flyer, I saw that the pianist was Aya—the same Aya who used to wear ruffled organza dresses to our master class. Now she was wearing jeans and a coral blouse open at the neck onstage. When she was done, she ran off, not toward her mother, who was waiting in the wings, but toward the woman seated next to me. Aya shot me a huge grin. "Hi, Ally. Would you like to meet my teacher?"

*Your teacher?* I sat up in my seat, paying full attention.

"Dr. Kong, this is Ally Katz. We used to be in Miss Pringle's studio together."

Dr. Kong flashed a reserved smile in my direction. "I studied with Miss Pringle when I was in the doctoral program."

"We all studied with Miss Pringle?" I said with surprise.

"Yes, we did," she answered me. "Philip Glass once said, 'We're always two or three teachers away from Beethoven.' In Juilliard, I like to think of it as Miss Pringle."

Then she turned to Aya. "You did a really nice job, Aya. You should feel very proud of yourself." Then she put her hand out. "It was very nice meeting you, Ally."

As I left the auditorium, I turned once again, and saw an Aya I had never seen. Not the girl who'd won competitions at eight, playing concertos that a twenty-year-old should be performing. No, what I saw was a joyful girl giving her teacher a hug.

Later I asked around about Dr. Kong.

"The word on the street," Hannah told me, "is that she came from Korea to study with Miss Pringle and switched a year later to study with someone else."

"Really?"

"Really," said Hannah. "And we know about that, don't we? Miss Pringle never spoke to her again."

That night I told my parents, "I want to audition for a new teacher."

"Go for it," Dad said.

"Do you need us to make any calls?" Mom asked.

"I'll do it this time. I'm old enough to make my own choices."

Mom looked at me with a mock severe glance. "*Some* choices."

"O-kay," I groaned. "Some."

I got Dr. Kong's e-mail address and set it up for the following week. My mother and father didn't drill me on what I was preparing or how many hours I was putting in every day. And when I did practice, they left me alone.

I told Opal and Brad in art class. "I think I finally found the right teacher."

"That's nice," said Opal, distracted by her drawing.

Brad gave me a different kind of look, like, *I hope you know what you're doing.*

"That's nice?" I repeated, giving Opal a shove.

"Okay, what's the deal?" Opal asked, putting down her charcoal.

"Well, her name is Dr. Kim Kong, and—"

"Kim Kong?" Opal repeated.

"Yeah."

"Hmm. You'd better not monkey around with her."

Brad jumped in without missing a beat. "Why did King Kong join the army?"

"Why?" Opal asked.

"To learn gorilla warfare," he answered, and Opal groaned.

I tried to outdo them. "What do you get if King Kong sits on your piano?" They both stared at me blankly. "A flat note."

Both of them looked puzzled, and I sighed. "Thanks for your support."

Opal picked up her charcoal and made little ape sounds.

"Very funny." I shook my head as we went back to drawing.

A few days before the audition I told my parents at dinner, "I'm canceling my therapy session with Lyn this week. I don't have the time."

My mother put down her fork. "Make the time. Especially now."

Dad agreed. "It's not all about the music. It's about everything you do. Even the time in between doing nothing."

"A grace note." And this time when I said it, it was a good thing.

We all smiled together. We were a family of musicians and spoke in a language that was often said in sounds and voices and rhythms and not always words.

I played my repertoire for them when we finished our meal. They applauded.

"Any places that need work?" I asked.

Mom looked at Dad. "Doug?"

"I can't think of a spot."

"Oh, come on," I insisted. "It was absolutely perfect?"

Grandma, who was lurking in the hallway nearby, came into the living room. "Stop walking on eggshells, you two."

They both glared at her.

"What?" Grandma said, glaring right back. "You think she's going to melt? No one ever died from the truth."

"But they could get hurt," said my mother.

"And they can grow if it's done the right way. She's asking both of you. Answer!"

Mom and Dad looked at each other, then Dad reached for the music.

"A little more emphasis here." He pointed to a passage.

"I'd watch the phrasing in this measure," Mom added.

"That's more like it." Grandma slapped her hands together. "Constructive criticism."

The day of the audition I was scared out of my mind. "If this doesn't work out, what am I going to do?"

"Continue," my father said.

Before I went inside Dr. Kong's studio, I rotated my arms in wide circles, like we did in gym, and flexed my wrists vigorously in the air, shaking them out to get circulation in my fingers. When I came inside the room, Dr. Kong bowled me over when she said, "Play anything you want. Classical, jazz, something you made up, anything."

"Really?" came out of my lips. "No scales?"

"Scales are for your practice. If you don't know your scales by now, don't bother to audition." She smiled. "I'd rather hear you play something beautiful. Let your imagination go."

I played for her for a whole hour. Maybe more. Not one of these ten-to-twenty-minute jobs. "The last piece," she inquired, "what was that?"

"A little something I wrote."

"You're studying composition, too?"

"I'm going to begin private lessons this term."

She grinned and opened a loose-leaf notebook, flipping to a page with a schedule. "I teach in Philadelphia on Tuesdays. At Curtis."

"Oh," I said, surprised, "I didn't know you could teach in both places."

"I'm a single parent—I need to. It's better than some of my friends who fly to Boston or Cleveland to teach." She thought out loud, directing her finger down the column of names on her schedule. "Let's see, I have to pick up my daughter from day care . . . give a lesson . . . How does Monday after school sound? Four? Is that good for you?"

"Y-yes," I stammered, "that works for me. Mondays are great. Then I'll know what to work on for the rest of the week."

She put my name down in her book. In ink. It made it official. "Mondays it is."

I let out an enormous sigh of relief. You could almost hear it crosstown.

Dr. Kong placed her hand on my arm. "You did very well."

I let out another breath. "I did?"

"You did."

I was so relieved I began to cry. I was mortified, but she acted like nothing had happened and handed me a tissue as I sniffled. "Next week we'll choose a new piece together. Still, think of some composers you would like to play."

"Great," I said, giving my nose a final blow.

I smiled to myself as I was leaving. Dr. Kong might turn out to be the best teacher I'd ever had. And she wasn't a cold fish, as I'd thought that day in Morse Hall. She was studied. Paced. But warm.

Needless to say, my mother was thrilled when I ran into the apartment and cried out, "I was accepted!"

"Oh, Ally!" She hugged me. "And you did it on your own!"

"Not really. I had a little backup," I teased her.

Mom was so joyous, I saw her take out an opera score later that evening—one she had performed when she had first joined the Met.

When I texted Opal and phoned Brad, both were excited for me, but no one understood how I felt better than Hannah did, which made absolute sense—she had been there herself. "It's going to free you to become the pianist you were meant to be."

"I'll miss you at master class," I told her.

"We'll see each other."

"But you were my support there."

"Maybe you won't need as much this time around."

After my first lesson, I gave Dr. Kong a CD Dad had burned of my compositions. She thanked me and put it in her brown briefcase. "When you teach others, you teach yourself. You have to listen. I want to know everything you do involving music. Even what you write." She gestured to the CD. "Everything you do goes toward who you become. I have a student who also loves to make clothes. It's all about making something out of nothing, isn't it? Being creative."

I nodded, remembering how the CD had remained on top of Miss Pringle's piano untouched. I felt comfortable enough admitting, "I like math. Fractals."

"So do I. They're pretty shapes in nature, aren't they?"

"I think you and my math teacher would get along."

"Modern composers think math and music are related. Would you like to try Copland?"

"I'd like to try more modern. Cage. Reich. Glass. Adams. And Katz."

"Katz?"

"Ally Katz." I grinned bashfully.

"This all sounds ambitious," she said, but it didn't sound like a criticism or like she was discouraging me.

"I'm open to anything."

"So am I," she offered. "You're young."

"I'm thirteen and a half already."

She let out a chuckle. "There's a lot of time ahead."

We both smiled at each other as I left. "See you next week," I said, and waved.

I was in the elevator waiting for the doors to shut when Miss Pringle got inside with her entourage. My head began to pound. Some students I knew said hello, while others were new, probably admitted in the fall when I was away. Miss Pringle gave me a polite smile, as if I could be anyone. Not like I had studied with her for years, including my summers. In a strange way, it freed me. I looked at her holding her black purse, and my head suddenly stopped pounding. She could be anyone, too. It was like when I'd seen Alex on the stairwell with Tanya. I wasn't sad or angry. I had moved on.

"I see you've returned," she said.

"Yes." I took in a breath and then let it out.

"Whom are you studying with?"

"Dr. Kong."

"Aha. Kim," was all she said. Not *She studied with me and she's good.*

As the doors to the elevator opened, I said, "Well, bye, Miss Pringle," but she was already talking to someone else.

I think that's when I realized I was a pianist. Or maybe that was when I *became* one. I didn't need her to succeed. Any doubts I had were cured like a bad case of chicken pox—like Grandma said, with maybe a scar or two left as a reminder. And with time, scars can sometimes heal.

By the following Saturday, I was back in the swing of things when I showed up for my private lesson with Dr. Rashad. "I'm thinking of working on the piece I told you about—the one the chamber coach I had last term said she'd let one of her groups perform. Can I show you what I've been doing?"

"Certainly! That's what I'm here for." I laid out the score with all the parts for the different instruments, and he scanned it. "Let's take it over to the piano." He made a few recommendations, then asked respectfully, "How does this seem?"

"I love your ideas."

"Then feel free to use them. I like what you did, too." He spoke to me as if I were a colleague—a real composer.

Dad and I continued to rehearse. "I'd like to set up a small gathering for us to do the sonata together at the end of January in another musician's home. Would that be okay?"

"Don't we need more time?" I asked, getting jittery.

"It'll be ready. And if it's not, we'll postpone it."

"Do they need hors d'oeuvres?" Grandma asked.

"Grandma," I sighed, "if they need any, I'll ask Brad."

"I'm fired? Just like that? Now that you're a big deal in the concert circuit again?"

"Swedish meatballs," I said. "Make those teeny-tiny ones."

"My rolling fingers are ready." She wiggled her fingers in the air. "You're not the only one who knows how to work those digits."

One afternoon I came home early because there were teacher meetings before the long weekend for Martin Luther King Jr. Day. I found my mother standing by someone at the piano, and when she noticed me, she got a deer-in-the-headlights look. Finally she said, "I'm taking voice lessons again. This is my vocal coach, Geoff Veroni. Geoff, this is my daughter, Ally Katz." I smiled and went to my room to get out of their way.

"How long has this been going on?" I asked when he left before dinnertime.

"Just started," she said.

"Why didn't you tell me?"

"I guess I'm scared, too."

I hugged her.

"Don't think we'll be hogging the piano. I'll be studying at his place. He was getting it painted, so I suggested we do it here for today."

A week later, at dinner, she announced, "I've decided to try out for a fledgling opera company downtown and get some arias under my belt again before I go for *the* company—we won't mention any names."

"That's great, Mom!"

Dad and I looked at each other. He moved his hand next to hers.

Over the next few weeks Mom and I almost had to fight each other for time at the piano.

"So much for not hogging," I teased her, nearly pushing her off the piano bench onto the rug on the floor.

On the last Sunday of the month, Dad hailed a cab to take us to his friend's on the Upper East Side. I had the sonata in hand. Mom held my other one as we crossed the street. Instead of pulling away, I left my hand in hers. Grandma was carrying a large plastic tub filled with meatballs, and Mr. DiMaggio transported her mandelbrot, its almonds falling off the top onto her pink-glass dessert plate. When we arrived, Brad and Opal were already munching on carrot and celery sticks, swirling them in a tofu curry dip Mr. Clark had whipped up. They were offering some to a little girl standing next to Dr. Kong. She must have been Dr. Kong's daughter—she looked exactly like her, and had a fold of fabric from Dr. Kong's skirt bunched in her pudgy hand.

After a while I went over to the grand piano and played a few notes to get a feel for the keyboard. The owner came over, and I prayed I didn't sound heavy-handed on the piano. "I had it tuned especially for this. I hope it's to your liking."

"Oh, thank you." I lifted myself halfway off the black leather-tufted piano bench, and he motioned for me to sit back down and relax.

"The former owner told me that Horowitz once performed on this piano."

"Horowitz?" I withdrew my hands as if the keys were on fire.

"Lang Lang played on it a few weeks ago when he was in town, to test out his performance before he did it at Carnegie Hall." The man carefully drew my hands back toward the keys. "Maybe his good fortune will rub off on you."

To think the great Vladimir Horowitz and Lang Lang, who had played with leading orchestras around the world in major concert halls, had touched the keys where my hands now rested totally freaked me out. Was that supposed to calm me down? Well, it didn't. When the clock struck three, I wiped my palms on the long Indian skirt I was wearing. Silver sequins, like Eduardo's coins, glistened on the shimmering silk as if reminding me to let go. As Dad tuned his violin, I remembered how I'd always thought Emma and I would premiere this together. Then the image of her was gone as my father smiled assuredly at me. Mom, Grandma, Dr. Kong and her daughter (whose name was Minsu), and Hannah with her mother were sitting together near the front. Dr. Rashad had told me he'd be busy with a presentation of one of his pieces and couldn't attend, but he'd wished me good luck and given me a mug that said, *Beethoven Rocks*. It was filled with new pencils, ready for writing. Opal and Brad were off to the side with Mr. Clark, whose hair was beginning to grow back. Others were on white folding chairs scattered around the room talking quietly, waiting. Dad rosined his bow, lifted his violin, and met my eyes briefly. We began.

Halfway through I had a slip. Tinier than one of Grandma's meatballs. And it stayed that way—tiny. Unlike the New Year's Eve party where I'd played in public again for the first time, this was in front of my teacher and other serious musicians from my school, but I went on. I survived. Without a net.

When it was over, there was a burst of applause. Hannah gave me a thumbs-up. Tears streamed down my mother's face. Her hand was at her throat, as if she were trying to catch her breath. I saw my father's eyes were filled, too. And Grandma, who was not one for being left out, took the tissue she had balled in the bottom sleeve of her sweater and wiped her eyes as Mr. DiMaggio stood behind her and patted her shoulder. I had played the Beethoven. I was finally done with it.

"Encore!" Opal hooted, and I shot her a look.

But everyone backed up her request. So I played the encore I'd never gotten to play at my recital with Miss Pringle— the Massenet *Thaïs*. And I added a little bit of Gershwin. Miss Pringle would have had a heart attack. Then I moved over, leaving an empty space next to me on the bench, and stretched my arm out toward my mother in this small, intimate audience. She shook her head, but I patted the bench, and Dad motioned for her to go.

Dad played the beginning to her aria from *La Bohème*. When she heard the first few notes, she froze, so I kicked into gear and did the rest by ear, I had heard it so many times. At first she gulped and shook her head emphatically, but we kept on going. So she started, reluctantly, and the three of us did it together.

When she was done, she apologized to me in a whisper. "Oh, Ally. I don't think I was ready."

I said to her, "Ma, you sound just like me. Is anyone ever ready?"

We both sat there and smiled.

Someone brought me flowers this time. Brad. A dozen red roses.

I gave one to my father, one to my mother, one to my grandmother, one to my new teacher . . . the list went on until there were people all over the room holding roses. And of course, I gave one back to Brad.

At the reception afterward, I told Hannah, "It's sweet you came to mine when I didn't attend yours."

"Ally, I'm not keeping a scorecard," said Hannah. "Although my mother is." We both laughed.

Grandma pulled me aside. "I'm all *farklempt.* Filled with pride and joy."

Grandma's meatballs were a hit. "To die for," I overheard one woman say. When Brad asked Grandma, "What's in them, Mrs. Katz?" she answered, "Trust me, you don't want to know."

"But I do," he pressed on.

She got as red as a corned beef and said in a hushed tone, "Ketchup and grape jelly." Then she really lowered her voice.

"And a touch of Manischewitz wine." She looked over her shoulder, as if she had just pulled a fire alarm and the principal was coming down the hall. "Don't tell anyone I spiked the meatballs."

"Scout's honor," he pledged, raising his hand in a salute.

"Are you an Eagle Scout?" I asked him after Grandma had moved off.

"Never."

"So much for honesty. Are you going to tell your father the recipe?"

"Not if you want me to keep it a secret," Brad promised.

I knew Grandma was a sharer, so I said, "If your dad becomes famous off them, he has to give her credit. And a piece of the action."

"Deal." Brad firmly shook my hand.

Ms. Johansen-Williams, who'd been seated all the way in the back, came up to me and handed me a small head of broccoli with a large white satin ribbon tied around the stem. "I know it's an odd bouquet," she said, "but it's—"

"Fractals," Dr. Kong completed her sentence. "Expanding patterns."

They smiled widely as I introduced them to each other.

"I did a paper on Benoît Mandelbrot when I was in high school," said Dr. Kong.

"Did I hear mandelbrot?" said Grandma, walking by with her dessert plate. "It's the almonds."

We all laughed. Ms. Johansen-Williams followed her, and I said to Dr. Kong, "I told you that you'd like my math teacher."

"I do. And I like your grandmother, also." Then Dr. Kong handed me a flat package tied with a gold ribbon. First I read the card: *Beethoven has endured throughout parts of three centuries and will last beyond our time. Music is a meditation, a reverie, a respite from madness.* A tear dripped down my cheek as I unwrapped the package. It was Scott Joplin's ragtime music, the notes all jazzy. She put her arm gently around me, and I threw my arms around her. "I thought it might be fun to mix it up a little," she said.

"The icing on Beethoven."

She looked at me, perplexed.

"A world without music is like having a cupcake without any icing."

"Or sprinkles," Minsu added in her tiny voice. "I like the green ones."

I looked down at her and smiled. "So do I."

That hole in my heart I had been trying to fill—I think I filled it today.

# February

Music is a zone of joy.
—Jamie Jones, music and mathematics author

The next day I IM'd Emma.

```
I did our sonata with my father. I can
put it to rest.
Until I want to take it out again.
Someday. Maybe.

So you went back to the piano?

I did.
```

And Emma responded after a long pause:

```
I'm returning to the music program
this summer.
I want to learn the Bach "Chaconne."
It's gorgeous.
If you come back, I'm not sure we
should be roommates.
Maybe I'd be willing to give it a try.
```

To which I said:

```
I understand. I'd like that.
Honestly, I doubt I'll ever be back
there.
I might try out a math program this
summer.
```

Emma zipped back:

```
Starting over is sometimes good.
```

You don't know what you've got until you've almost lost it—whether it's a friend or music or a life. And then if you get it back, it's more meaningful. It feels like the whole world is open and this time you can learn how to navigate it in a better, smarter way. A second chance. Me, my mother, my father, my grandmother, Eduardo, Mr. Clark, Emma—everyone should have a second chance. (Well, I'm not so sure about Miss Pringle.)

The next Saturday, I asked my chamber coach, "Can we do a casual reading of my piece? So I can actually hear it and then work out some of the kinks?"

"Sure, Ally. I can make that happen."

Everyone set up the chairs in a circle and I distributed the short score on their music stands. "I'll play the piano part for now," I told the group.

"Who else would?" asked the flutist, looking perplexed.

"My friend Hannah."

"The girl who won the competition?" she asked.

"Yes. I'm sure she'll sit in for me and we'll perform it in the spring."

"You wrote this?" the violist asked.

"Why?" I asked defensively.

"Because I think it's an amazing thing to do."

"Oh . . . thank you. Thanks," I repeated, relieved and surprised.

Afterward I stopped by Dr. Rashad's classroom. "My quintet read my piece."

"How did it go?"

"It was the first time. You know. Lots of stops and starts. We'll work at it."

"I'm sure you will." His face beamed. We settled down and went over the sections, rewriting where it didn't seem to work.

As I was racing down the long hallway from my composition lesson so I could be on time at Dr. Kong's room—she didn't have her own studio yet and shared it with two other teachers—I saw Eduardo at the other end of the corridor.

I screeched to a halt. "Eduardo? You're back? No one told me." I hit the side of my head with my hand. "Of course you're back—you're here."

"I feel like I'm still in Venezuela. I returned a week ago. Miss Pringle got me a lawyer."

"Now you can finish what you began—your master's."

"And then audition for the doctoral program."

"I never got a chance to tell you that your Rachmaninoff this past summer was inspiring. Hearing my teacher perform at a concert was a real trip."

"I'll have to remember that teachers can have such an impact on their students."

If only he knew the half of it.

"I heard about your grandmother. I'm sorry."

He kicked at the carpet with the toe of his boot as if there were something on it, then let out a long, deep sigh.

When he didn't say anything, I went on. "I was hoping you'd return. I had wanted to continue lessons with you."

He seemed surprised. "Not with Miss Pringle?"

"No," I said, almost in a whisper.

"Sorry I wasn't here for you."

"You had more important things to take care of."

"I'm still sorry."

I dug in my wallet and handed him a coin. He flipped it in the air, tucked it in the pocket of his jeans, and smiled slightly. "Thanks."

He was about to walk away when I added, "Eduardo, my chamber music group from last term is going to be doing a reading of a piece I wrote at the Composers' Forum. Will you come?"

"Of course I'll come. I missed your recital. I owe you."

I smiled, because he didn't owe me anything.

"I'm looking forward to seeing where you go," he added.

"Me too," I said. *Me too*.

I continued on my way, late for my lesson. When I entered the room, Dr. Kong lifted her eyes from the keyboard and said cheerfully, "I want to tell you again how much I enjoyed the concert your father and you gave. It was a lovely afternoon. And if Minsu wasn't bored, asking a hundred times, 'Is it time to go yet?' then it must have rated."

"There were a lot of goodies to eat."

"It wasn't just the cookies." She glided her fingers across a few keys.

"Thanks." My eyes twinkled. "I'm doing another concert. . . ."

"Another one?"

"A chamber piece I've been working on for a while. The one I wrote."

"You're one busy young lady."

"Well . . ." I awkwardly shuffled from foot to foot.

"In terms of what we'll be doing, would you like to try some Mendelssohn?"

"Felix is cool." I thought of how Erik had been playing him over the summer and how Emma had teased him about how romantic his music was. I was ready for romance.

"I see you're on a first-name basis," she said, and chuckled.

"What about some Baroque music, too? I did some transcriptions in graduate school for one of my professors."

I wrinkled my nose without realizing it, but she saw my reaction.

"Okay, we'll try something else."

"I said I'd be open to everything, so I'll try it."

I opened the music score, but she closed it. "Another time. It's like reading a book or seeing a film. It depends on what you're in the mood for and what's happening in your life. Even how old you are. It's got to be the right time." She handed me a bunch of scores by other composers and we sat on the floor surrounded by music.

During the week, my father brought home little peat containers with potting soil and several packets of seeds. "I'd like to get a head start on spring." We filled each one with dirt and poked holes for the seeds. *Number four on my list: gardening with my father.*

When Brad saw the aluminum trays on the windowsill, he got a gleam in his eyes, noticing a peat pot labeled *Basil.* "Herbs?"

"Yep," I answered.

"So, Nature Girl, I think there's going to be major sauce action when these babies ripen." He pointed toward three types of tomato seeds.

On President's Day, lessons were canceled, so Brad and I went to the planetarium. Brad wrapped my hand in his when the lights went down. The constellations twinkled on the ceiling above us, and I pointed to the North Star. "The brightest one in the sky."

"People always think that," said Brad. "It isn't. But it guides us. A good thing if you're lost."

"I always thought it was the brightest," I said, kind of disappointed.

"A star that leads the way is even better. Especially when you don't know how to get to the place you want to go to."

I looked over at him, and from his face I got the double meaning of his words.

"What about a shooting star?" I teased him, remembering what he had written on the card he gave me at my May recital.

"To me you'll always be a star."

But I knew that wasn't enough. And it never would be.

It's wonderful having others believe in you, especially the people who love you. We all need that. But I also had to believe it, too.

And that took work. A lot of hard, hard work.

When I came home, I fiddled around with a new piece I'd started writing.

"To think I could be living with another Beethoven," said Grandma.

"You are—our cat," I said.

"Oh, you." She raised her hands toward the ceiling.

"Grandma, can I hire you as my press agent?"

Dad came up behind us and put his hands on Grandma's shoulders. "Hire her as your manager. She's relentless." Now it was my father's turn to do an eye roll at *his* mother.

"Relentless? How was I relentless?"

"You tried to orchestrate how long I practiced, where I played, but it didn't work," he teased her.

"Big talker," she said to her son. "I was never able to manage you. You were always your own person."

It was exceptionally warm on Tuesday, and as I was eating breakfast, some guy on the radio said, "It's a fluke today. Going up to seventy degrees by the afternoon!" A fluke is a stroke of good luck, an accident, a chance happening.

Whom you meet. Whom you don't.

The breaks you get. The ones you don't.

Kind of opposite to choices. And decisions.

Should I add it to my stack of flash card words?

"Temperatures in the mid-sixties, maybe reaching almost seventy! In February! A taste of spring is right around the corner. So put the top down on your convertible. I'm taking my old Impala out of the garage while I play some of those oldies. I've got the Beach Boys for all you boomers out there." It was a song I didn't know, but my mother sang along with the words and danced around the kitchen. My father sipped his coffee and watched until she pulled him out of his seat to dance, nearly dumping the contents of his mug onto his lap.

At first I turned red, embarrassed, as they danced, and then as I watched I thought how amazing it is how you can both love and hate your parents so intensely, and how those feelings can shift over the course of a day, an hour, or even a minute. The look on my face must have communicated something, because my mother stopped dead in her tracks. "What?"

"I love you," I said.

"*Su-ure* you do," she said, but she was smiling.

"Right this second I do," I said with extreme certainty.

"And later, when you come home from school, or tonight, I could be toast."

Grandma walked in. "Where's toast?"

Dad said, "My wife could be toast."

"Are you two fighting?" she demanded.

"They were dancing," I said with a groan.

Grandma wrinkled her brow. "Now I am *really* confused."

"Ally was just saying how much she loves me," said Mom.

"That's nice," said Grandma.

"And Mom said that I might not feel that way in twelve hours," I added.

"Twelve hours if I'm lucky and it's a good day," Mom said back, eyes twinkling.

Grandma laughed. "Your father," she told me, "used to drive me nuts. One minute I was the perfect mother, and the next I was never going to see another Mother's Day card again."

I looked over at him. He was staring innocently toward the ceiling. "I was an angel."

"Oh, suddenly he grows wings?" Grandma said. "Some angel. He never practiced."

I widened my eyes.

"Or listened when I told him he had to or else he'd lose his music scholarship, and we could afford zilch. I was a basket case until your mother took him off my hands."

"Gee, thanks a lot, Mom," my father said. "I love you, too."

"What I'm saying is, it never changes. We love. We hate. We love. That's life." Grandma put her hands on my shoulders. "And trust me, someday you'll be having this same discussion with your son or daughter. And if you don't want children, well, you'll love and hate your cat or dog or goldfish."

"At least you don't have to force a goldfish to practice," I said.

Grandma hugged me tighter than tight, then walked over to my father and hugged him.

He said to his mother, "I love you, Mom."

"I love you, too," she said, adding, "But not more than anything in the whole wide world anymore. Now I have a granddaughter also."

I ran over to them and added myself to their hug.

As we stood in front of our school that morning, patches of snow were quickly melting into gray slush. The early crocuses began to poke through mounds of dirt. Brad, Opal, and I took off our down jackets. By the end of lunch we'd taken off our sweaters, too, leaving long-sleeved cotton T-shirts. After school we went to Sheep Meadow in Central Park and sprawled in the middle of the vast lawn on our jackets beneath leafless trees, staring at the clouds drifting by in a clear blue sky. My head was on Brad's stomach, and Opal's was on mine, and we lay dozily in the sun, its heat on our faces. Then Opal jumped up as if she had been stung by a bee.

"I've got an idea! Follow me."

I looked at Brad, he looked at me, and we followed our nutty friend across the meadow. Opal began to pick up anything metal she could find—nails, aluminum soda tabs, discarded pens, pushpins, unmatched earrings, barrettes, paper clips. We explored the park like homeless people. I wondered where this was heading. "Opal, are you crazy?"

"Everyone's crazy."

"Yeah!" cried Brad, scooping up a pair of rusty scissors. "Everyone's nuts!"

"Watch out for tetanus!" I shouted to him. He found an old corkscrew, while I found a silver comb and nail file.

After we'd accumulated what Opal thought was enough, she took out a huge ball of string from her backpack and sat down on a bench.

"You carry that around with you? You *are* nuts," I insisted.

"Do you always have music in your head?" she asked me.

I nodded.

"Well, I've got art. It stays with me. Always."

"Another installation?" I said, understanding.

Opal gave me one of her crooked, playful little smiles. The three of us sat there twisting, tying, fastening all the objects we found to the string, and then tying it like the longest clothesline you ever saw between two trees. As the sun became hotter, people played Frisbee and rollerbladed, or jogged with dogs barking, chasing them, and children squealed as parents ran after them, scooping them up in their arms. Horse-drawn carriages carried tourists. I took off my socks, just to feel the earth, risking it, and went barefoot on the lawn, thawing for this one day from the long winter's freeze.

I ran my hand through the dangling metal, all sizes and shapes, making music like wind chimes in the air. The more

I did, the more people came, listening to the music I was making. I'd never felt so alive.

"I think I found my herbs," I whispered to Brad.

"What are they?" he asked, although I think he already knew the answer.

"For you it might really be basil."

He laughed out loud.

I remembered wondering what extra I could bring to my music to make it great. Now I knew it was the tiny things that spice up a single day. One moment among the chaos of many. Loving what you do each day. That knowledge had been in me all along—I'd just needed to find out that it was there.

"Einstein summed up life by saying, 'A table, a chair, a bowl of fruit, and a violin; what else does a man need to be happy?'" I told Opal and Brad. "He left out the rest of the quote. But then it's mine to put in, not his."

Opal and Brad looked at me expectantly.

"A piano. He left out a piano."

*Music is my air, too. And I need it to breathe.*

That is what I learned.

I thought of my mother.

I thought of my father.

The stories—the pictures in my head—were now mine to make.

And I was going to make them without fear.

# Mrs. Clark's Best Birthday Cake in the Entire World

*Children should not try making this recipe without the help of a grown-up. (That means YOU, Bradley Clark, until you are old enough!)*

3 cups bleached flour, sifted
1 teaspoon baking soda
1 teaspoon baking powder
3 extra-large eggs, separated
1 cup granulated sugar
¼ cup vegetable oil
juice of one lemon
1 cup honey

1 cup strong coffee
1 teaspoon maple syrup
1 teaspoon cream of tartar
1 tablespoon grated almonds
  (optional)
1 teaspoon powdered ginger
1 teaspoon ground cinnamon
1 teaspoon ground allspice

1. Preheat oven to 350 degrees.
2. In a large bowl, sift flour, baking soda, and baking powder.
3. In another large bowl, beat egg yolks and sugar until foamy.
4. Add oil, lemon juice, honey, coffee, and maple syrup. Mix.
5. In a separate bowl, beat egg whites with cream of tartar until stiff peaks form. (Make sure beaters are clean or stiff peaks won't form.)
6. Fold egg whites into batter with a spatula. Add grated almonds (optional), folding gently.
7. Grease two 9-inch round layer pans that are 1½ inches deep and one 10-inch round layer pan of the same depth.
8. Pour batter two-thirds full to allow cake to double in height.
9. Bake 25 to 30 minutes. (Test with toothpick to see if it is dry when removed.)

Yield: 3 round honey cake layers

*Note:* You can use various-sized pans and make each layer a different kind of cake—strawberry shortcake, lemon-poppy, carrot, chocolate—whatever you choose. My favorite is honey because your father is so sweet and the best husband in the whole wide world. (I leave out the nuts now because Brad's allergic.)

# Coconut-Vanilla-Raisin Icing

8 ounces softened cream cheese
1 stick unsalted butter, softened to room temperature
1 pound confectioners' sugar, sifted
2 teaspoons vanilla extract
¼ cup dark or light raisins
½ cup toasted pecans, chopped
½ cup coconut flakes

1. In a large bowl, blend cream cheese and butter with an electric mixer.
2. Add sugar and vanilla to mixture.
3. Fold in raisins, pecans, and coconut flakes.

Yield: Enough icing for 2 to 3 round cakes unless there is any pre-licking going on! (Brad, I know you and your dad are major "icing" fans, but leave some left over for the cake, okay?)

# Acknowledgments

I shall seize Fate by the throat:
it shall certainly not bend and crush me completely.
—Ludwig van Beethoven (letter to F. G. Wegeler, 1801)

This book could not have been written without the inspiration of many, particularly a long list of musicians, music teachers, librarians, and the meticulous copyediting department at Knopf, who generously gave of their limited time. Some people are openhearted—the rare ones—and it is an unexpected blessing when it comes, but I need to narrow it down to a few select individuals whom I owe so much. My editor, Michelle Frey, is a special person. She is warm, sensitive, intuitive, and smart. She goes over every line, every word, every comma, with a fine-tooth comb. I appreciate her care. Everything is okay in the world when I am doing a novel under her guidance and discerning eye. Her wonderful "sidekick," Michele Burke, is a great backup, and between the two of them, it works for me with ultimate joy! (Even when they make me take eighty pages out of the book or cut characters I have "befriended" and passages I am utterly attached to!) I am indebted to them both. My agent, Elizabeth Harding, is a calm, soothing ripple when I feel a storm. She always, and I mean *always,* helps me ride the wave. She is so sane! Dr. Ellyn Altman has been a sage in my life, who helps me to grow, delve, change, take risks, and teaches me to think carefully about things. I appreciate her infinite empathy and wisdom. To my son Alexander, it breaks my heart remembering how young, innocent, and sweet you were, and how I used some of that, turning it into fiction, of course— and now how you have a child of your own that I love. My husband, Steven, goes with the routine when I am writing a novel—how I disappear off the face of the earth for a very long time into another world. He is my best friend and makes me laugh when I need it. And even when I don't.

Mostly, this book could never have been written without the existence of my youngest son, Jonathan. My husband told me that Jonathan means "a gift from God." Jonathan is a gift in my life. It is a true gift when the baby you nurture grows up from that drooling infant into an impossible teenager and then into an adult whom you love having dinner with, learning from, and sometimes doing nothing at all with—just hanging out and enjoying a brilliantly talented, infinitely caring, and funny person. Thank you, most of all, for allowing me to witness, borrow, and partake in your journey as it intersects with mine.

# About the Author

Jane Breskin Zalben is the award-winning author-artist of over fifty books and has written and illustrated picture books, poetry, cookbooks, short stories, chapter books, and eight novels. Her books include *Leap, Paths to Peace: People Who Changed the World,* and *Baby Shower,* which received a starred review in *Booklist.* Her young adult novel *Unfinished Dreams* was a finalist for the William Allen White Children's Book Award. She was recent chair of the Original Art Exhibit at the Society of Illustrators and is best known for her world-recognized Beni and Pearl picture books, which have received various medals.

Ms. Zalben began piano lessons at seven years old and gave them up at thirteen, when she decided to audition for the art program at the High School of Music & Art instead of the music program. The last piano piece she played was by Rachmaninoff. She became first a painter of modern art, then a writer, too, but music will always have a very deep place in her heart. She lives in New York and invites readers to visit her website at JaneBreskinZalben.com.

You ask me where I get my ideas. That I cannot tell you with certainty. They come unsummoned, directly, indirectly—I could seize them with my hands—out in the open air, in the woods, while walking, in the silence of the nights, at dawn, excited by moods which are translated by the poet into words, by me into tones that sound and roar and storm about me till I have set them down in notes.

—Ludwig van Beethoven